A Murder of Convenience

A Murder of Convenience

The meandering

Chronicles of Brother Hermitage

by

Howard of Warwick

From the Scriptorium of
The Funny Book Company

The Funny Book Company

Published by The Funny Book Company
Crown House 27 Old Gloucester Street
London WC1N 3AX
www.funnybookcompany.com

Cover design by Double Dagger.

ISBN 978-1-913383-19-0

Scriptorial appreciation is due to:
Mary
Susan Fanning
Karen Nevard-Downs
Lydia Reed
Claire Ward

Also by Howard of Warwick.

The First Chronicles of Brother Hermitage

The Heretics of De'Ath

The Garderobe of Death

The Tapestry of Death

Continuing Chronicles of Brother Hermitage

Hermitage, Wat and Some Murder or Other

Hermitage, Wat and Some Druids

Hermitage, Wat and Some Nuns

Yet More Chronicles of Brother Hermitage

The Case of the Clerical Cadaver

The Case of the Curious Corpse

The Case of the Cantankerous Carcass

Interminable Chronicles of Brother Hermitage

A Murder for Mistress Cwen

A Murder for Master Wat

A Murder for Brother Hermitage

The Umpteenth Chronicles of Brother Hermitage

The Bayeux Embroidery

The Chester Chasuble

The Hermes Parchment

The Superfluous Chronicles of Brother Hermitage

The 1066 from Normandy

The 1066 to Hastings

The 1066 via Derby

The Unnecessary Chronicles of Brother Hermitage

The King's Investigator

The King's Investigator Part II

The Meandering Chronicles of Brother Hermitage

A Mayhem of Murderous Monks

Brother Hermitage Diversions
Brother Hermitage in Shorts (Free!)
Brother Hermitage's Christmas Gift

Audio
Hermitage and the Hostelry

Howard of Warwick's Middle Ages crisis: History-ish.
The Domesday Book (No, Not That One.)
The Domesday Book (Still Not That One.)
The Magna Carta (Or Is It?)

Explore the whole sorry business and join the mailing list at
Howardofwarwick.com

Another funny book from The Funny Book Company
Greedy *by Ainsworth Pennington*

A Murder of Convenience

Caput I: A Happy Wanderer

Brother Hermitage sat comfortably under a tree outside the workshop of Wat the Weaver contemplating the summer sun and the buzz of activity from inside. He had even laid down his slim volume of devotional texts for a moment and closed his eyes.

The voice of Cwen drifted over the ground as she gave instruction to the apprentices, most of whom were older than she was. Her natural talent and ability leant her a certain authority and the rest she got from being naturally authoritative.

There was no indication that Wat himself was at work, but then it was his workshop and he had moved on from any actual weaving. On the one hand this was a bad thing, as Cwen frequently pointed out, as a bit of labour from him might actually get more done. On the other hand, the sort of tapestries Wat had made in the past really did not want repeating.

Not that he would dream of doing anything like that anymore, he promised Hermitage. Unfortunately, many of Hermitage's dreams involved Wat's old tapestries and there wasn't room for that many naked people in one monk's head. The thought of Adam and Eve was uncomfortable enough; he didn't need a picture of them with several companions, doing things that were most assuredly never mentioned in the Bible.

Just at this moment, though, there was peace and calm, about which Hermitage naturally felt enormously guilty. He knew that he was no weaver and so could not contribute to the work that put bread on the table. Neither could he offer spiritual guidance to those busy at their looms; he had tried that once and the response had been quite insulting.

Wat and Cwen assured him that he didn't need to do anything, but that could not be right. He may not need to do anything at the workshop, but he needed to do something. He was a monk of commitment and sincerity and as such could not simply sit around.

He could go and offer his services to the people of Derby, but they always seemed so busy whenever he tried. And they said that they already had all the service they needed from the priest.

He had long since given up trying to help that man. It was hard enough to even find him, let alone do anything constructive.

Wat and Cwen argued that as he was King William's own Investigator, he should consider that that was what he did now. That there was no investigation at the moment was not his problem. He just had to wait. One would come along.

That was a worry to accompany his guilt, which made for a rather sour dish. Investigating murder for the Norman king was not what he wanted to do at all.

They then said that he was being rather selfish for thinking that he could do what he wanted, rather than what was expected.

He knew in his heart of hearts that a murder would come along, it was only a matter of time and circumstance. He could stay sitting under this tree or even climb into its branches to hide and a murder would find him.

It could be the king sending word directly. It could be some other Norman who wanted a death resolved. It could be a passing Saxon with a murder that just had to be solved. He wouldn't even be surprised if two people walked by on the road, only for one of them to murder the other right in front of him.

At least that would be easy. Most of the time, he had not the first idea who had done what to whom until the moment came to reveal the truth. And frequently, the revelation was as much a surprise to him as it was to those involved.

Somehow, when all the facts had spent long enough washing around inside his head, they would coalesce into the only possible conclusion. He just wished that he had a bit more idea about how the washing was going before the conclusion slopped out in front of him.

He frequently told himself that the next time an investigation reared its ugly head, he would organise himself properly to begin with. By that means, he would know what he was doing from the start. He would develop a clear plan, establish a route of progress, and then gather the relevant facts in an ordered and comprehensive manner. He might even write some of them down. All of this would mean that the conclusion became increasingly obvious over the course of time, rather than come as a bit of shock right at the end.

This was all well and good, but it was a scheme that lasted about as long as it took someone to say, "there's been a murder". Before he knew it, he was confused. He followed this by getting completely lost and ended up in a bit of a panic. Then, those involved in the whole sorry business would start suggesting that he had something to do with it all. They didn't seem to realise that he had no idea what was going on, never mind what he was doing about it.

It almost seemed that these stages were essential before he could say, "aha" and reveal who did it. Perhaps increasingly personal threats and the associated sense of dread prompted his mind to get on with it. This had worked thus far, but it was not a comfortable process to rely on. And surely, the investigation would arrive when it didn't work at all.

Wat and Cwen seemed happy to assume he would get there in the end; he did not share their confidence. Surely, one of these days, not having a clue what was going on would last the entire investigation. He would start that way and end there as well. Someone would ask who did it, and he would have to say, "no idea".

Perhaps that would be that. End of investigation, back to being a monk. The weavers urged him to have confidence in his own ability. Yes, he may not know what those abilities were, or how to harness them, or even tell whether he was using them or not, but they always got their man or woman.

Telling a man of faith to have faith shouldn't really be necessary. But no matter how many times they told him, he still couldn't muster it.

He tried to tell himself that the current period of calm was only preparing him for the next onslaught. Either that, or it was a reward for the previous harrowing experience.[1]

The moment would come, he knew it. He was still a young monk and so the moments would probably be many. He didn't like to think about that and so took up his devotional text once more.

As he did so, he cast his eyes along the road and noticed a lone traveller coming their way.

A murder was his immediate thought. Ridiculous though he knew it to be, anyone on the road in this part of Derby was bound to be bringing a murder; or was about to be murdered themselves. He had tried to warn people that his presence promoted death, but no one listened.

As the man drew closer, Hermitage felt some relief. He

1 *A Mayhem of Murderous Monks;* and harrowing, to boot.

could hear a jolly whistle and saw that the step was jaunty. This was not a man weighed down by information about some unnatural death.

He was well equipped for the road as well, carrying quite a large pack on his back and a sturdy stick in his hand. A felt cap on his head and a fine pair of boots on his feet said that this was an experienced man of the road. He doubtless had a clear destination in mind and was making good progress towards it.

'Halloo,' the fellow called, raising an arm in greeting as he spied Hermitage.

Hermitage lifted his own hand in reply. 'Good day to you.'

'And a good day it is,' the man replied, turning his face to the sun. 'A fine day to be on the road.'

'Indeed,' Hermitage agreed.

The man now drew level with Hermitage and came to a halt. He was a mature and strong-looking fellow, probably about thirty years of age, with the darkened skin of someone who spent most of his time out of doors. A much paler Hermitage, who spent as much time as possible indoors, took pleasure from the fact that this would doubtless be an idle exchange of conversation, instead of anything more worrying. He got to his feet and ambled over to the edge of the track.

'We have had fine weather for many days now,' the traveller observed.

'We have. The crops will be ripening well.'

'Aye, that they will.' The fellow doffed his cap. 'Raegnald,' he introduced himself.

'Good day, Master Raegnald.' Hermitage bowed. 'I am Brother Hermitage.'

'Brother Hermitage, you say?' Raegnald's tone was one of surprise.

'I know,' Hermitage acknowledged. 'An odd name for a monk, but the one I was given by an old abbot.'

Raegnald nodded happily. A bit too happily, really. Hermitage wondered if this Raegnald might be a bit of a strange fellow who could do something unexpected at any moment.

He did.

'You are the very Brother I have been looking for.'

'Really?' Hermitage was overly cautious. He had been caught out like this before. A so-called merchant once told him that he was the very monk he had been looking for. The next thing he knew was that he had handed over the monastery alms he had been entrusted with. All he got in return was the promise of delivery of a fine gold cross that would sit very well in the chapel. He never saw the merchant again and had to explain to his abbot, whose berating of Hermitage lasted all through Lent.

'That's right,' Raegnald confirmed. 'This would be the workshop of Wat the Weaver, then?' he asked as he considered the buildings.

'Erm, yes,' Hermitage said slowly.

Now his concern was that this Raegnald was seeking Wat. At least his chances of getting any money out of Wat were non-existent. Anyone's chances of getting money out of Wat were pretty non-existent, even the people to whom he owed money.

Or perhaps the motive was even less wholesome. Wat's old trade was still the talk of many parts of the land. News may not have reached Raegnald's ears that the works of Wat the Weaver were pious and decent now.

'Good, good,' Raegnald smiled. 'Might I have a word, do you think?'

'With Wat?' Hermitage asked very carefully.

'With all of you. Brother Hermitage, Wat the Weaver and Cwen.'

'You know of us?'

'Everyone knows of you,' Raegnald said enthusiastically. 'I heard all about you and realised that you are the very people for me.'

Now Hermitage's heart sank. It was an investigation after all. There could be no other reason why the three of them would be needed or any other reason why their names would be known.

He clung to the hope that this may still be to do with tapestry. After all, he had guided the workshop on the accuracy of their religious images; or rather had managed to remove the more blatant inaccuracies and downright fantasies. Could this Raegnald be seeking a pious work and had come here on recommendation?

'King's erm, what was it?' Raegnald asked.

Hermitage's resignation swept through him. 'Investigator,' he sighed wearily.

'Investigator?' Raegnald repeated the word. 'Yes, that was probably it.'

Still, Hermitage thought it impossible that Raegnald had brought murder along the trail with him. The fellow was too happy and seemed carefree. If he had a murder that needed investigation, he would be far more sombre.

And he was a Saxon. What was a Saxon doing getting information about the Norman King's Investigator? Hermitage had investigated Saxon deaths, but they were never brought to his door in such a jolly manner.

'Perhaps you'd better come in,' Hermitage said, holding an arm out to direct Raegnald towards the workshop.

'Too kind, too kind, Brother,' Raegnald burbled happily.

No, this could not be murder. In theory, investigation could apply to any matter that needed tracking. After all, that was the Latin root of the word. Something was lost, perhaps. Or stolen? Could there be an investigator of robbery, he wondered? He'd only done murder up to now; the thought of doing something harmless like a robbery was quite refreshing.

As he thought about it, he concluded that this probably wasn't even Raegnald's investigation, that was why the fellow was so happy. He had been sent by someone else.

Which brought Hermitage back to the possibility that this could be murder after all.

He recalled his experience in Shrewsbury when virtually the whole town was incredibly happy about the murder. That didn't mean things had gone at all well, of course.[2]

They entered the workshop and Hermitage called out to Wat, who was most likely in his upstairs chamber, a remarkable luxury that was a reminder of just how profitable Wat's awful trade had been.

'Up here, Hermitage,' Wat confirmed his location.

Hermitage led the way up the narrow stairs and made the introduction.

'This is Master Raegnald. He's come looking for all of us, apparently.'

'Oh dear,' Wat said, offering Raegnald a sympathetic smile. As this was replied to with a hearty handshake, Wat looked confused.

'Wat the Weaver, eh?' Raegnald beamed. 'Well, I never.' He took a step back and appraised Wat. 'You'd never know to look at you.'

---

[2] *Hermitage, Wat and Some Nuns*: a happy murder

'Erm, know what?'

'All them tapestries.' Raegnald gave a dirty snort. 'I saw one once, you know.'

'Did you?' Wat gave Hermitage a rather worried look. Perhaps this Raegnald was going to be hard to get rid of.

'Oh, yes. A wonder, it was.'

'Was it?'

'Where do you get your ideas?'

'He doesn't anymore,' Hermitage stepped in quickly.

Wat nodded. 'Decent images these days. Saints, don't you know.'

'Saints, eh?' Raegnald leered.

'Pious saints suitable for the Norman nobility.'

'Oh, right,' Raegnald was disappointed.

'Well, Raegnald,' Wat moved quickly on. 'Take a seat. Shall we have ale?' It sounded like this was a good excuse for Wat to have some ale, rather than a genuine enquiry.

'I'll go and find Cwen,' Hermitage said as he turned for the stairs.

'And the ale,' Wat called after.

Cwen was in the workshop, busy at her loom, and those of several of the apprentices. When Hermitage said that she was needed in Wat's chamber for a visitor, she huffed her frustration at being taken away from her work.

As they left the room, the apprentices sighed their relief at her being taken away from their work.

On the way, Hermitage stopped to fill tankards with ale from the barrel.

'Who's the visitor, then?' Cwen asked.

'A fellow called Raegnald.'

'Hm, doesn't sound Norman.'

'No. Definitely Saxon.'

'And he wants all of us?'

'That's right.'

'It'll be a murder, then.' Cwen said this as if a new bale of wool had just been delivered.

'I don't know. He seems to be a very cheerful fellow, which would be odd if he does bring a murder to our door. I wondered if it might be something else. Robbery, perhaps?'

'Investigate robbery?' Cwen asked. 'Who on earth would want to do that?'

'It would be better than dealing with the dead.'

'I suppose so.'

'Or he brings word on behalf of someone else.'

'Someone he doesn't care for very much. Not bothered that they're dead.'

'There's only one way to find out.' Hermitage had filled the tankards now and Cwen took two of them as they made their way back to Wat and Raegnald.

Once the tankards were distributed and sups of ale taken, Hermitage had to get to the heart of the matter. Not because he wanted to, but because he was already feeling it weigh on him.

'So, Master Raegnald. You seek the King's Investigator?'

'That's right. Heard all about you.'

'Really?'

'Oh, yes. I keep my ear to the ground now that the Normans are in charge, and I picked up all about the King's Investigator. It's remarkable.'

'I suppose it is.' Hermitage knew it was remarkable, just not in a good way.

'And, erm,' there was no putting it off. 'Why do you come? Perhaps some robbery, or attack, or other mystery that needs resolution?' he asked hopefully.

'Oh, no, nothing like that.'
Could Hermitage really get his hopes up?
'It's a murder.'
No, he couldn't.

Caput II: Business As Usual

'A murder,' Hermitage repeated the word, mainly to force it into his thinking.

'That's right,' Raegnald beamed happily. 'I heard talk of the King's Investigator dealing with all these murders and knew exactly where to go.'

'Where did you hear it?' Cwen asked.

'London.'

'From the Normans?' Cwen's voice took on a tone of impending threat.

'That's right,' Raegnald didn't seem concerned.

'What are you doing listening to the Normans?' Cwen was blunt.

'Pays to listen,' Raegnald explained without explaining.

Cwen's folded arms made it clear that this was not sufficient.

Raegnald leaned forward in his chair as if the walls might be listening. 'I used to do a bit of business with the king, the old king.'

'Harold?'

'Oh, no.' That name gave Raegnald a bit of a shiver. 'Edward.'

'What sort of business?' Cwen asked suspiciously.

'Nothing mysterious,' Raegnald relaxed now that the names of the kings had been spoken. 'Messages, missions, that sort of thing. Confidential, a lot of it. All the sorts of things kings have to deal with, I suppose. I mean, it's all very well us talking about how the king made Odda of Deerhurst Earl of western Wessex, isn't it?'

'Did he?' That great appointment of state had passed Cwen by.

'Oh, yes. Year of our lord Ten-fifty-one, it would have been.'

'That's very interesting,' Hermitage said. The others all looked at him. 'The monastery of Deerhurst was made alien in ten-sixty.'

They still looked at him.

'It was granted to the abbey of Saint Denis in France. Making it alien, you see. Not under the control of an English house.' He tailed off as he saw that no one else seemed to find this interesting at all. 'Odda founded a chapel there,' he added as a final contribution.

Raegnald carried on from where he had left off. 'But how does this sort of thing actually happen, I hear you ask?'

'I don't think you do,' Wat muttered.

'The king is in London and old Odda is in Deerhurst.'

'I suppose he would be.' Cwen acknowledged.

'Word has to be taken.' Raegnald tapped the side of his nose. 'And I do the taking. Me or someone like me, there were a few of us. Didn't do monasteries and churches very often,' he acknowledged Hermitage. 'The bishops had their own people for things like that, but I helped out now and again.

'Anyway, first of all, I have to inform Odda that the king might be thinking about the possibility of looking for an earl of western Wessex. Then I judge his reaction and report it back to the king.

'It wouldn't do for the king to announce it at court only for Odda to say, no thank you.'

'Is he allowed to say no thank you?' Wat asked.

'Well, no, not really. Not unless he wants to start a rebellion and get himself executed.'

'At least it's a choice.' Wat supped some more ale.

'Next, word goes back again that the king is minded to appoint Odda. We've gone from thinking to minding, see. It's a big step.'

'And lots of going back and forth to Deerhurst,' Cwen commented.

'That's right. And it's a tidy step, I tell you. Nearly to Wales, it is. Then I take word back to the king that Odda will accept. Then it goes back to Odda that the king will appoint him. Only then do Odda and the king actually get together.'

'Seems like a lot of trouble,' Wat observed.

'It is,' Raegnald agreed. 'And trouble has to be paid for.'

Wat nodded at that statement.

'So, with Edward gone and Harold spending all his time fighting wars, business tailed off. Now the Normans are here, they might want my services again. Got a lot of useful information, I have.'

'Which you'll sell to the Normans,' Cwen sneered.

'Not selling tapestry to the Normans then?' Raegnald asked amicably.

Cwen could only snort in Wat's direction.

'You heard talk of the King's Investigator, from the Normans?' Hermitage didn't like to think of being talked about by the Normans. He kept hoping they'd forgotten all about him.

'That's right. Couple of the high-ups it was, Le Pedvin and de Sauveloy.'

Now it was Hermitage's turn to shiver at names.

'Surely they can't have been saying anything good?' Cwen asked. 'Not those two.'

'Well, it seemed to be more of an argument, really. They

were trying to blame one another for some problem or other.[3] The monk is the King's Investigator, Le Pedvin said. Then he went on about how you'd dealt with all these murders.'

'He thinks I'm useless,' Hermitage protested.

'Well,' Raegnald, was a little sheepish. 'That did seem to come up quite often.'

'He mentioned me by name?' Hermitage had rested many of his hopes on the fact that William and Le Pedvin never seemed able to remember who he was, just that they had a monk who dealt with murder.

'Yes, that's right. And then another, name of John, told me all about you.'

'Ah.' Hermitage understood now. John had been a true friend during the horrible business at the Tower of London. In all the other horrible businesses, he'd had to rely on Wat and Cwen alone. He released a small sigh as he realised that they were now going to have to tackle the horrible business Raegnald had brought.

'You have a murder for us to investigate, then?'

'That's right.' Raegnald still seemed far too cheerful for one with murder in his life. 'At least, I suppose so.'

'You suppose so? Are you not sure?'

'Well, I've never done this sort of thing before.'

Hermitage had sympathy for that position; he wished he was in it. 'Can you tell us who the victim is?'

'Of course.' Raegnald sounded surprised by the question. 'What sort of murder would it be if you didn't know the murdered person?'

'It could be a stranger,' Hermitage said.

'Really?'

'It does happen.'

---

3 *The King's Investigator parts I and II,* blame aplenty

'Well, I never. Not in this case, though. It's Nigel of Lincoln

'Nigel of Lincoln, I see. And who was Nigel of Lincoln?'

'Who was he? Oh, well, he was a complete rogue, apparently.' Raegnald gave a quite inappropriate snort and a wink.

Hermitage's best-laid plans of having a best-laid plan were already falling apart. Raegnald seemed particularly poorly informed about the murder that he had brought to the door.

'Can I ask? Do you bring word of this murder from someone else? On someone's behalf, if you like?'

'Yes, I suppose I do, really.'

That explained something, Hermitage thought. 'You'd better tell us what you know, and we'll see what can be done.'

'Good show,' Raegnald nodded.

Hermitage chanced a little scowl that he would like their visitor to take this a little more seriously.

'Nigel of Lincoln, then. Do you know when he died?'

'When he died?' Raegnald now seemed to be the confused one.

'Yes. When did the murder take place?'

Raegnald looked around at them all with a bit of a puzzled expression. 'That's rather down to you, isn't it?'

'Down to me?'

'Isn't it?'

'You mean we need to determine the time?'

'Of course.' Raegnald seemed to think that this should be obvious.

'I see. And the location. Was Nigel in Lincoln at the time?'

'That's down to you as well.'

Hermitage did not like being lost this early. He tried to lay out what he knew, which was pretty much nothing.

'We have Nigel of Lincoln, who may have been a rogue. He may or may not have been in Lincoln, murdered at a time that we do not know.'

'That's it.' Raegnald confirmed.

'Are you even sure there is a murder?' Hermitage asked in some frustration.

'I wouldn't have come all this way otherwise.'

'I suppose not. It doesn't give us much to start the investigation with.'

'You've got the name.'

'We have,' Hermitage sighed. 'Nigel of Lincoln, murdered.'

Raegnald nodded some more. 'Yes please.'

Hermitage stopped thinking altogether. 'Yes please?' he managed to repeat. 'What do you mean, yes please?'

'I mean, yes, I would like Nigel of Lincoln murdered, please.' Raegnald grinned at them all.

'What?' Hermitage felt that his loss for words might be permanent.

Cwen had a very thoughtful look on her face. 'You want Nigel of Lincoln murdered?'

'That's it,' Raegnald agreed with a jolly nod.

'And you want us to do it for you?'

'Right again.'

'Because we investigate murders.'

'Exactly.'

'Can I ask, what you think investigating a murder means?'

Raegnald shrugged. 'Doing it.'

'Doing a murder?'

'That's it.' Raegnald was happy that they were all talking about the same thing now. 'I never knew there was such a service. Come over with the Normans I expect. Good, isn't it?'

'Good?' Hermitage could only breathe the word.

'Do you want to tell him?' Cwen asked Hermitage.

Only just managing to contain himself, Hermitage explained. 'Investigation is from the Latin,' his voice was shaky. 'Vestigo, vestigare, to track. I investigate, track murders if you like. More specifically, I track murderers. I find out who did it.'

'Really?' Raegnald's face became confused.

'Absolutely. And bring them to justice.'

'Well, that's no good to me, is it?' Raegnald was now looking quite disappointed.

Cwen leaned forward. 'So, just to make sure we're all completely clear. You have come here asking Hermitage to commit a murder for you?'

'That's it. On recommendation of the Normans. Never thought it would be a monk and some weavers though. Probably lowers suspicion, eh?'

'I am an investigator,' Hermitage spelt it out, still struggling for breath. 'I track killers and bring them to justice. That's what I've done for the Normans. Investigation is not going out and killing people.'

'You want an assassin,' Wat suggested.

'Assassin?' Raegnald scowled. 'Sounds a bit foreign to me. Don't want foreigners coming over here doing our murders for us.'

'You should not want anyone doing murders for anyone,' Hermitage insisted, feeling very agitated at this ridiculous situation. 'I have never heard of such a thing. And to think I would be involved? It's awful.'

'All right, all right,' Raegnald complained. 'No need to go on about it. Simple misunderstanding, that's all. The Normans said that you'd dealt with all these murders for them. What am I supposed to think?'

'Not that you can have one of your own,' Hermitage instructed. Then he recalled something else that Raegnald had said. Something that had been driven from his mind by the appalling conclusion to this whole discussion. 'You said you'd come on someone's behalf. Who?'

'I can't go into that,' Raegnald replied. 'Wouldn't be right.'

'Wouldn't be right?' Hermitage couldn't stop his voice rising. 'You come here asking a monk to go out and murder someone, and this wouldn't be right?'

'I can't go giving away confidences like that. My reputation would be ruined.'

'It's not that great at the moment,' Cwen observed.

'I think you had better leave, Master Raegnald.' Hermitage even sounded firm to his own ears.

'Please yourself.' Raegnald shrugged. 'What a waste of time this has been.' He stood and considered them once more. 'You're sure you won't reconsider? Have you ever thought about a change of trade? If you've tracked down all those killers, you must know how to do a good murder by now.'

'No,' Hermitage insisted. 'We will not reconsider.'

'I'd make it worth your while.'

'No,' Hermitage got in before Wat could say anything. 'In fact, I will tell you this. We now know that you want Nigel of Lincoln murdered. We further know that someone has put you up to this.'

'Doubtless, a Norman,' Cwen said.

'Exactly. You are trying to get into the service of the Normans and have probably heard that one of them would like this Nigel killed. The king, perhaps?

'You also heard about the investigator of murder. You put two and two together and made five.'

'Four,' Wat corrected.

'Yes, I know it's four. It's four if you add it up correctly. I'm saying that he has added it up wrong.'

'Oh, right, I see. Carry on.'

'Thank you. Furthermore,' Hermitage went on, 'you are right. I have investigated a lot of murders and know how it's done. I will use all of this knowledge to stop Nigel of Lincoln from being murdered at all.'

'Oh, I say,' Raegnald complained.

'And if I should fail in this, I will know that you are involved. You and some shadowy Norman. Both of whom can be brought to justice.'

'This is completely unfair,' Raegnald moaned. 'I wouldn't have said anything at all if I thought you were going to be all difficult about it.'

'Difficult about it?' Hermitage contained his shriek of complaint. 'We are talking about a man's life.'

'Quite a nasty man.'

'It doesn't matter.'

'And you should have thought before opening your mouth,' Cwen added.

Hermitage now realised that there was a key question he should have asked quite a while ago. 'Why do you want Nigel of Lincoln murdered?'

'Why?' Raegnald didn't seem to think that was important.

'Yes, why? Or why does this Norman want him murdered?'

'Why does anyone want someone murdered?'

'Anger, revenge or greed,' Wat spoke up. 'I've always said those are the only reasons.

'You only said it a few weeks ago,' Cwen pointed out.

'Still true. Either someone is angry with Nigel, they want

revenge on him, or he has something they want.'

Raegnald clearly thought that this was interesting to everyone but him.

'Why do you want this Nigel killed?' Cwen repeated the question in her inimitable manner; indomitable. 'And who sent you?'

'Ha,' Raegnald seemed to think this was quite funny. 'I'm not going to tell you that, am I? I wouldn't have done before, and now you won't even do the murder for me. I think I shall go about my business and bid you good day.'

'The business of murder,' Hermitage accused.

Raegnald only shrugged and gave them a cheery wave over his shoulder as he skipped down the stairs.

'And our business will be to stop you,' Hermitage called after.

Caput III: Send An Apprentice

'We should have tied him up,' Cwen said, angry at not having thought of this earlier. 'Three of us and one of him, we could have had him easily.'

'I'm not sure that would be any good,' Hermitage mused.

'In fact,' Cwen ignored him, 'there might still be time.' She jumped for the stairs. 'Gather some of the apprentices and we can go after him. Get him while he's on the road.'

'And then what?' Hermitage asked.

'We hold him. Make him talk.'

'I'm not sure he would.'

'The key word was "make",' Cwen pointed out.

'We would not do him harm,' Hermitage replied to a huff from Cwen. 'And as I said, what good would it do? Someone clearly wants this Nigel dead and Raegnald may only be one of those out on the mission. If we follow your plan, he might tell us of some others and we would end up with a workshop full of would-be murderers, none of whom will tell us what they are actually up to.'

'They'd tell me everything,' Cwen grumbled at the lack of action.

'There is more than just Raegnald going on here,' Wat agreed. 'He's obviously not a man for doing the deed himself, he thought we'd do it for him.'

'And what a ridiculous idea that was,' Hermitage was still trembling from the suggestion.

'There are those who would. He just got the wrong ones.'

'Idiot,' Cwen summed him up. 'It'd be like walking up to someone at the market and asking if they'd help you rob a merchant, only to find out you've asked the sheriff.'

Wat supped more of his ale until the tankard was empty.

He then reached over to Raegnald's discarded cup, checked the contents and poured them into his own. He supped again. 'Raegnald obviously hasn't told us the whole tale. He overheard de Sauveloy and Le Pedvin, but were they the ones talking about Nigel? Or were they just talking about Hermitage?'

Hermitage didn't like that idea.

'So there could be a whole band of Normans behind this,' Cwen added.

Wat nodded. 'The question is not why does Raegnald want Nigel dead, the question is why does anyone want him dead?'

'And we don't know, because we just let the one who had the information walk away.' Cwen folded her arms at Hermitage. 'We've as good as sent Nigel to his death.'

Hermitage did feel bad about it when Cwen said it like that.

'It's as Hermitage said,' Wat went on. 'I don't think it would make any difference. Someone wants Nigel dead. Knowing the reason why might not help. And we're not even sure that Raegnald knows himself.'

'It would be something,' Cwen complained.

'He could just be an enemy of the Normans. You know, fought at Hastings but got away. William doesn't like people getting away with anything. Perhaps he's fomenting rebellion? He was rude to William's wife? Who knows? If word has gone out that the Normans want him dead, I don't hold out much hope for Nigel.'

'Which is why we must help,' Hermitage said.

Cwen looked at him askance. 'King William's own investigator is going to stop William doing his own murders? I'm not sure he'll be pleased about that.'

'We don't know it's William himself, do we? It could be de Sauveloy and Le Pedvin up to their own business. Or one of the many others, doing it for their own evil ends.'

Wat pointed a finger at Cwen. 'No comment about the Normans having evil ends.' She shrugged.

'And William has not sent me word about any of this,' Hermitage persisted. 'I would simply be acting on my own initiative.'

'I don't think he'll like that either,' Cwen said. 'And anyway, you're always the one who wants to keep as far away from murder as possible. You don't want to investigate. You keep trying not to.'

'This would be preventing a murder.' Hermitage was very satisfied with that idea. 'It would be much better than us turning up once everyone is already dead.'

'Oh, it's us now, is it?' Cwen asked with a smile.

'We would be preventing the death of an innocent man.'

'We don't know he's innocent,' Wat said. 'He could be horrible like Raegnald said. You could end up saving the life of a monster. Perhaps he's a killer himself. He goes around jumping on Normans and killing them; that's why William wants him dead.'

'If that were the case, I'm sure Raegnald would have mentioned it.'

'If he knows,' Cwen put in. 'If he's only eavesdropping around the Norman court, he could have got completely the wrong end of the stick. He's nosing about and hears someone say, "who will rid me of this troublesome Nigel," or something like that. He then hears about Hermitage and thinks this will get him in good favour. Off he goes to ask nicely for a murder.'

Hermitage shook his head and tried to get back to the facts;

what few of them they had.

'All we know is that Raegnald wants Nigel dead. He indicated that this was at the behest of the Normans, but that's all we know. The first step we have to take is to find this Nigel and warn him.'

'If he's not already dead,' Wat said.

Hermitage thought that unlikely. 'Raegnald would hardly come here asking us to kill a dead man. He's also unlikely to do the deed himself if he asked a monk to do it for him.'

'We don't know how long he's been on his mission. Someone else could have got to Nigel first.'

'Then we have to find out.'

'We don't even know where he is,' Cwen said. 'Or was.'

'Lincoln would seem a sensible place to start.'

'Again?' Wat moaned. 'Traipsing backwards and forwards to Lincoln looking for a dead man who might not even be there?'

'We've only been twice,' Hermitage pointed out.[4] 'And a man's life is at stake.'

'I suppose,' Wat said despondently. 'Oh, wait a minute though.'

'What is it?' Hermitage hoped that Wat had thought of something they'd missed.

'Gunnlaug.'

Hermitage couldn't immediately see what Gunnlaug the apprentice had to do with any of this.

'He can go.'

'Gunnlaug?'

'That's right. We've got the tapestry of some saint to send to Godrinius.'

[4] Twice being *The Heretics of De'Ath* and *The Hermes Parchment*; very little traipsing, really.

'Saint Matthew,' Hermitage scowled. He remembered Godrinius of Lincoln, and not in a good way. The fellow seemed to be a merchant of very questionable morality. He had only ordered a tapestry so that he could display it to the Normans and look pious; it was much easier than being pious. 'He must have had his work months ago.'

'Wanted another one.' Wat didn't care why people wanted his tapestries, as long as they paid for them.

'It's nearly ready,' Cwen reported.

'Only nearly?' Wat complained. 'What have you been doing?'

'Weaving tapestry while one of the weavers is missing,' Cwen said.

'Missing?' Wat was shocked. 'Which one's gone missing?'

'You.'

'Oh.'

'Yes, if the owner of the workshop ever bothered doing some of the work, we'd be a bit further ahead.'

'Work, shop,' Wat explained. 'You do the work, I mind the shop.'

'There isn't a shop to mind,' Cwen said very clearly.

'When's it going to be done then?'

'Actually,' Cwen said, 'it is done.'

'Why did you say it wasn't?'

'It was a chance to have another go at the laziest weaver in the workshop. If I was in charge of you, you'd know about it.'

'I do know about it, that's why you're not in charge.'

'Can we just sort out how we're going to find Nigel?' Hermitage asked, thinking that a possible murder was slightly more important than Wat and Cwen's squabbles.

'Yes, Cwen,' Wat said in a very critical manner. 'We've more important things to deal with.'

Cwen stood, walked over to him, held her tankard above his head and then pointedly tipped it over. Wat squirmed, but the tankard was empty.

'Yes, Wat,' she copied his tone. 'Organise delivery of the tapestries we've made, will you? We have to find out something important.'

'Who wants Nigel dead,' Wat said.

'No,' Cwen corrected. 'We have to find out what it is you're actually good for.'

Hermitage looked at them both with concern and shook his head.

'Don't worry, Hermitage,' Cwen said. She patted Wat on the head and gave him a kiss on the cheek. 'He's harmless, really.'

'Gunnlaug?' Hermitage reminded them.

'Yes, right. He can take the tapestry to Lincoln and find out about Nigel for us. Save us making the trip.' Wat clearly thought this an excellent plan.

'Or we could take the tapestry?' Hermitage suggested.

'Cwen's busy in the workshop,' Wat said. 'Won't get anything done without her in charge.'

'Don't you forget it,' Cwen said.

'And anyway,' Wat went on. 'Nigel may not even be in Lincoln.'

'If he is and he's alive, what then?'

'Gunnlaug can give him the warning.'

'This seems a heavy burden to give an apprentice,' Hermitage said. 'None of this is his problem, after all.'

'He'll love it,' Wat assured him. 'Add a bit of spice to the journey.'

. . .

'Are you mad?' Gunnlaug asked as he stood before Wat, Cwen and Hermitage in the upper chamber.

Actually, he stooped before them as he was a very large apprentice indeed. He was a lovely boy; caring, thoughtful and very creative, but he was huge. The first impression people got was that there was something of the Viking about him. There was probably something of two Vikings about him, one on top of the other, and this massive presence made everyone think twice before approaching him.

This would be particularly useful on the road to Lincoln, where robbers and ne'er-do-wells might be waiting. Any robber or ne'er-do-well with an ounce of sense would leave Gunnlaug to his business.

Unfortunately, Gunnlaug was very clear that his business did not involve looking for dead people.

'We don't know that he's dead,' Wat explained. 'In fact, we're reasonably sure that he isn't. We don't even know if he's in Lincoln at all. You only have to ask. You can manage that, surely?'

'A Norman killer wants this Nigel dead and you want me to stand in the way?' Gunnlaug now helped himself to a seat.

They had had to explain the whole situation to the apprentice. Asking him to go and find out if Nigel of Lincoln was dead only prompted more questions than they could avoid.

'Raegnald wasn't a killer,' Cwen reminded him.

'No, he wanted to hire one though.'

'He won't even be there.'

'You don't know that.'

'All you have to do,' Wat said slowly, 'is discretely ask about Nigel of Lincoln. You don't need to cause a fuss.'

'Discretely ask about the man the Normans want dead? That's not going to draw attention then, is it?'

Hermitage thought that Gunnlaug had a point.

'Ask a Saxon,' Cwen suggested. 'Ask Godrinius.'

'I wouldn't advise that,' Wat put in quickly. 'Not overly trustworthy, is Godrinius.'

'There you are,' Gunnlaug clearly thought his case was made. 'Why can't you go?'

'What's the point? You're going anyway, to deliver the tapestry. It really would look odd if four of us turned up to do that.'

'You don't all need to come,' Gunnlaug said. 'I deliver the tapestry and one of you ask about the dead people. In fact, if one of you were going, I wouldn't need to. There you are.'

'Gunnlaug,' Wat said firmly. 'Someone has to take the tapestry to Lincoln.'

'And I'm not doing it,' Cwen said. 'There'll be no work done at all if I'm not here.'

'And I can't go, Wat added. 'It would be bad for business if Wat the Weaver is seen delivering his own tapestries.

'You are going to Lincoln to deliver the tapestry to Godrinius. You will find someone to ask about Nigel, or simply keep your ears open and see what you can pick up. You bring word back to us and we will take it from there. We're not asking you to take a sword and fight your way through a horde of Normans.'

Gunnlaug's huge chest grumbled his complaint, but he seemed to accept that he was being given an instruction by his master. Hermitage was sitting closest to the apprentice so only he heard the muttering. 'Don't see why you couldn't come,' Gunnlaug was clearly talking about Wat. 'Don't do anything useful around here anyway.'

Only now did Hermitage see what the solution was, and he felt bad about his selfishness. 'I'll take it,' he said.

'Pardon?' Cwen didn't seem to understand.

'I will take the tapestry to Lincoln and ask about Nigel.'

The others all looked at him and there was a moment of profound stillness in the room.

Then, as one, they all burst out laughing.

'What?' Hermitage asked.

'You?' Cwen said between her chortles.

'Yes.' Hermitage was disappointed at the response.

'You wouldn't last a mile before the tapestry and everything else was gone,' Wat said.

Gunnlaug's laugh was deep and booming. 'We'd have to come and find you then, never mind Nigel.'

'I would manage,' Hermitage protested.

'Hermitage,' Cwen had calmed herself. 'It's very kind of you to offer, but it really would be best if Gunnlaug went.'

Gunnlaug nodded at this.

'I could go with him.'

'I'd rather not have you to look after,' Gunnlaug said.

'You wouldn't have to look after me,' Hermitage protested, now feeling moderately irritated. 'I am the King's Investigator, you know.'

'And how many times have you been accused of the murder yourself and thrown in a cell to wait for execution.' Wat asked.

'Not that many,' Hermitage grumbled.

'No, no,' Gunnlaug was now shaking his head with mirth. 'I'll go.' He stood from his chair and returned to the stairs. 'I'll get the tapestry and be off straight away.'

As he made his way back to the workshop, his voice came back to them. 'Brother Hermitage will go, oh my, har, har,

har.'

'I don't see why this is so funny,' Hermitage protested.

Caput IV: Waiting Room

'I am the King's Investigator,' Hermitage protested. He'd never boasted about the role in his life but thought that a King's Investigator ought to be able to find out about a murder on his own.

'You are, Hermitage,' Cwen assured him. 'And you do it very well; the thinking bit of it. You get all the information and have a good old think and come up with who did it. We can't do that. We're even surprised when you do it.

'But we all have our talents. Yours is thinking and saying "aha", right at the end, and ours are running about and chasing killers and the like. We can't all be good at everything.'

They went to the door to see Gunnlaug off while he still chortled to himself and gave Hermitage little shakes of the head. The tapestry for Godrinius was carefully rolled in his pack and his best pair of sturdy boots was on his feet; his only pair of sturdy boots was on his feet, and Wat said he wanted them back when this was over, having had to pay for the things.

It was going to take him two days to get to Lincoln and another two to get back. The handover to Godrinius should be a straightforward business, although Wat did warn that if Gunnlaug came back without the money, he had better keep walking; he could send the cost of the boots when he found another job.

'This is your first real test,' Wat told him. 'It's all very well knowing how to make tapestry and present it properly, it's quite another to get the payment out of the customers. Most are fine, but others are not. Godrinius is not. If he can get away with not paying the king his taxes, taking a tapestry for nothing will be meat and drink.'

Gunnlaug nodded at this and waited for Wat's words of wisdom.'

'You're a big fellow, threaten to hit him.'

'Wat!' Cwen interrupted. 'Just don't hand over the tapestry until you have the money. Let him look at it and examine it by all means, but no "taking it away to have a look under a better light". No, "just getting his tapestry man to check it over while you wait". Don't let it out of your sight until he's paid.'

Gunnlaug nodded his thanks to Cwen and rolled his eyes at Wat. He gave Hermitage a final laugh and set off.

'A week,' Hermitage moaned. 'It's going to take the best part of a week to hear anything of Nigel. If there's anything to be heard at all. That's a week in which he could be murdered.'

'Don't worry,' Cwen comforted him. 'Raegnald will only be just ahead if he's even gone to Lincoln at all and isn't wandering the streets of Derby asking if there are any killers for hire.'

'And even if he did get to Lincoln ahead of Gunnlaug, he wouldn't do anything, would he?' Wat added. 'He came here asking the King's Investigator to do his murder for him, he's not going to suddenly decide to do the deed himself.'

'He might have more luck finding a killer in Lincoln,' Hermitage suggested.

'Oh yes,' Wat sounded mocking. 'A den of killers is Lincoln. Hanging around on every street corner, I expect.'

It's easy for you to mock,' Hermitage said.

'Yes, I know.'

'But if we'd gone ourselves, we'd have been there in two days. As it is, we have to wait four or five. And then, if we decide we have to go, it will be two more.'

'And if word comes that Nigel of Lincoln isn't even in Lincoln, we'd have wasted four days going there and back for nothing.' Wat pointed out.

'Oh, this is impossible,' Hermitage sagged. 'One might call it a dilemma.'

'You might,' Cwen scoffed slightly. 'Go on then.'

'Go on, what?'

'Tell us what a dilemma is. You know you want to.'

'From the Greek.' Hermitage wasn't really seeking an etymological exploration just at the moment, which was unusual. He just thought it the most appropriate word. 'It means a double proposition. In our case, we should stay and we should go.'

'Well, we've done both.' Wat seemed to think that was the end of the conversation. 'Gunnlaug's gone and we're staying. There you are. Now it's only a lemma.

'Lemma?'

'It was a dilemma, now we've taken one of them away.'

Hermitage couldn't be bothered to argue the point, which was also unusual.

That first day of Gunnlaug's absence, Hermitage kept himself active. He constantly walked up and down the road outside Wat's workshop, wondering whether he should set off after the apprentice regardless of his instructions. At one point, he found himself half a mile away from home before he turned around and came back.

Having come back, he realised that it was now too late to follow, as Gunnlaug would have strode far ahead on his long legs. That didn't stop him going about a quarter of a mile before turning back once again.

He told himself that all this toing and froing could have

been usefully spent actually moving along the road instead of covering the same bit of it over and over again.

It was too late now, but if he had set off decisively when it wasn't too late, he would be with the weaver by now.

Or was it too late? If he was going to do it, he should do it now. Right now, this very moment. If he didn't do it now, he would be looking back in another few hours, telling himself that he should have gone when he first thought about it.

A few hours later he told himself that he should have gone when he first thought about it. Then he should have gone when he thought about it the second and third times. But he hadn't. He was still here, and Gunnlaug would be miles away by now.

He waited outside until the darkness began to fall and took the problem away from him. Or rather, made it explicit that the whole situation was not entirely his fault.

And the evening and the morning were the first day.

On the second day, it was definitively too late. There was simply no way he would be able to catch up now so there was no point worrying about it; at least that's what Wat said.

Hermitage worried about it anyway but told himself that one of the days was gone now. Gunnlaug could be back in three if he had made good progress. Of course, if he were lying in a ditch somewhere, having been attacked by robbers, that would be all Hermitage's fault.

Cwen said that anyone capable of getting Gunnlaug into a ditch against his will would probably have chopped Hermitage into little pieces at the same time.

He tried to distract himself by returning to his work on the post-Exodus prophets. True, the work thus far had involved a lot of reading and assimilation of ideas, but that was an essential stage. He already had several thoughts about what the work would look like in the end but there was no point starting it until he knew the path he was going to tread.

It would be like following Gunnlaug; if he began down the track and only had to turn back because he had gone wrong, time would be wasted.

Which meant that the first thing to do was lay down the track itself. He would need to plan the task ahead of him so that he could organise his activity in the most productive manner.

And he really needed to complete his reading before he could even make a start on the planning. Woe betide him if he came up with a marvellous route to completion, only to find some later piece of information threw the whole thing into disarray.

Needless to say, he couldn't really read effectively unless he planned which volumes to consider.

He was not a proud man in any normal sense of the word; the idea that he would consider himself or any of his achievements better than others simply didn't occur to him. Through his horrible investigations though, he had amassed a small library of texts about which he was grateful, not proud.

This gave him the next problem, which was organising the best order in which to read. He really couldn't start to formulate the concepts that would lead to the overall outline plan before he had addressed the structure of the research that would generate the initial draft of the overarching themes.

By this time, he was quite effectively distracted.

Of course, he couldn't even read effectively if he didn't have some peace and quiet; peace and quiet that always made him quite drowsy.

Cwen woke him for the noonday meal.

'I bet you didn't sleep this much in the monastery,' she said as they ambled to Wat's upper chamber.

'Certainly not, and I am quite ashamed about it.'

'Probably got a lot of catching up to do.'

'I suppose there is no word of Gunnlaug?'

'You've only been asleep for two hours Hermitage, not three days.'

'He hasn't returned then?'

'Why would he have returned?'

'I don't know. Some trouble on the road, perhaps.'

'It would be nothing like the trouble he'd get from Wat if he didn't deliver that tapestry.' She paused on the stairs. 'Didn't come back with the money, I mean.'

Wat was kneeling on the floor when they entered the chamber, scribbling some tapestry ideas on the floor with a piece of chalk.

'Look,' he said, pointing proudly.

They stepped over and peered down at the drawing. To Hermitage's eye, it was a wonder. He had no skills in this area at all, even though his scribing was to a reasonable standard. He couldn't draw at all. His fellow monks, all of whom could scribble sometimes outrageous images in the margins of their texts, sneered at his awful attempts.

He'd tried to draw the usual sort of thing, a goose dressed as a bishop preaching to a rabbit in armour, but it looked more like two donkeys fighting over a duck. He didn't bother after that.

Wat's drawing was beautiful and was probably something he'd scratched out in a couple of moments. It was perfectly clear what this image was and there wasn't a donkey in sight.

'Oh, Wat,' Hermitage expressed his disappointment.

'What now?' Wat replied, looking at his own work with admiration. 'It's very good. Everyone's got their clothes on.'

'That's something, I suppose. But it is a violent scene.'

The image was obviously one of two figures having at one another with mighty swords in their hands. One of them had had such success that the other's head had come off.

'Are you proposing to make a tapestry of this?'

'Absolutely. Should be very popular.'

'With the Normans,' Cwen complained.

'Who are the ones buying tapestry at the moment,' Wat pointed out.

Hermitage shook his head slowly. 'I'm not sure we should be encouraging them to glory in death.'

'You want me to do saints,' Wat said.

'That's right.' At least Wat had taken that lesson to heart.

'There you are then.' He pointed to his sketch. 'Fighting saints.'

Hermitage had to pause for a moment to let that sink in. 'Fighting saints?'

'That's it. You told us all about Saint Michael and his mighty sword.'

'Well, yes.'

'And here he is. Vanquishing away.'

'Who's the one without the head, then?' Cwen asked.

'Don't know,' Wat shrugged. 'Gabriel?'

'Gabriel?' Hermitage squeaked. 'The archangel Michael did not cut the head off Gabriel.'

'One of the others.'

'One of the others.' Hermitage's despair was not so much at this appalling idea, but that Wat had come up with it after they had spent so much time together.

'Who did he smite then?' Wat asked.

'Satan.'

'There you are, it's Satan. Michael smiting Satan. You can't complain about that.'

Hermitage could see that, in principle, he could not complain about that. In practice, there was quite a lot to complain about.

After the meal, Cwen made her excuses and went back to the workshop while Wat carried on with his sketching. Hermitage stayed to try and impart some improving words, which he knew might take some time.

And the evening and the morning were the second day.

The third day was positively fretful. Even though there was still a day to go by any sensible reasoning, Hermitage managed to convince himself that Gunnlaug would have got ahead of himself and could arrive a whole day early.

'How's he going to do that then?' Cwen asked as she stood by her loom.

Hermitage had moved down here after being told by Wat, in the nicest possible manner, to go away.

'How is he going to take a whole day off a four-day journey?'

'Oh, I don't know. Maybe Godrinius came to meet him.'

'Godrinius doesn't even know he's coming. There's a tapestry on the way, but he doesn't know when.'

'The murder of Nigel may have driven the people from the town,' Hermitage said with rising panic.

'For goodness' sake, Hermitage.' Cwen turned from her work. 'There is nothing you can do but wait. Constantly fretting over what might, or might not, have happened is going to achieve nothing at all. I know that it's pretty much all you can do, but you've got to wait.

'Anyway, you're the one who doesn't want to be an

investigator and doesn't want to deal with murder. Why are you thinking the worst? Gunnlaug could come back from Lincoln and report that Nigel is alive and well.'

'That will be even worse!'

'Worse? How can he being alive be worse?'

'It means that he's going to be killed. If he was already dead that would be terrible, and we would have to find out what happened. If he's alive we have to try and keep him that way.'

'Why?'

'Why? What do you mean, why?'

'Just because Raegnald came here thinking that you would do his murder for him doesn't mean we have to be involved. The Normans are probably killing people every day and we don't go off and interfere with them.'

'Because we don't know about them. We know about Nigel and how the Normans want him dead. It is our duty to prevent that if we can.'

'To be honest,' Cwen said as she turned back to her loom, 'we don't even know the Normans want him dead. All we do know is that some Saxon called Raegnald would prefer him that way. He indicated that it was to do with the Normans, but would you trust a man who wants people murdered?'

'I suppose not.' Hermitage really must stop believing what people told him.

'It could be entirely personal. Raegnald hates Nigel and wants him dead. He spins a yarn about the Normans wanting it done but then makes the mistake of asking you.'

'Which will only mean that he goes off and asks someone else. Someone more open to committing the odd murder.'

'The Normans,' Cwen said.

'Yes, they'd do it.

'Exactly. Have you ever known the Normans to not kill

someone they want dead?'

'I suppose not.'

'They had a go at Harold and he was the King of England. Some unknown Nigel of Lincoln is hardly going to bother them, is he? So why involve Raegnald?'

'He just overheard that they wanted it done and is trying to ingratiate himself with them.'

'Yes, so he said. But if the Normans really wanted it done, we'd be talking about dead Nigel by now. And they wouldn't have brought your name up at all.'

This was a whole new area of worry for Hermitage, and if there was one thing he could do with his time, it was worry.

And on the evening of the third day, Cwen told him to go away.

Caput V: News of The News

The fourth day dawned bright and early, as most days do, and Hermitage was awake to see it arrive. He was also standing on the track looking expectantly to the east to see Gunnlaug rise with the sun.

Wat and Cwen merely shouted at him from the upstairs window. Gunnlaug would not be back until at least sunset, if then. He might even be another day if he had tarried in Lincoln or had trouble with Godrinius.

Hermitage didn't think he could stand another day; Wat and Cwen were of a similar mind.

Now he had a fresh conundrum; should he start walking towards the east to meet Gunnlaug? And if so, how far should he go before deciding that Gunnlaug wasn't coming? He took a couple of hesitant steps in that direction before stopping. He looked at his feet and concluded that it was about time he took charge of the things.

'Wat, Cwen,' he called. 'I am going to walk along the track to meet Gunnlaug.'

'Good,' the voices called back.

Well, that was clear. Wat and Cwen were happy for him to go, and he wanted to do it himself. His feet would just have to do what they were told.

After a mile or so, he came to a junction which solved his conundrum for him; there was no way he was going to be able to make his mind up between two roads. Any seasoned traveller, in fact, anyone who travelled anywhere at all would know that one road led east, on towards Nottingham, Newark and then Lincoln, while the other went north, in completely the wrong direction.

Indeed, anyone who had never even been here before

would be able to tell north from east. The position of the sun, the way the moss grew on the trees, the bend in branches from the prevailing wind; all of these were indicators of direction that would aid even the most confused traveller.

Consequently, Hermitage was stuck. The only thing he could do was sit here and wait. Actually, he was very confident that he knew which road was the right one; well, reasonably confident. The problem was that he too easily put himself in other people's places and foresaw all manner of problems.

Gunnlaug could have been diverted. He might have had to change road to avoid robbers. He could have lost his way and ended up on the wrong road. Perhaps he'd headed north for his own reasons.

Whatever the situation, Hermitage was not going to commit to one road and almost certainly miss Gunnlaug as a result. He would wait.

The many passing travellers who knew exactly which road they wanted considered Hermitage with wary eyes. A monk who simply stood by the roadside watching them was a worry. There was absolutely no doubt that he would want alms. There was a strong possibility that he was mad and might accost them in some manner. There was also the slight risk that he might be from an impoverished monastery and was looking for new monks to swell the population; whether the people he approached wanted to be monks or not.

Hermitage greeted all alike with a nod and friendly smile, which made them cross the road almost immediately.

The morning wore on, and there was no sign of Gunnlaug. He told himself that this was perfectly understandable and that he had been rather rash to have expected anything this early. He should probably make himself comfortable for the wait.

As noon passed overhead, he wondered whether he should have brought some food with him. A simple loaf would have been sufficient. Still, the abstinence would do him no harm at all.

He had taken up position under a tree hard by the junction of the roads so that he could see all who passed by in any direction. By afternoon, his hunger must have been obvious as one man, leading a single goat by a rope around its neck, paused, considered Hermitage, and then handed over half a loaf and an apple; both gifts to which the goat took great exception.

Hermitage was about to protest that this was unnecessary but the man moved quickly on. Giving aid to starving monks was one thing, stopping and talking to them was quite another matter.

The afternoon wore on and Hermitage took simple pleasure from watching the world move around him. As the shadows lengthened, he began to think about setting off back to the workshop.

The whole point of his expedition had been to meet Gunnlaug on the road but waiting out after dark on his own might not be wise. The Normans may well be rulers of the country now, but they were not rulers of the countryside. Even a penniless monk would not be safe from those who roamed the land thinking they could do what they liked; occasionally doing it to penniless monks.

When he judged that there was just enough light left to make his return journey, he picked himself up, took one last look to the east and turned for home.

'There you are,' Cwen said as she strode purposefully towards him.

'Ah, Cwen, hello. There was no need to come and get me, you know. I'm perfectly fine.'

'I'm sure you are. It's simply that we don't want to wait any longer.'

'I would have been back before dark.'

'It's not that. We don't want to wait any longer before Gunnlaug tells us what happened in Lincoln.'

'Gunnlaug?' Hermitage was confused.

'He's been back for a couple of hours. We thought you'd be behind him.'

'What?' Hermitage looked around the roads again, wondering how this was possible.

'Probably asleep under your tree when he came by,' Cwen explained.

'Oh, really.' Hermitage expressed his frustration; frustration at Gunnlaug for passing by, himself for not noticing and the tree for conspiring in the whole debacle.

'There's no point in him telling us and then having to repeat it for you.'

Hermitage shook his head as he trudged along at Cwen's side.

'We did find out the most important thing though,' Cwen said.

'Really? We know what happened to Nigel?'

'No, we got Godrinius's money.'

. . .

Wat and Gunnlaug were looking quite impatient by the time Cwen and Hermitage got back.

'Asleep under a tree?' Wat asked.

'I think so,' Cwen nodded.

Hermitage couldn't really deny it as he didn't remember very much of the afternoon.

'Well, you're here now. So, Gunnlaug, what did you discover?'

They were back in the upper chamber once more, this time with evening ale instead of morning ale. Wat was clearly treating Gunnlaug very well, probably because he had returned with the payment.

The apprentice looked at them all and leaned forward on his stool as if about to begin a great tale of wonder and excitement.

'He's gone.'

'Oh my, we are too late,' Hermitage wailed. 'We should have gone ourselves. I knew we should have gone ourselves.'

'What good would that do?' Cwen asked. 'We wouldn't have got there any quicker than Gunnlaug.'

'But we would have been on hand to pursue any immediate clues. Two more days have passed now, the trail will be cold.' He turned to Gunnlaug. 'When did he go?'

'At least a couple of days, they think.'

'They think?'

'Well, yes,' Gunnlaug seemed a bit confused now. 'No one noticed until they wanted him for some town business.'

'The poor fellow,' Hermitage now felt even worse. 'To depart in such a manner.'

'Still, there we are,' Wat said brightly. 'He's gone now. Nothing more we can do about it.'

'Apart from find out who killed him,' Hermitage said in some shock at Wat's callousness.

'Killed who?' Gunnlaug asked.

'What do you mean, killed who?' Cwen asked. 'You did ask about the right Nigel?'

'I didn't have to ask, it was the talk of the town.'

'Really?' Hermitage thought that sounded interesting.

'Yes, he was under-scribe to the wapentake court, apparently.'

'A modest position,' Hermitage observed.

'And guardian of the wardrobe for the shire reeve. Crier to the Ealdorman as well.' Gunnlaug started to count off on his fingers. 'Doorkeeper to the Dean, almsman to the chapter of canons, keeper of the curfew...,'

'Busy fellow,' Cwen observed.

Gunnlaug nodded. 'And those were only the jobs he did every day. If ever there was a position available with a title, Nigel would have it. Or so they said.'

'And now that he is gone, all those functions have gone with him,' Hermitage said.

'Well, quite. The place was in quite a mess. No one to open the door for the Dean or mind the shire reeves' robes.'

'Perhaps he had too many jobs?' Wat suggested. The others looked at him to explain. 'All those titles and positions, he sounds like an important fellow. Or rather, more like a fellow who thinks he's important. We all know the type; tell someone they're the Lord of the Manor's knight of the undergarment and they think they're the Earl of Leicester. Always telling other people what to do without any real authority. Try that on a passing Norman and see what happens.'

'They are all very minor roles,' Hermitage said. 'Why would anyone want to kill a Dean's Doorman?'

'He shut their foot in the door?' Wat offered.

'Why is he killed?' Gunnlaug asked, apparently quite sincerely.

'That's the question,' Hermitage said.

Cwen was looking very hard at Gunnlaug. Nobody lasted long with Cwen looking at them very hard.

'What?' the young man asked.

'When you say Nigel of Lincoln is gone,' Cwen said.

'Yes?'

'You mean he's dead, yes?'

'No, I mean he's gone.'

'What do you mean, gone?' Hermitage asked.

'You know, not there anymore.'

'He's not dead, then?'

'Don't know. Could be, I suppose. But he's definitely gone from Lincoln.'

Hermitage was struggling to readjust his thinking. 'Where's he gone?'

'If they knew that, he wouldn't be gone, would he?'

'Well, why's he gone?'

'Same answer.'

'So, he's not there anymore?'

Gunnlaug looked to Wat and Cwen for some help with this line of questioning.

'And no one knows where he's gone?' Hermitage had to repeat the question.

'That's right,' Gunnlaug spoke quite loudly and very plainly. 'In fact, that's what Godrinius's man said to me.'

'What did he say?' Hermitage asked hopefully.

'That no one knew where he had gone.'

'Oh.'

'Can I go now?' Gunnlaug asked. 'It's been a long day.' He cast a sideways look at Hermitage. 'And it's not getting any shorter.'

Wat gave a nod of the head that indicated Gunnlaug was free to leave.

'So,' Hermitage said when the apprentice had left. 'Nigel of Lincoln has gone, eh?'

'I believe that was the main theme of the message,' Wat said.

'Where and why, that's the question, or rather, questions.'

'Where? Don't know,' Cwen said. 'Even the people of Lincoln don't know, and they were there at the time. Why? Also don't know.'

'It's a bit suspicious though, isn't it?' Hermitage asked. 'Raegnald turns up here asking for Nigel of Lincoln to be murdered, next thing is, Nigel has vanished.'

'Probably very wise of him,' Wat said with another sup of the ale. 'If the Normans wanted me dead I think I'd disappear as well.'

Hermitage came to a clear and concise conclusion. 'We have to find him.'

'We have to what?' Cwen asked.

'He is in danger.'

'I think he knows that. Hence the going away. If we find him, he won't be gone away anymore, will he? And then the Normans can kill him. Which will be our fault.'

'I don't mean we have to bring him home or anything. He could have been taken by someone who wishes him harm. That's why we need to find him.'

'Probably too late,' Wat said casually. 'If the people who want him dead have got him, he'll be dead. If he's got away from the people who want him dead, we had better leave him alone.'

'Anyway,' Cwen said, 'it's dark now and as we don't even know what he looks like, it's probably not the best time to start searching.'

'Not that we can anyway,' Wat noted. 'The man has gone.

Where would we even begin? He could have headed north, south, east or west, or any point in between. We've got no hope.'

'We go to Lincoln and ask around,' Hermitage responded.

'Ask all the people who have already said that they don't know where he's gone?' Cwen asked.

'Someone will know something. A man of such importance can't just vanish without leaving a trail behind. He would have been seen, or spotted packing his things, or passed on the road. We just have to ask.'

'No we don't,' Wat was quite firm. 'As I said, if he's dead, he's dead and there's nothing we can do. If he's not, the last thing he'll want is someone finding him; let alone that someone being the King's Investigator.'

'But if he's dead we need to find out who did it. And if he isn't, we need to find out who wants him dead.'

'You mean you do,' Wat said. 'I think this investigation business has started getting to you.'

'Sleep on it, Hermitage,' Cwen said. 'After all, you must be worn out with all that dozing under trees.'

Hermitage had to agree that there was nothing to be done tonight. He would think about it all again in the morning. He would also think what to do about the way his days were going just at the moment.

By this time of night, he should have performed at least seven acts of worship interspersed with hours of prayer and labour. All he'd done was go for a walk and have a sleep.

As they made their way towards the stairs there was a clattering from below and Gunnlaug reappeared. The young man looked flushed and concerned.

'What's amiss?' Wat asked anxiously, clearly thinking there was some problem in the workshop.

'There's someone creeping about outside,' Gunnlaug reported.

'Creeping about?'

'I went down to the outhouse and there was someone in the bushes.'

'A deer?' Cwen suggested. 'Fox, badger?'

'They'd have run off. This just went very still and I'm sure I saw a pair of eyes.'

'My God,' Wat cried.

'What is it?' Hermitage asked. He'd never seen Wat so fretful before.

'It's Godrinius. He's come to steal his money back.'

Caput VI: Into The Bushes

'How do you know it's him?' Hermitage asked as they made their way to the back of the workshop.

'It's a favourite trick of his. He gives you what he owes, then sends one of his men to follow you and steal it back. They obviously weren't willing to tackle Gunnlaug so they've come to the workshop in the middle of the night.'

'Followed from Lincoln?' Hermitage asked, an entirely different possibility presenting itself. 'What if it's Nigel?'

'Nigel? What would he be doing coming here?'

'He heard of Gunnlaug asking about him, could see that there was someone concerned for him and so followed him back.'

'Why?' Cwen asked.

'Safety. He needs somewhere to go. He's clearly well known in Lincoln so couldn't hide there.'

'And just how did he hear about Gunnlaug? Sitting in the tavern not being spotted, was he?'

'Let's just find this creeper and deal with him,' Wat was decisive.

At the back of the workshop, a large door opened to the outside. This was the route for getting large pieces of equipment in and out as well as being the regular exit for the privy and the outhouse.

The outhouse itself was a solid and well-built structure that housed supplies as well as finished works. Rumour was also strong that it was the hiding place for much of Wat's wealth. His constant denials only confirmed that it must be true.

Wat led the way out, cautiously peering around the door as if suspecting someone was waiting there to attack. The way was clear and so he stepped carefully forward.

The others followed for a moment before Wat realised that Gunnlaug was behind him and ought to be in front. Quickly swapping places, he pushed the apprentice to lead the way as they progressed towards the outhouse.

'Where did you see the eyes?' Cwen whispered.

Gunnlaug pointed out into the darkness and the four of them crept onwards.

'Who's there?' Wat called out after they'd gone a few more paces.

'What are they likely to say to that?' Cwen asked. 'Only me, Godrinius's favourite thief?'

'You might as well come out,' Wat continued loudly.

'Which is almost certain to make anyone run away,' Cwen commented.

'If you don't come out,' Wat called, 'we'll send this woman in to talk at you until you surrender.'

Cwen clipped him round the head.

'Come on,' Wat urged. 'There are four of us, you might as well make yourself known.'

Much to Hermitage's alarm, there was a shaking and rustling from the undergrowth and a patch of the darkness moved. This patch resolved itself into a figure not much lighter than the night. It stepped forward, adjusted its robes and stood before them.

'Oh, great,' Wat sighed. 'Another monk.'

Hermitage could see that this was not just another monk. This fellow wore the habit of his own order of Benedictines but was an altogether higher class of monk than a humble brother or even a prior.

Despite the dark, it was clear that the habit was immaculate, even though it had been dragged through a hedge. The cloth was of the very highest quality and hung around the man as if it had been tailored to perfection. The blackness of the dye was as good as anything Wat would use and lent a profound air of authority to this man.

The scapula and cowl were perfectly laid around his shoulders and back, and the cincture around his waist looked like it had been made by the king's own rope-maker.

Finally, the sandals that peeped from underneath this fine collection of garments appeared to be more like court shoes than the footwear of a humble monk. But then, Hermitage had already concluded that this was no humble monk.

To confirm his suspicion, the monk gave them a bow of the head that made it quite clear it was they who were being honoured.

'I imagine you're keen to explain what a monk is doing in my bushes?' Wat stood with folded arms.

'I will speak with you indoors,' the monk said with deep gravitas.

'People generally knock on the door when they want a conversation.'

'My business will become clear.' The monk gestured towards the workshop as if he owned it and was inviting them in.

'It had better,' Wat grumbled as he followed the man back into his own home.

'Is there somewhere we can talk?' the monk asked when they were back in the workshop. 'In confidence.' This clearly meant that Gunnlaug was to be excluded.

The young apprentice seemed to be quite grateful for this and quickly departed with mutterings that if weaving was going to be like this, he'd become a thatcher; and he wouldn't even need a ladder.

Wat led the way through the workshop and back to the upstairs chamber. He pointedly did not offer ale this time.

'Well?' he asked.

'I am Father Baldice.'

'Father Baldice?' Hermitage questioned with a frown. 'Are you an abbot?'

'No,' Baldice replied conspiratorially. 'I am, in fact, a priest.'

'A priest?' Hermitage expressed his surprise. 'Where is your cloak? You seem to be dressed as a simple monk.'

Baldice nodded at this observation. 'I am in disguise,' he said quite mysteriously.

Cwen could not contain her snort of laughter at this.

'Well, Father Baldice, What do you want?' Wat cast a glance towards Hermitage to see if the name Father Baldice meant anything.

Hermitage could only shrug that he had never met the man before, nor heard of him. This was not unusual as there were so many monasteries, monks and priests in the country that no one could know them all. But Father Baldice did stand out rather. Not only did he go around disguised as a monk, but he did it very poorly. His clothes were of such good quality that there as no way he could be a monk. Hermitage suspected he was something high in the church hierarchy, which nicely explained why their paths had never crossed.

'The King's Investigator,' Father Baldice said with a nod towards Hermitage.

'Funnily enough, I didn't think you'd come here to ask about tapestry,' Wat said.

Hermitage's heart sank. He was already worrying about the fate of Nigel and what he could do about it, and here was more trouble being brought to his door. Well, brought to

Wat's door, but it still found its way to him.

'You've got a murder, then?' Cwen asked.

'Heaven forfend,' Baldice said in a calm and confident manner.

Hermitage couldn't think why anyone would want him if they didn't have a murder to be resolved. The wretched things had become his meat and drink.

'So why the bushes?' Wat pressed.

Father Baldice looked around the room as if making sure that they were not being overheard. He then leaned forward on his stool and beckoned them to draw near.

Wat and Cwen pointedly ignored the beckoning, but Hermitage couldn't help himself.

'I bring information,' Baldice said.

'You bring it very slowly,' Cwen observed.

'Information that will aid the King's Investigator in his work.'

'Don't think he has any at the moment,' Wat said.

'Just so,' Baldice nodded. 'We understand one another, then.'

Wat looked at Cwen and Hermitage in turn. 'I think we've found an idiot in our bushes.'

'A very well-dressed one,' Cwen added.

'The King's Investigator has no work at the moment,' Baldice repeated the words quite slowly and very deliberately.

Wat considered him carefully. 'Well.' He clapped his hands. 'It was lovely to meet you, Father Baldice, thanks for coming and all. Do feel free to knock on the door next time. Would you like to leave through the front, or do you want to use the bushes again?'

'You do not understand,' Baldice said firmly.

'You're right there,' Cwen agreed.

'The King's Investigator has no investigations at present.'

'Do you do this often?' Wat asked. 'Go into peoples' homes and say the same thing over and over again? Folk must jump for joy when they see you coming.'

Baldice sighed, clearly frustrated that they weren't being very cooperative. 'There is no need for the investigator to look into anything.'

'Lovely.'

'Not here,' Baldice said, looking as if he were saying something significant. 'Not in Derby.'

'Not here, not in Derby. This is good news.' Wat rolled his eyes at Hermitage.

'Not in Nottingham, or Newark either.'

'We should have the whole country done by morning.' Wat slumped in his chair.

'Not even in, say, Lincoln?' Baldice added as if coming to the end of his list.

'Oh,' Cwen said this in a very knowing manner. 'Now we get down to business.'

Hermitage could only hope so. Mention of Lincoln seemed to be a bit of a coincidence. How did a cleric in the bushes know about Nigel of Lincoln?

Cwen was nodding. 'And no need for the investigator to look into anyone particular either, I imagine. Anyone called Alwin, say, or Chad, or Wilfrid. Or even Nigel?'

Baldice smiled confidently.

'Nigel of Lincoln?' Hermitage confirmed.

'Nigel of Lincoln?' Baldice seemed to be considering this name as if he'd never heard the words put together before. He gazed at the ceiling. 'Nigel of Lincoln, you say?'

'That's the one,' Cwen confirmed. 'Perhaps the King's Investigator should not bother himself looking into anything to do with Nigel of Lincoln?' This seemed to be an idle suggestion and Hermitage really wasn't clear what was going on. He was used to that, though, and would wait for revelation.

'That is entirely a decision for the investigator himself.' Baldice did his nod once more. 'But it sounds like a wise course of action to me.'

'I expect it does.' Cwen looked at him as if hoping to see his very soul. 'Just who are you, Father Baldice?'

'Simply a humble servant.'

'The only true word in that sentence is "a",' Cwen said. 'There's nothing simple or humble about you. Best-dressed monk I've ever seen and very well informed. If you're serving anyone, it will be a very important person.

'And how did you know about Nigel of Lincoln?'

'I don't.' Baldice did not seem put out by this interrogation. 'It was you who mentioned the name.'

'After you'd suggested Hermitage stay away from Lincoln. And that investigating anyone called Nigel might be a mistake.'

'All of which only took place after we find you skulking around my outhouse,' Wat said. 'What's a humble servant doing out there in the dark?'

Baldice didn't seem inclined to answer this question.

Hermitage surprised himself by coming up with a pertinent question. 'Do you know a fellow called Raegnald?'

'Raegnald?' Baldice tried out the sounds as if tasting a foreign dish.

'Yes, Raegnald.'

Baldice appeared to be thinking carefully about this; either that, or he was really thinking carefully about it. 'Sounds like a Saxon name.'

'It is,' Hermitage confirmed. 'Do you know him?'

Eventually, Baldice shook his head slowly. 'I can't say that I'm familiar.'

'Which doesn't answer the question,' Cwen pointed out. 'And I don't know what else would bring you to our bushes in the middle of the night. It's hardly a resting spot on the way to Jerusalem.'

'He could have followed Gunnlaug,' Hermitage suggested, quite pleased with two insights coming together so quickly.

Wat and Cwen looked at him with interest, and he took some sinful pleasure from watching Father Baldice shift in his seat.

'As you say Cwen, how else would he know to come here? Either Raegnald told him, or he was in Lincoln and overheard Gunnlaug's discussions about Nigel.'

'And what was he doing in Lincoln?' Cwen asked Hermitage the question but stared at Baldice.

'We don't know. He could live there. He could have gone looking for Nigel.'

'He could have gone there to kill Nigel,' Cwen suggested.

'What?' Baldice did speak up now.

'Don't sound so surprised,' Wat said. 'This place is turning into a regular stopping-off point for people who want Nigel of Lincoln dead. You might have to get to the back of the queue.'

Hermitage nodded to himself that this made sense. 'First Raegnald comes here asking for Nigel to be murdered.'

'Murdered? Shocking,' Baldice seemed to have recovered some of his control. He didn't really sound very shocked though.

'Exactly. At the behest of the Normans, he said. We send to Lincoln and find that Nigel has gone.' Hermitage reached another helpful conclusion. 'Then Father Baldice turns up, suggesting that we might not want to investigate any death.'

'I don't think I've said that,' Baldice protested.

'It's what we've heard,' Cwen retorted. 'And who but a killer would want an investigation stopped?'

'Perhaps he was sent by his master, whoever that is, to make sure Nigel was properly killed,' Wat suggested. 'And he doesn't want any investigation to show up his part in it all. Another one trying to impress the Normans?'

Baldice was gently shaking his head as if entertained by this nonsense.

'But what does he find? Nigel has gone. Not murdered, just gone. Well, this is a disaster. No one in Lincoln knows where he's gone either.

'Then a clue arrives in the shape of Gunnlaug.'

'Big shape,' Cwen observed.

'Exactly. A young man to attract attention wherever he goes. Father Baldice observes him and overhears some of the discussion. So, he follows Gunnlaug back here, having nothing useful to find out in Lincoln.

'When he gets here, he discovers that this is the workshop of Wat the Weaver.'

'And the King's Investigator,' Cwen concluded.

'Just so. Which further means that he is well informed. Probably by the Normans.'

Cwen took up the tale. 'And the last thing he wants is Nigel's disappearance being investigated and all this coming out.'

'My my,' Baldice said. 'What fanciful tales you do tell. All part of the creative spirit, I suppose.'

'We can be highly creative when we feel like it,' Cwen said with a horrible leer at Baldice.

'Well,' the priest said with some finality as he stood from his chair. 'I think that just about covers everything.'

Hermitage could only gape. He was fairly sure that nothing had been covered at all. In fact, he wasn't even clear what had been discussed. He'd drawn some very interesting conclusions about this Father Baldice but hadn't got a single thing out of the man.

'More bushes to hide in?' Wat asked.

Baldice simply looked very knowing and confident. 'I shall bid you farewell.'

'In the middle of the night,' Wat noted.

'Early evening,' Baldice corrected. 'And still far to go. I must say, this has been fascinating.'

'Yes, hasn't it,' Cwen said.

As he headed for the stairs, Baldice laid a hand on Hermitage's shoulder. 'You will take my words to heart, Brother.'

Hermitage still didn't know what any of the words meant, but he gave a non-committal sort of shrug.

'I'll bid you goodnight.'

'It was nice to meet you Father Baldice,' Cwen called after him. 'We never forget a face.'

'Wasn't that interesting?' Wat said when they settled again. 'First Raegnald wants Nigel dead, most likely at the behest of some Normans. Now we have a priest on the trail as well.'

'A very well-to-do priest,' Cwen added.

'He was, wasn't he?' Hermitage said thoughtfully.

'Is it significant?' Cwen asked.

Hermitage nodded. 'We've only seen priests and monks that well-presented when they are senior in the church hierarchy.'

'Oh Lord,' Wat said with some sincerity.

Hermitage knew Wat well enough to see that this was not a prayer. He raised his eyebrows in question.

'If the church hierarchy has gone to the trouble of hiding in my bushes,' Wat explained, 'all hope is gone. If important people in the church want him dead, Nigel really has no chance at all.'

Caput VII: Off With Their Heads

'The church wants him dead?' Hermitage was shocked at the very idea. 'Where did you get that from?'

Wat sighed. 'Father Baldice of the bushes made it quite clear that he does not want Nigel investigated.'

'But we don't know who this Baldice is. Yes, he appears to be a high-ranking cleric, but he may not be acting on behalf of the church.'

'Who else?'

'It could be the Normans? Maybe it's personal.'

'At least he didn't ask you to do the murder,' Cwen said. 'That's an improvement.'

'Whatever Baldice's motives,' Wat sounded quite weary, 'we know that he does not want the King's Investigator poking his nose into Nigel of Lincoln.'

'And he took the idea of Nigel's murder very well indeed,' Cwen added.

'We now have two people who don't have Nigel's best interests at heart.' Wat said. 'At least Raegnald was honest about wanting him murdered. Baldice strikes me as the sort of man who could dip his hands in a bucket of blood and come out with no blood on his hands.'

'Oh, my,' Hermitage's confusion was getting the better of him. Obviously, he didn't want a dead body lying in front of him with a knife sticking out of it, but why did things have to be so complicated? And for all they knew, Nigel was alive and well and had escaped the fate that was seeking him out.

'We really have to find him,' he said, his own mind made up, despite all the earlier arguments about why they should do no such thing.

'Oh,' Wat shook his head and sounded worried. 'Bad idea.

Bad idea for everyone.'

'Bad idea? Why?'

'We've been over this. Everyone wants Nigel dead but now he's vanished. If we find him he'll be un-vanished. Soon after that, he'll be dead. If Baldice could follow Gunnlaug, I'm sure he could follow us. And Raegnald? We don't really know where he's gone. For Nigel's sake, we need to leave him alone. Never mind the danger to us.'

'What danger to us?'

'The danger of us getting too close to someone the world wants dead. If we happen to get in the way or are seen to be a problem, we could be next. Particularly with so many important people wanting him gone.'

'And that's assuming we could even find him,' Cwen said. 'We've no idea where he went. If he managed to get out of Lincoln without anyone noticing, he obviously knows what he's doing; what with being such a well-known local.'

'But if we do nothing, he could be unaware of just who is after him.'

'Don't think you need to know who wants to kill you,' Wat said. 'Just that someone does. That's enough motivation to make sure you don't get spotted.'

'We must save him,' Hermitage persisted.

'He's already saved himself.'

'We don't know that. All we do know is that he is in danger. He may have simply left Lincoln for his own reasons and be completely unaware of those following him. Or he does know about them and is in a frightful panic about what to do. He could need our aid.'

'It's all speculation,' Cwen was not convinced. 'The only things we do know are that some people want him dead and he's not around anymore.'

'And so we must help. Once he is safe with us, we can find out what is going on.'

'Ah,' Cwen sounded as if the truth had now been revealed. 'You want to know why they want him dead.'

'Well, of course.'

'And you won't know that unless you talk to Nigel.'

'Possibly.' Hermitage had to admit to himself that the most irritating feature of this whole situation was that he didn't know why Nigel was being marked for death. Knowing why things happened was far more interesting than knowing what the things were.

'But we have to give what help we can. We know people are after him and they wish him ill. It is our duty to do what we can.'

'There's really no point trying,' Wat said. 'Cwen's right.'

'Thank you.'

'This time, she's right. We have no idea where Nigel went. We can't just go wandering off into the countryside in the hope of bumping into him.'

Hermitage had to admit that was true. It was a two-day journey to Lincoln and Gunnlaug had already reported that Nigel was not there. Where else to go? Perhaps Nigel had even escaped by sea. He could have fled east and taken a boat across to Denmark, where the Vikings were. No, maybe not Denmark.

South into the fens? Would Nigel find safety with Hereward and his men?

Even though he knew that there was nothing he could do, he still felt bad that he should just sit here and wait for events to be reported to him. One of these days someone would walk along the track and stop for a conversation; "have you heard about dead Nigel of Lincoln?", they'd say. "Murdered, he was, and no one went to help."

His indecision was even worse than his time out on the track. Then, he had known where Gunnlaug had gone and still couldn't bring himself to follow. What chance did he have now?

'We'll just have to wait and see what the morning brings,' Cwen said.

'News of dead Nigel,' Hermitage sighed.

'In which case, we'll know that there was nothing we could have done,' Wat said brightly.

...

Hermitage's night was fitful, and he had expected no less. Before bed, he considered several of his texts to see if there was any guidance to be found. The evil of murder was absolutely clear, what anyone was supposed to do about stopping one was less well covered. Of course, it was a sin to stand by and let evil be done, but as he had no idea where the evil was, he couldn't see what to do about it.

With all of this swilling around inside his head, he slept for what felt like moments before waking once more to the darkness.

It must have been in one of these short moments that Wat arrived at his bedside and shook him awake.

'Come on, Hermitage,' Wat hissed. 'Wake up, for goodness' sake.'

'What? What is it?' Hermitage was almost certain that the messenger of the Lord had arrived to chastise him for dropping off. When he saw that it was Wat, he relaxed. He knew that if the Lord wanted a messenger, he wouldn't choose Wat the Weaver.

Wat held a finger to his lips. 'There's someone trying to get in.'

'Trying to get in?'

'From outside.'

Hermitage could only assume that anyone trying to get in would do it from outside.

'Father Baldice?' he swung himself from his cot, straightened his habit and shook the sleep from his head.

'Don't know. Cwen and the apprentices are watching the workshop entrance, you and I have got the front.'

Hermitage considered the front of his habit before realising what was meant.

'Who would be trying to get in?' he asked quietly.

'That's what we're going to find out.'

'How do you know there's anyone out there?'

They had made their way towards the front door now and were keeping their heads down for some reason. Perhaps they just assumed whoever was outside could see through wood.

'Noises,' Wat explained. 'Someone trying the doors.'

'Which are all shut?'

'Of course, they are. Otherwise, they wouldn't be trying to get in, they'd be in.'

'What do they want?'

Wat simply looked at Hermitage.

'Ah, right. We don't know.'

'They certainly haven't announced it.'

Just at that moment, there was a rattle of the door.

Wat beckoned Hermitage with a finger. 'You go to the door, pull back the bolt as quick as you can and fling it open.'

'Why me?'

'Because the sight of a monk will put whoever this is off

their guard, if it doesn't actually scare the life out of them. I'll hide behind the door and grab him.'

Even with Wat close at hand, Hermitage was not comfortable about flinging doors open in the face of night-time intruders. 'What if there are lots of them?' he whispered.

'Run,' Wat said unhelpfully. He pushed Hermitage towards the door. 'Quickly, before he goes away.'

'Wouldn't we prefer it if he went away?'

'I'm not having people trying to break into my workshop. If one of them gets away with it, the whole town will be having a go. We need to catch him.'

Hermitage could only swallow helplessly.

'Go on, you never know, it could be Nigel. He's found his way here looking for help and you won't even open the door.'

Hermitage knew that this was an argument with little merit, but it did prompt him to step forward.

Another shove from Wat got his hand on the bolt.

'One, two, three,' Wat counted quietly. 'Now.'

Hermitage shut his eyes, heaved on the bolt and pulled the door open.

A slight and dark-cloaked figure tumbled into the entranceway and sprawled on the floor. Wat immediately leapt from his hiding place and grabbed the shape by the scruff of the neck. He heaved upwards and staggered back as he easily lifted the body from the ground.

'Get off me,' a voice squealed from within the now tangled cloak.

'Absolutely not,' Wat replied, giving the intruder a good shake. 'Is this the best Godrinius can send?'

'Godrinius?' Hermitage asked.

'The thief come to take his money back, I suspect. A little

one to sneak into my workshop. Go and tell Cwen and the others that we made a capture.'

Hermitage gave the pair a nervous glance but was more worried that Wat might do something, rather than be done unto. He scurried off to fetch Cwen.

Moments later they were back in the entrance hall, but Wat was nowhere to be seen.

'Has he been taken?' Hermitage worried away. 'He seemed to have the situation under control when I left him.'

'Up here, Hermitage,' Wat's voice called down from the upper chamber.

He and Cwen exchanged puzzled looks but climbed the steps to see what was going on. It was unlike Wat to invite anyone upstairs, let alone people who tried to break into his workshop with ill-intent.

When they got to the top, Wat was sitting by the fireplace and the new arrival sat opposite, back towards the stairs.

Hermitage could see why Wat had quickly overpowered the newcomer.

The cloaked one was particularly small. Perhaps that was the point, a person who could climb through windows would be more useful than someone of Gunnlaug's size. And presumably, the intention was not to get caught.

The figure turned as Hermitage and Cwen stepped forward.

'Oh,' Hermitage said, stopping in his tracks.

'Exactly,' Wat said.

'This is Godrinius's thief?' Hermitage asked, quite appalled at the idea.

'No,' Wat replied. 'This is Nigel of Lincoln's daughter.'

That was a relief. Hermitage didn't like to think of young children being used as robbers. Next, he wondered what

Nigel's daughter was doing here.

'And what have you given her to eat and drink?' Cwen asked pointedly.

'Give me a chance, I've only just sat down.'

Cwen huffed and stomped off back down the stairs.

Hermitage took another chair and joined Wat. 'How old are you, child?' he asked.

'Nine,' the girl replied. Then she frowned, 'Or ten, one of them.'

'Nine or ten, are you not sure which?'

'It's my birthday, but I've lost track of what day this is.'

'It is Wednesday.'

'I'm still nine then,' the girl sniffed. 'I've been travelling for days.'

'From Lincoln?'

The girl nodded and then dropped her head.

'And you arrived in the middle of the night?'

'I had to keep out of sight, so I've been moving after dark. I had to steal food and hide during the day.'

'Because of your father?'

The girl just sniffed again.

'What is your name?'

'Alyssa.'

'Well, Alyssa, what can you tell us?'

'I woke up one morning last week and my father had gone.'

'Gone?'

'Vanished.'

Cwen now reappeared with a bowl of stew from the kitchen, a piece of bread and a mug of ale. She presented this to Alyssa who immediately started devouring the lot.

As the stew had come from Mrs Grod, Wat's cook, Cwen had been careful to remove all the meat; or rather the bits of things that Mrs Grod called meat. The apprentices might be used to the food but to inflict it on a young girl was too cruel.

Alyssa continued through her mouthfuls. 'And there were people asking where he was and saying how they wanted him. At first, I just said that he wasn't in, but they kept coming back. I overheard one of them saying they would keep me and that would make him come back. So I left.'

'That was very brave of you.'

Alyssa shrugged.

'Your father left no word?'

'None, but that wasn't unusual. He's always out at something or other. Meeting people, dealing with business.'

'And who looks after you?'

'I look after myself,' Alyssa said with pride.

'But you have servants?'

'Yes, but they do everything for my father.'

'We have heard that he is an important figure in Lincoln.'

'Yes,' Alyssa agreed. 'He told me that as well.'

'But this time he didn't come back,' Cwen said.

Alyssa nodded. 'I wandered around town listening to people, no one notices a child. There was lots of talk of him being killed.'

'How awful,' Hermitage sympathised.

'So you ran away.' Cwen clearly thought this had been a good idea.

'And you got this far and saw the workshop? You thought it would be a good place to steal some food?' Wat didn't sound too upset at this theft.

This time Alyssa shook her head. 'No, I was heading here all along.'

'Really?

'I heard all about the King's Investigator. And how he stays at the workshop of Wat the Weaver.'

'Did you?' Hermitage was surprised to hear this. Had his reputation really spread so far? At least now they had to help Nigel. How could any of them turn down a request for aid from a young child?

Alyssa took another bite of bread. 'That's right.'

'So you've come here for our help.'

'Well,' Alyssa looked at them one by one. 'The investigator's help, obviously.'

'Of course.' Hermitage realised that Alyssa would not know that he was the investigator.

'Yes. I want him to do what he's renowned for.'

'We will see what can be managed.'

Alyssa nodded. 'I want him to find those who want to harm my father.' She took on a look of determination and strength.

'Quite,' Hermitage agreed.

'And then descend from the clouds with his mighty sword and chop their bloody heads off.'

Caput VIII: Never Work With Children

'You're the investigator?' Alyssa sounded and looked extremely disappointed.

Hermitage had taken a lot of criticism and disparagement in his short life. Abbots, priors, other monks; they had all had their comments to make and none of them had been encouraging.

To take it from a nine-year-old girl really was too much.

'But you're a monk.' Alyssa clearly couldn't reconcile a monk with an investigator.

'I am,' Hermitage confirmed.

Alyssa considered him carefully. 'Are you allowed to chop peoples' heads off?'

Hermitage took a breath. 'Investigation is not cutting peoples' heads off,' he explained patiently.

First Raegnald, now Alyssa. One moment he was supposed to do the murders himself, now he was supposed to kill the killers. What next?

He wondered if there was any way of letting the world know what investigation meant. If everyone were free to make their own minds up, words would become meaningless. Perhaps he could write a text that listed all sorts of words and what they meant. Some sort of dictionarium, perhaps. Then everyone would agree what they were talking about.

Of course, it would rely on people being able to read, so perhaps wouldn't be so much use. And it would probably take about a hundred years to get such a book produced in a scriptorium, and then there would only be one copy. Not such a good idea after all, but at least the thought had been a distraction.

'But you find out who does murders, yes?' Alyssa persisted.

At least she had got that bit right.

'That's correct.'

'And then you chop their heads off.'

'No.' Hermitage tried to sound very firm about this.

'What do you do with them then?'

'It depends on the circumstances.'

Alyssa frowned at this. 'I don't think people who go round killing other people should not have their heads chopped off.'

'That is for others to determine,' Hermitage said. 'I simply find out who did it.'

Alyssa was still not encouraged. 'You done a lot of these then?'

'Quite a few.'

'And how many heads have you chopped off?'

'None at all,' Hermitage was finding this line of questioning and this child quite annoying.

'Well, that's not much good, is it? All them murders and not a single head chopped off.'

There seemed to be no arguing with this child. Perhaps getting her to think about other things would take her mind off heads and chopping.

'Why are you worrying about murders anyway?' Hermitage asked. 'You say your father has gone but all you have is talk in the town of murder. To leap to the conclusion that your father is dead is unjustified, let alone thinking about punishment and chopping things off.'

'And if we chop peoples' heads off too soon,' Wat put in, 'they won't be able to tell us anything.'

Alyssa seemed to reluctantly accept that this might be a problem.

'Did the people who came say why they wanted your father?' Hermitage asked. 'In fact, did they actually say they wanted to kill anyone?'

Alyssa looked to the floor and mumbled her reply. 'Maybe not directly. But I heard them talking about murder.'

'Surely, if he was a significant figure in the town people asked for him all the time?'

'Maybe,' Alyssa shrugged. 'But they was rude about it.'

'Rude?' Hermitage thought it was quite a step from being rude to committing murder. 'And the talk in the town,' he went on. 'Did you overhear anyone saying why your father might have been murdered?'

'Only that there was strangers looking for him.'

'And strangers commit murder?'

'I don't know, do I?' Alyssa snapped. 'You're supposed to be the investigator.'

'Don't know?' Hermitage found this most frustrating. One moment the child was demanding executions, the next she'd become sullen and unhelpful. 'What did these strangers actually say?'

'Say?'

'Yes, child. What were their words? You have come here demanding that people have their heads cut off simply because they came and asked for your father and that they were rude. And now you can't say what they were asking. Were they threatening?'

'My father's gone, all right?' Alyssa snapped.

'I am sure that many fathers have,' Hermitage replied. 'That doesn't mean they've been murdered.'

'I hate you.' Alyssa now folded her arms and glared at Hermitage.

'What?' Hermitage now felt that he had jumped into a completely different conversation. Moreover, it was already halfway through and he had no idea what was being discussed. All he could do at this was pass the glare on to Wat and Cwen along with his complete confusion.

Wat just looked bemused and had nothing to offer.

Cwen leaned forward and addressed Alyssa directly. 'You stupid child. Are you going to explain properly, or do you need a slap?'

Hermitage gasped at this utterly heartless approach.

Alyssa gave Cwen a look that seemed to be shocked, defiant and challenging, all at the same time.

Cwen shifted in her seat and watched as Alyssa twitched backwards, clearly recognising that the slap was more promise than threat.

Cwen spoke slowly and carefully. 'What did these people say? It's quite a simple question.'

Alyssa dropped her gaze in surrender but carried a look that said she'd remember Cwen and probably come back when they were more evenly matched; or when it was dark and she wouldn't be spotted until it was too late.

'How many were they?' Hermitage prompted. Surely counting people was something this difficult child could manage.

'Three,' Alyssa replied.

'Three people.' Cwen sounded as if this was a complete waste of time; a complete waste of time that was all Alyssa's fault.

'What sort of people were they?' Wat asked. 'Merchants, soldiers, tradesmen?'

'A priest, perhaps?' Hermitage asked with interest.

'No, no priest,' Alyssa confirmed. 'They looked rough. Not soldiers, they didn't have uniforms or anything, but one of them had a scar on his face.'

Hermitage grimaced at the thought.

'And what did they say?' Cwen reminded the girl of the question she was supposed to be answering.

'They was nice at first. They asked if father was in. When I said no, they pushed in and looked anyway.'

'Did they say why they wanted him?' Wat asked. 'Did they use any of his titles?'

'Titles?'

'You know, did they say, "where's the guardian of the wardrobe, or the Ealdorman's crier?", or did they use his name?'

'They just said, "where's your father?"'

'And when they couldn't find him, they were angry?'

'That they were. They said I must know where he was, but I didn't. They grumbled a bit as they left but said they'd be back. That's when I heard one of them talking about taking me.'

'What did they say?' Cwen repeated the words quite loudly. 'You know, what words did they use?'

Alyssa gave Cwen a glare and a stiff reply. 'You must know where he's gone, girl. You'd better have a think about it and come up with an answer. Because if you don't, we might just take you instead.'

'Which is what made you run away?' Hermitage said.

Alyssa nodded. 'I also saw some man watching the house at night.'

'One of the men who had come asking?' Hermitage enquired.

'It was night,' Alyssa spelt out quite rudely. 'It gets dark at night.'

'It'll get dark in your head in a moment,' Cwen snarled. 'This is a very interesting tale, but I don't see what it's got to do with us.'

'You've got to help,' Alyssa instructed them.

Cwen thought about this for a moment. 'No, don't think so.'

'But, the King's Investigator?'

'He deals with murders and dead people. Your father's just run off. Sounds like that's up to him.'

Hermitage knew that he should not mention the fact that Alyssa was just the latest in a line of people interested in her father's death, but he couldn't see why Cwen was being so dismissive. He glanced at her but got a warning look in response.

'He could be dead,' Alyssa managed to say, some genuine distress now poking through her hostility. 'The people in the town said he might have been murdered.'

'People in towns say all sorts of things,' Cwen said. 'And you're one of the rudest most impudent children I've ever met. All of which are extremely good reasons for us to send you on your way.'

'I can't go home,' Alyssa now wailed and burst into tears.

Cwen sat back and her look now became sympathetic. 'And you really have no idea where your father went?'

Alyssa just shook her head.

'Did he usually tell you where he was going?'

'Sometimes.'

'Do you know exactly when he left?' Hermitage asked. 'Did he just go as normal and then not come back?'

'I woke one morning and he wasn't there. That's not unusual. He didn't come back that night, but he often stayed out. The next day the men came asking.'

'And he left no clue?' Hermitage asked.

'No what?'

'A clue. An indication of where he might have gone. No

message for you, no sign, nothing at all?'

Alyssa just shook her head.

Hermitage took a breath and looked at the others. No one had anything to offer.

'So,' Cwen spoke up. 'He could have gone anywhere. North, south, east, west, who knows?'

Hermitage tried to imagine what he would do if people came asking for him. People frequently did come asking for him and most of the time he wished he could run away. The question was, where would he go if he could actually do it? Wat's workshop was his haven; there wasn't anywhere else he would feel as safe.

A church or a monastery, probably, if he had to choose. He never got on terribly well with his fellow monks but if someone were trying to kill him, they would surely offer him sanctuary; unless it was them trying to kill him, of course.

Sanctuary, now that was a thought. If he were under threat he might retreat to the church and seek sanctuary. But then, the church seemed to be as interested in his death as anyone so perhaps that wasn't a good idea.

'Did your father know anyone away from Lincoln?' he asked.

Alyssa looked on the verge of saying, "don't know", once more but at least appeared to be thinking about it.

'Do you have any other relatives anywhere?'

'They're all in Lincoln.'

'Might he have gone to one of them? So that they could hide him?'

'Not our relatives.,' Alyssa seemed quite sure about this. 'They don't like father.'

'Really?'

'Jealous.'

'Is that right?'

'Jealous of his position and his role in the town. They're always trying to get around him for advancement or favour, but he says no.'

'Someone not giving his friends and family preferential treatment?' Wat said. 'He is unusual. And not popular for it, I imagine.'

'Could this be simply a town matter?' Cwen speculated. 'If enough of the people your father has upset got together, they might arrange some trouble for him.'

Hermitage gave a cough at this. Through various facial contortions, he tried to remind Cwen about Raegnald and Father Baldice.

'And they could have gone out of town to get help,' she said, obviously understanding the problem. 'Was your father involved with the church at all?' she asked very nonchalantly.

'The church?' Alyssa didn't seem to understand the significance of the question.

'Could he have gone there for aid or shelter?'

'He did have a few positions with them, I suppose.'

'They weren't jealous of him as well?'

'The church?' Alyssa clearly couldn't understand that.

That just brought another silence during which Hermitage, Wat and Cwen exchanged hopeless glances.

'This really isn't getting us anywhere,' Cwen complained. 'How are we supposed to do anything if we don't even know where he's gone.'

'I thought the investigator was a tracker of murderers,' Alyssa said. 'At least, that was the word. Can't you track him?'

Hermitage smiled as sympathetically as he could. 'Investigation certainly means tracking, but it's not like tracking an animal. It's more about following clues. And I'm afraid we have very few of them. Your father has gone, some men were asking for him and that's about it.'

Alyssa nodded to herself. At least she now seemed to be understanding the problem.

Another silence prevailed while everyone tried to think of anything useful to say. Eventually, Alyssa sighed heavily and spoke.

'There's always Nottingham, I suppose,' she said.

Hermitage held his breath, hardly daring to hope that this might be something useful. In which case, why hadn't she mentioned it before?

'Nottingham?' Cwen was the first to repeat the name of the town and she did so with barely controlled restraint. 'Tell us about Nottingham.'

'It's not far from here.'

Cwen's teeth were gritted. 'Yes, I know that. My question was more about why you are mentioning Nottingham?'

'Because of the castle.' Alyssa said this as if everyone should know what she was talking about.

Cwen leaned too close to Alyssa's face. 'Your next sentence had better be a complete explanation.'

Alyssa looked more puzzled than anything. 'My father travelled to Nottingham to see the Norman Lord. He was summoned. Something about a new position. I suppose it's possible that he might have gone there. I mean, if people were after him.'

Cwen leaned back. 'So you decided to come here looking for the King's Investigator, and not go to Nottingham and ask if your father was in. In fact, to get here from Lincoln you had to pass by Nottingham!'

'All right, all right,' Alyssa snapped. 'I just forgot.'

'Forgot? You think your father's been murdered, you run for your life, and you forgot that he might be in Nottingham?'

'It's an easy mistake to make,' Alyssa defended herself.

'No,' Cwen disagreed. 'No, it isn't. It's an incredibly difficult mistake to make. You'd have to work very hard indeed to make a mistake like that. Well done.' She now threw her hands up in the air and slumped back in her chair.

Alyssa looked at them all. 'It's not my fault,' she complained rather quietly.

'Wrong again,' Cwen replied.

'She is only a child,' Hermitage had to defend Alyssa who was looking completely defeated.

'She's a child idiot,' Cwen concluded.

'At least we know where to look,' Hermitage said.

'Right,' Wat interrupted loudly and jumped to his feet. 'Off to bed with you now, Alyssa.' He nodded to Cwen that this was going to be her job. He got a scowl in return, but Cwen did rise and beckon that Alyssa should follow.

'You've obviously had a bad time of it and a good night's sleep will do you the world of good. We can talk again in the morning,' Wat nodded and smiled.

Alyssa rose tiredly and, completely subdued now, followed Cwen down the stairs.

'Right, Hermitage,' Wat clapped his hands and they sat once more. 'Before we go any further, let's be completely clear about Nigel and Nottingham.'

Hermitage nodded that it would be good to make a plan for once, instead of having to respond to events all the time.

'We are not going to Nottingham and we are not looking for Nigel. There we are.'

Caput IX: Here Pursey Pursey

'But,' Hermitage began.

'I knew you'd say that.'

'We know where he may be.'

'Good for us. Listen.' Wat looked Hermitage in the eye and explained carefully. 'Castle, Nottingham, Normans, bad. If Nigel has gone to Nottingham castle, one of two things will have happened. Number one, his new Norman friends will have welcomed him with open arms and he is safe and well.'

'But,' Hermitage tried again.

Wat held up a hand. 'Two, his new Norman enemies have already killed him. Either way, there's not much we can do, is there?.

'But,' Hermitage said as he felt it was expected. Unfortunately, he didn't have anything to come after his but. Wat's points were good ones. If Nigel had gone to Nottingham he may have walked straight into the people who wanted him dead; at least, according to Raegnald. 'He was offered a position by the Normans.'

'According to Alyssa, who doesn't seem to be the most reliable witness of what was going on in her own house.'

'Why would they want to kill him if he'd been offered a position?'

'Why do Normans do anything that they do? Perhaps one group offered him the position and another group thought it was a bad idea?'

'Hardly grounds for murder.'

'"I'm a Norman, you're not," that's usually sufficient.'

Hermitage knew that was true. They couldn't simply leave the matter there though. There was Alyssa to consider. She had a right to know what had happened to her father. And Raegnald, he couldn't come asking Hermitage to commit a murder for him without the truth being discovered. And then Father Baldice. Could they all simply be ignored while Hermitage, Wat and Cwen returned to their daily business?

Wat looked perfectly happy to return to daily business.

'The very least we can do is go to Nottingham,' Hermitage said with confidence.

Wat slowly shook his head. 'No,' he said thoughtfully. 'If we try really hard we can do an awful lot less than that. Nothing, for example.'

'Nothing?'

'Stay here, do nothing, see? That's got to be the least we can do.'

'What about Alyssa?'

'She could go to Nottingham, I suppose.'

'She's a child.'

'A child who managed to get all the way here from Lincoln. Nottingham will be easy.'

'Wat, you can't.' Hermitage used his most serious and critical tone. 'You cannot send the child of a possibly murdered Saxon from your door.'

'She can leave by the window if she likes.'

Hermitage ignored the comment and carried on as if the plan were agreed. He'd seen Cwen do this on several occasions and it always seemed to work for her.

'We don't need to go anywhere near the castle or the Normans. We just go to Nottingham and see what the gossip of the town is. There may be word of Nigel, particularly if the Normans have killed him. That sort of thing does get talked about.

'If we set off early, we shall be there by noon. A few hours of careful observation and return by evening.'

Wat narrowed his eyes. 'You talk as if it's decided. Have you been listening to Cwen?'

'And I'm sure you wouldn't want Alyssa staying here permanently,' Hermitage said, feeling quite bad about using the child as a bargaining tool.

'Why would she do that?' Wat sounded positively alarmed.

'Where else is she going to go? She can't return home, her father is missing, She'll have to stay here.'

'Cwen can look after her,' Wat said. 'No need to disturb the workshop.'

At that moment Cwen reappeared at the top of the stairs. She looked at them both, her face frozen. 'That child has got to go.'

Wat considered this for a moment as he looked out of the window. 'If we left now we could be in Nottingham by dawn.'

. . .

The next morning, without any explanation to Alyssa about their plans, the four of them took to the road.

'We shall go to Nottingham and see what we can discover,' Hermitage said as Wat and Cwen walked on ahead.

'I only thought he might be there,' Alyssa said. 'I didn't say he was.'

'It is the best information we have. And you never know, this position he was offered may have something to do with his disappearance.' Hermitage hadn't thought of that until he said it. Could it be that Raegnald and Baldice and the men in Lincoln were all connected through this new role of Nigel's? 'Do you know what it was?'

'No,' Alyssa's reply was blunt.

'He didn't tell you?'

'He might have done.'

'What do you mean, he might have done?'

'He goes on and on about all sorts of things but they're all boring.'

'Boring?'

'He's been made an under something-or-other today. Tomorrow he's got to officiate at a ceremony. Then he's got to do some writing in court.'

'It sounds a busy life'

'A boring one.'

'Surely, being invited by a Norman lord to take on some new task would be of interest?'

'Not to me.'

Despite his disapproval of Wat and Cwen's attitude towards Alyssa, he was starting to feel that a weight would lift from him when she wasn't here anymore.

'Can you not remember anything he might have said? He must have talked about it at some length.'

'Oh, he would have done that all right.'

'Well, did he seem pleased or worried?'

'Worried?'

'Was this position something that gave him concern? Had it been thrust upon him and he had no choice? After all, if the Normans ask you to do something, you can hardly say no.'

Alyssa contorted her face into a visage of extreme disinterest. 'He seemed to think it was a good thing. Didn't stop going on about it.'

'There you are then.' Hermitage smiled. 'And what, exactly, did he go on about.'

'Don't know.'

Hermitage breathed deeply and tried to control himself.

He also tried to remember what it was like to be a nine-year-old. His recollections were no help as all he could come up with was how exciting books had been. He did recall that this enthusiasm did annoy virtually everyone around him.

He also recollected his own singular disinterest in the world of adults. The workings of the land, all of them, crops, animals, construction, repair drifted through his attention like a fog. His father and the others around him talked of nothing else but the latest litter of pigs, or which trees would be ripe for felling that winter. If he had been asked to repeat what they'd said, he wouldn't have had a clue either.

None of this stopped Alyssa from being the most annoying child he had ever met. And most of the children he met annoyed him.

'Did he even mention a title?' Hermitage tried. 'Did he say what the position was, even if you can't recall the details?'

Alyssa shrugged.

'Have a good think about it,' Hermitage prompted as gently as he could manage. 'What was the most annoying thing he kept going on about, perhaps?'

Alyssa sniffed. 'There was something about a purse.'

'A purse?' That sounded interesting.

'I like purses,' Alyssa informed him.

'I see. Do you remember what it was about the purse? Was he going to get one?'

'No,' Alyssa snapped. Hermitage seemed to have hit a soft spot.

'What, then?'

Alyssa looked at him and her reply burst out. 'I asked if I could have a look at the purse and he told me not to be stupid.' Her anger at this was explicit. Hermitage had been called many things in his youth, but they had all washed over him. It was clear that Alyssa had bottled the wash and it was regularly flooding out.

'It wasn't a real purse?' Hermitage asked.

'He said he was looking after it. Why couldn't I see it?'

Hermitage nodded that he understood now. 'Sometimes, a purse doesn't mean a real, actual purse.'

'That's stupid.'

'It probably is,' Hermitage agreed. 'But when there's talk of, say, the king's purse, it doesn't mean the king actually has a purse, it simply means his money.'

'Money?' Alyssa seemed interested in money as well.

'That's right. Once upon a time, I suppose it might have been kept in a real purse, hence the name. These days, that wouldn't be practical. The king has so much money, an actual purse would have to be enormous.'

Alyssa nodded now as if she could well imagine an enormous purse full of money.

'When someone is paid by the king, it's said that the money comes from his purse. You know, building a church for example. Well, it might come from the king's purse, but can you imagine how big a purse would have to be to contain a whole church?'

Alyssa laughed at this. She actually laughed. Hermitage was quite surprised to see a smile on her face and reminded himself that this was a nine-year-old girl who had been through a horrible trial. It should be no surprise that she was wary and difficult.

'Do monks have purses?' she asked.

'Monasteries do,' Hermitage said. 'Things have to be bought and paid for and the abbot has a purse. In the case of a monastery, the purse often is a real purse, quite a small one, monasteries not having much money, you see.'

Alyssa nodded.

'So,' he went on. 'Just as the king has a purse, and a monastery has a purse, so do the other lords and nobles of the land. Doubtless, whoever commands Nottingham castle has a purse from which he pays for supplies. Perhaps your father was being asked to look after this?'

Alyssa shrugged.

'Did he look after money for other people? In the town perhaps? Was that sort of thing part of the work he did?'

'Probably,' Alyssa was back to her grumpy self.

Hermitage could see that this was an interesting development. If Nigel of Lincoln was used to managing purses and did it well, it was quite possible that he would come to the attention of the Normans.

And if he was given such authority, he would immediately be of interest to anyone who wanted to see the inside of the purse and get at its contents; the metaphorical purse, that is. But would anyone want to kill him for it? Perhaps Alyssa was right and there were people jealous of his role. In this case, the role of looking after a purse full of Norman money. If ever there were a motivation for murder, money would be it.

Had someone in the Norman court been snubbed when the job went to Nigel? Had de Sauveloy and Le Pedvin decided that getting rid of him was necessary and had discussed the prospect within earshot of Raegnald?

What of Father Baldice's interest? Naturally, the church would be interested in Norman money. There was no one else to endow institutions, after all. Did they want their own man in control?

He had to talk to Wat and Cwen. This would be a very interesting area to explore once they got to Nottingham.

They didn't need to explicitly ask about Nigel, all they needed to do was talk about money; everyone loved to talk about money.

And if this was all about money, it was quite possible that Nigel really had been killed. That was hardly a topic to raise with Alyssa.

'I, erm, just need a word with the others,' Hermitage said. 'Back in a moment.' He was grateful that Alyssa didn't follow and was happy to keep her own company, although she did give Cwen's back a hard stare. It seemed that animosity between the two was mutual.

'Wat, Cwen,' he said when he caught up. 'I have some interesting information from Alyssa that may well aid us in our investigation.'

'Right,' Wat said, hopefully. 'You've discovered Alyssa has relatives in Nottingham and we can leave her there?'

'She's decided to go back to Lincoln?' Cwen asked.

'No, no, nothing like that. It is to do with Nigel and what may have taken him to Nottingham.'

'I've told you,' Wat said impatiently. 'Nigel is really no concern of ours. If he got a role with the Normans and went to Nottingham, that's enough for us. The only reason for going there at all is to get rid of her.' He nodded his head back towards Alyssa who was now kicking stones along the track.

'And if we find he's dead,' Cwen picked up, 'we just have to tell her to find another relative to go and live with. If the men who were bothering her find out Nigel is gone for good, they'll leave her alone.'

'But it might explain what has happened to Nigel,' Hermitage insisted.

'Oh, investigation, you mean.' Wat sounded quite

disheartened at the prospect.

'Which we don't really need to do,' Cwen added.

Hermitage shook his head at their reaction but knew that his next words would change the situation completely.

'It's all to do with the Normans' purse,' he said.

Wat stopped walking. Cwen sighed heavily.

'What purse?' Wat asked.

'The purse of the castle keeper, probably.'

'Why haven't we heard about a purse until now?'

'Because Alyssa didn't think it was important.'

'A purse? Not important?' Clearly, Wat couldn't follow this at all.

'I got her to talk about anything her father might have said. He mentioned something about a purse he was being asked to look after. In Nottingham, for the lord of the castle.'

'That would be quite a big purse, then,' Wat speculated.

'Good job we're not interested in finding out about Nigel, isn't it?' Cwen said.

'Now, let's not be hasty.'

'Hermitage,' Cwen tutted. 'What did you have to mention purses for?'

'It could be motivation for murder.' Hermitage was ashamed to be excited at the prospect. 'Not the money itself, necessarily, but the role Nigel was given.'

'But we know someone who is motivated by money itself; Wat the Weaver.' She turned to Wat. 'I suppose that now we need to do all we can to help the poor child, God bless her.'

'We are going to be in Nottingham,' Wat pointed out as if it had only just occurred to him. 'Finding out about Nigel wouldn't do any harm.'

'Unless it's the sort of harm Nigel might have come across;

a bit like death?'

'We don't even know he's dead. He could be fine.'

'And as soon as we find out, we go home,' Cwen informed him. 'Unless of course…,' she looked very thoughtful.

'Unless what?' Wat asked.

'He needs any help choosing some tapestry to buy with his big purse?

'

Caput X: Enter Aethelthryth

Entry into Nottingham was a straightforward process, as long as one didn't mind being glared at by Norman guards, who seemed to think they could spy the soul of anyone who passed if they stared hard enough.

Of course, Cwen did mind being stared at by Norman guards, or anyone else, come to that, so Hermitage and Wat had to hurry her by with apologetic glances.

They had followed the Roman road east out of Derby, but that went off in the wrong direction after a while and so they crossed onto drovers' trails until they came within sight of the River Trent and could follow its path.

Hermitage found it odd that a place of Nottingham's size had no discernible Roman presence, but then he supposed they couldn't be everywhere.

And where the Romans might not have bothered, the Normans certainly had.

Glowering down on them from the highest point for miles around was an all-too-familiar sight: a Norman castle. It may only be made of wood, but it must have been cut from particularly threatening trees. In this case, the Normans hadn't needed to make the local folk create the hill on which it stood, the rock was ready and waiting for them.

The main fortification sat atop the hill, surrounded by its own high fence. Towards the bottom of the hill, a further fence encompassed a wider area and had a gathering of buildings inside, doubtless stores and sleeping quarters for the soldiers.

Quite noticeably, and probably sensibly, the local Saxons were keeping well away from all this. Their own habitation almost constituted a completely different town, separated by a distance of open land from the invaders.

Of course, the Saxons had been here first, and the Normans wanted the high ground for their castle. The fact that this kept the two parties apart probably suited everyone.

It did present a problem to the current situation though. The Saxons, not being close to the castle, might not be privy to the detailed goings-on within. Similarly, the Normans would keep themselves to themselves and not go spreading their gossip amongst the locals; if any of them could actually understand one another anyway.

'Where do we go?' Hermitage asked. 'The Saxons may not know anything of business over there.' He nodded towards the castle.

'Well,' Wat said thoughtfully. 'Let's think about it, shall we? Here we are, four Saxons wandering into the town. Should we go to the big Norman castle and start asking questions, or do we stay with the Saxons?'

'All right.' Hermitage got the criticism straight away. 'But if we don't find anything we may have to approach the castle.'

'You can,' Cwen said, sounding quite callous.

'Me?'

'Yes, you're King William's investigator. They might be quite pleased to see you.'

Hermitage swallowed. 'Perhaps we should thoroughly question the Saxons first.'

'Yes, let's.'

Leaving the Normans to do whatever it was they did in their castles, the four of them made for the Saxon settlement. At least it seemed that the Normans hadn't worked out that Nottingham meant the village owned by Snotta, a good old Saxon name if ever there was one.

Perhaps, when they discovered the truth, they'd rename it

Williamham, but until then, it retained its Saxon origins.

It also retained its Saxon dwellings, which, Hermitage had to admit, looked quite primitive compared to the Norman constructions.

Simple, wooden-framed huts were dotted about, their thatch roofs in various states of repair. A single large building constituted the centre of the town and had probably been the home of the local thegn. They would soon find out whether the thegn had survived the arrival of the new masters.

It did appear to be a busy and thriving place, but the arrival of four strangers would be noticed by any town, and so the stares they got were understandable.

Hermitage was grateful that no one seemed to recognise them from their last visit.[5] That had been an eventful affair and memories for events could be long.

'Wat the Weaver,' a voice cried out.

Hermitage stopped feeling grateful. At least the voice sounded more interested than threatening. Many of the voices that greeted Wat the Weaver were quite threatening.

They stopped and looked over to see a cheerful, well-dressed looking man coming towards them.

When he arrived, he clapped Wat on the shoulders in a familiar manner and then stood back to appraise him.

'Are you allowed in Nottingham anymore?' the fellow asked brightly. 'And Cwen,' he went on without waiting for an answer to his question.

'Hello, Aethelthryth.' Cwen sounded quite weary at this meeting. 'Although I imagine that's not what you're called anymore.'

Aethelthryth quickly looked around and made gestures to keep their voices down. 'Not a popular name these days,' he

[5] *The Case of the Clerical Cadaver*, just passing through.

explained. 'I'm trying out William.'

'We've already got a William,' Cwen replied.

'Yes,' Aethelthryth agreed. 'And I've noticed people tend not to believe me.'

'Looking and sounding like a Saxon could be what does it.'

Aethelthryth nodded mainly to himself. 'Anyway, what brings you here? Not got Normans of your own to be ruled by?' He now seemed to notice Hermitage and Alyssa. 'A whole merry band, I see.'

'Perhaps we could go somewhere to talk?' Wat asked.

'Do we have to?' Cwen complained.

'Come on,' Wat urged her. 'We know Aethelthryth is a largely dishonest, thieving cheat, but if anyone knows what's going on in a town...,'

'Now, that's unfair,' Aethelthryth complained. 'I paid you right and proper.'

'You paid most people you dealt with,' Cwen agreed. 'But none of them was right or proper.'

Hermitage knew that he was going to find out what all this was, and he knew that it would not be comfortable listening.

This accusation hardly seemed to bother Aethelthryth at all. He gave a nonchalant shrug and pointed towards the large hall, stepping off to lead the way.

'He's a merchant, of sorts,' Cwen explained to Hermitage as they followed. 'Buys and sells. Well, more selling than buying, mostly. Quite frequently selling things he hasn't bought in the first place.'

'Including tapestry?' Hermitage enquired.

'Most definitely tapestry. More specifically the works of Wat and Briston.'[6]

---

6 *The Tapestry of Death* goes into the works of Briston in horrible detail.

'Oh dear,' Hermitage felt embarrassed at the very words. It was clear that these were the old works, the ones that did not bear speaking about, let alone looking at. He certainly didn't want any discussion of the topic with Alyssa walking at his side.

'He told all sorts of people that he had tapestries he could let them have.'

'And he didn't?'

'No, he didn't.'

'Then why would he say he did?'

Cwen sighed. 'To get them to pay him?' She said this as if it should be obvious.

'But when he didn't have the tapestries wouldn't there be trouble?'

'Oh, there usually was.'

Hermitage wasn't following this at all.

'The trouble was for Wat and Briston who were blamed for not supplying the tapestries they'd promised.'

'Had they promised them?'

'No.'

'Then? Oh dear, I feel I am not cut out for this sort of thinking.'

'Aethelthryth would tell Wat and Briston that trouble was coming their way if they didn't let him have some tapestry. Usually, trouble from someone quite important. Of course, he would pay them as soon as he got paid himself.'

'But he'd already been paid?'

'Now you're getting the hang of it.'

'And he got the tapestry and still didn't pay them.'

'That's it.'

Hermitage had to pause for a moment's thought. 'What an awful fellow,' he concluded.

'Rich one though and knows everyone.'

'Hardly reason to have any dealings with him at all, I'd have thought.'

'Oh, once he'd done that a couple of times Wat and Briston could manage him. You know what Wat's like about money.'

Hermitage did and couldn't imagine how anyone managed to live like this at all, let alone sleep at night.

Cwen finished the tale. 'They made Aethelthryth actually agree a price for the tapestries first, usually before they were even made. Then, he goes out into the world and promises the tapestry that isn't yet made for his own price. When the time arrives to settle up, he comes to Wat to buy the tapestry for much less. And Wat refuses.'

'He refused to sell a tapestry?'

'Hard to imagine, I know. And risky. Wat says that the price has gone up to more than what Aethelthryth has already sold it for. Wat having his own sources of information.'

Hermitage's head was starting to swim.

'Things settled down after that. They each knew where the other stood.'

Hermitage was just appalled by the whole sorry tale. He glanced down at Alyssa and shook his head that so young a child should hear of such dishonesty.

Alyssa was nodding thoughtfully. 'I'd think I'd like to be a merchant,' she said.

They arrived at the hall now and Aethelthryth led the way in.

It was more like a farmyard than a dwelling of any sort, let alone one fit for a thegn. Animals were tethered here and there, and the smell might be a natural one but it wasn't very nice. The place was thick with smoke from a fire that was burning almost exactly not below the hole in the roof, and various people seemed to be going about their business as if they were in the market square.

'What's going on?' Hermitage asked.

'The thegn went south with Harold,' Aethelthryth explained. 'So he doesn't need the hall anymore; if the Normans would let him keep it anyway. No sense in letting it go to waste.'

This hall in particular, seemed to be going to ruin, as far as Hermitage could tell.

'Anyway, now that we're out of sight, what's going on?' Aethelthryth rubbed his hands in greedy expectation of something interesting.

'This is Alyssa,' Wat said, gesturing to the girl who was still using Hermitage as some sort of shield from Cwen.

'Hello Alyssa,' Aethelthryth nodded.

'Daughter of Nigel of Lincoln,' Wat said with significance.

'How nice for her.'

'Name mean anything to you?'

'Alyssa?'

'No, Nigel of Lincoln.' Wat was irritated.

'Nigel of Lincoln, eh?' Aethelthryth sounded as if he were contemplating this question deeply. After a few moments, he slowly shook his head. 'Couldn't say.'

'Couldn't say? You either know of him or you don't. There's a possibility he could have come to Nottingham.'

'Lots of people do.' Aethelthryth nodded to himself at this truth.

'For some position at the castle,' Wat specified.

'Oh,' Aethelthryth was much more concerned now. 'I don't know anything about the castle. Normans live there.'

'You don't say?' Wat took half a step closer to Aethelthryth. 'Alyssa is looking for her father.'

'And you're helping?' Aethelthryth seemed surprised at this, which was probably quite understandable.

'We are,' Wat said.

Aethelthryth gave a helpless shrug as if he would love to help but really had nothing to offer.

'A position,' Wat said with a deliberate pause, 'to do with the castle purse.'

Even Hermitage could see Aethelthryth's eyes light up at this.

'I bet you know about the castle purse.'

'Possibly.' Aethelthryth tried to sound nonchalant but had lost a bit of control.

'What with the lord of the castle needing to get supplies.'

'And you being a supplier,' Cwen added.

'Nigel of Lincoln,' Aethelthryth repeated the name.

'That's the one.'

'If only I had something to help my memory,' the man tutted at himself for his absent-mindedness.

Wat took his purse from his belt and absent-mindedly jangled it in his hand.

Aethelthryth's eyes only had one target.

'I might have something that could help you remember,' Wat said.

Hermitage had thought that tales of tapestry and deceit had been bad enough, but here were Aethelthryth and Wat trading over a man's life. It was now obvious that Aethelthryth did know of Nigel but would only tell for money; disgraceful. And Wat was prepared to offer the money. He didn't know which of them was worse.

'Anything coming back to you?' Wat chinked the coins in

the purse.

'Now that you come to mention it,' Aethelthryth said cautiously, clearly wanting to see the money before he said any more.

'That's excellent,' Wat said with a smile, deliberately putting the purse back at his waist. 'Because Brother Hermitage here is King William's own Investigator and he really wants to hear it.'

'What?' Aethelthryth squeaked and actually jumped away from Hermitage as if in fear of plague.

'King William,' Cwen repeated. 'You know, the Norman.'

'Of course, I know. What do you mean he's the King's investermator?'

'Investigator,' Cwen corrected happily. 'And he does it for the king. It means to track. It's from the Latin.'

Hermitage could only offer a sympathetic and apologetic smile. This had clearly come as a great shock to Aethelthryth, which was probably as intended.

'I don't care where it's from. What are you doing with the King's what-do-you-call-it?'

'Investigator,' Wat repeated. 'It's a long story. Mostly we deal with murder, don't we, Hermitage?'

Hermitage gave a reluctant nod.

'Murder?' Aethelthryth's shriek said that he really was having a hard time with this.

'That's right. Someone gets murdered and Hermitage has to work out who did it. We help.'

Aethelthryth had clearly concluded that the next murder might be him. Wat was clearly happy with the conclusion. 'So, Nigel of Lincoln. You said you remembered something?'

'Yes, yes,' Aethelthryth nodded and gabbled. 'Of course. Anything to help the King's, erm, invigilator.'

'Investigator,' Cwen corrected again. 'Shall I write it down for you?'

'No, no, that won't be necessary.'

'But you do know of Nigel?'

'He was here.'

Alyssa stepped forward and glared at Aethelthryth, who backed off as if faced with an army of imps. 'He came to the castle, some appointment or other, from what I heard. A Saxon going in that place voluntarily gets noticed.'

'An appointment to do with a purse?'

'Could be, I don't know the details.'

'And where is he now?' Alyssa demanded.

'Gone.'

'Gone?'

'Vanished, they say. He met the lord of the castle and then he was gone.'

'Gone where?'

'No one knows. Or if they do, they're not saying. Here, you could track him.'

'Yes, thank you very much,' Wat sneered a little.

'Did he come out again?' Cwen asked. 'After he'd met the lord?'

'I don't know.' Aethelthryth clearly wanted the questioning to stop; he'd also like to go away now and never to have met these people in the first place.

'A Saxon coming out of that place would get noticed,' Cwen pointed out.

'No one's talked about it. And there comes a point at which looking the other way is for the best.'

'Hm,' Cwen didn't sound satisfied.

'That's all I know. Honestly. I wouldn't lie to the King's, erm, man, would I?'

'Yes,' Wat said nonchalantly. 'You probably would.'

'But I'm not. It's the truth.'

Wat considered Aethelthryth very carefully and seemed to reluctantly conclude that there was nothing more to do.

'Can I go now?' Aethelthryth asked with sincerity.

'I suppose so,' Wat replied. 'But don't leave Nottingham, the King's Investigator may want another word.'

Hermitage though that was a bit odd as he hadn't said a single word so far.

'So,' Wat said with heavy resignation when Aethelthryth had skipped out of the hall. 'I suppose that's that. We know Nigel came here, but where he's gone might forever remain a mystery.'

Hermitage couldn't see that at all. 'We know where he went,' he said. 'We only have to go and ask the Normans.'

Wat visibly sagged where he stood. 'I knew you'd say something stupid like that.'

Caput XI: Up To The Top Of The Hill

'Nigel went to the Normans,' Wat said as if this was a final conclusion of all questions. 'And he went willingly. For all we know, he's in there still, alive and well and looking after the lord's purse.'

'And if he isn't?'

'If he isn't, then he isn't.'

Hermitage frowned as that made no sense at all.

Wat gave a sideways look at Alyssa, clearly not willing to say what the other possibility was. 'If the Normans have done something, there's not much we can do about it. And if Nigel's left again, we're back where we started.'

Cwen spoke up. 'I thought you were the one with the deep abiding interest in this purse?'

'That was before I saw where the Normans were keeping it.'

'They might want a nice tapestry for their castle,' Cwen said sweetly.

'They only have to come and ask.'

'Is this Wat the Weaver speaking? The man who persuaded Dunston of Etwall to buy four tapestries?'

Wat just made a grumbling noise.

'The Dunston of Etwall who sneezed every time he got near wool?'

'Happier times,' Wat mused. 'And Dunston was a harmless Saxon landowner, not a murderous Norman.'

'My father could be in the castle,' Alyssa pointed out quite vigorously. 'We can't come this far and not find out.'

'Off you go then,' Wat said quite heartlessly.

'Wat!' Hermitage chastised.

'It's a good idea,' Wat said, obviously thinking quickly. 'If any of us go up there we'll have trouble. Alyssa could go and say she's asking for her father, Nigel. It's perfectly reasonable.'

'And if anything has happened?' Hermitage asked pointedly, also trying to avoid saying anything too worrying in front of Alyssa.

'What could have happened?' Alyssa asked.

'We don't know,' Hermitage said. 'That's the point.'

Alyssa didn't look satisfied with this answer. 'I'll go and ask, I don't mind.' This statement was a clear accusation that Wat did mind but shouldn't.

'There you are.' Wat was content.

'We are not sending a nine-year-old child to knock on the door of a Norman castle on her own.'

'That's fine. You can go with her.'

'What?'

'You are the King's Investigator, they won't mind you.'

'And you are a monk,' Alyssa pointed out.

Wat seemed to have grasped this suggestion with both hands. 'What's the point of being King's Investigator if you can't knock on a castle door and ask a simple question?'

Hermitage had a horrible sinking feeling about this. He looked to Cwen for support. She just shrugged back as if it wasn't actually a bad idea.

'You can do what you do best,' she said. 'Tell the truth. You'll like that.'

Hermitage couldn't help but gape.

'You're Brother Hermitage, the King's Investigator, and you are helping this young child find her father, Nigel of Lincoln. You heard he came to the castle and wondered if he was still there.'

It all sounded straightforward the way Cwen said it.

'The truth and nothing but the truth. What can go wrong?'

Hermitage knew perfectly well what could go wrong. He could be murdered. If the people in the castle had killed Nigel, they wouldn't hesitate to do the same to anyone who came asking about him.

He couldn't let Alyssa hear his worry, but then neither could he take the child into such danger.

He immediately imagined the castle door being thrown wide to reveal Raegnald, probably standing on the body of Nigel.

'Erm,' was all he could say.

'We'll come to the bottom of the hill with you,' Cwen said helpfully.

'And wait,' Wat added.

'Coming to our aid if there is trouble?' Hermitage asked.

'Well, we'll wait, anyway,' Wat said. 'See what happens.' He gave a grin which was no help at all.

Hermitage was resigned to the course of action. It sounded perfectly reasonable, and he always had trouble arguing against perfect reason. That didn't mean he had to like the idea and he didn't.

'We'll probably be spotted long before we get to the castle itself.' He couldn't immediately see why this would be a problem, but he was keen to come up with as many as he could.

'That'd be good,' Wat said. 'Then the soldiers can escort you, won't be such a surprise for whoever opens the gate.'

'Oh, dear.'

'Come on,' Cwen encouraged. 'It's the only way to find anything out for sure. And you won't come to any harm. King's Investigator, remember? William?'

Hermitage nodded silently.

'Just mention the name and everything will be fine.'

. . .

The walk to the castle hill was like a long walk across an open space towards a castle sitting on top of a hill; a castle full of people who wished him harm. He knew they wished him harm because they wished everyone harm.

Alyssa seemed quite excited at the experience, but then she probably had some hope of finding her father.

Quite a long way before the hill began, Wat and Cwen paused and said that they would wait here. Behind this tree. Where they couldn't be seen.

'I don't see why we can't all go,' Hermitage said. 'After all, Wat and Cwen are known as well as I.'

'We don't want the Normans to think they're being attacked,' Wat said in all seriousness.

'By a monk, a girl and you two?' Hermitage asked incredulously.

'You know what they're like.'

Hermitage did know, and that was the main problem.

'Go on,' Cwen urged. 'The sooner you start the sooner it'll be over.'

Hermitage could only think that if he never started it wouldn't have to happen at all.

With a shove in the back from Cwen, he began his awful journey. As he trudged along, Alyssa almost skipping at his side, he tried to think what he was going to do when the Normans said, '"Ah yes, Nigel of Lincoln, we killed him, you know. Would you like the body?"

He supposed that that would be a resolution of the whole question, but what would it do to Alyssa? The first thing he had to do was mention the fact that she was Nigel's daughter. That way, the Normans might be more circumspect in delivering any bad news they had.

He had to confess he had never met a circumspect Norman, so all he could do was hope.

They had only progressed a few paces up the incline towards the first wooden fence when the gate opened and a troop of soldiers came out. Surely they hadn't despatched half-a-dozen men to deal with one monk and a small child.

The soldiers didn't immediately pay them any attention at all, which was obviously good. Perhaps this was a routine patrol and their meeting was a complete coincidence. It seemed too much to hope, but there was no point turning around and running away now.

Monk and child walked slowly up the hill while soldiers marched down. Actually, they didn't march down, they more sort of ambled down and looked quite disorderly, if Hermitage had been asked to comment; which he hadn't, and he wouldn't anyway.

The space between the two groups shortened and Hermitage swallowed hard, waiting for the instruction to halt and explain themselves.

With the men almost upon them, Hermitage put his arm around Alyssa's shoulder and drew her close. Her earlier cheerfulness had dissipated at the sight of some real live Normans.

Walking two-by-two as the path was quite narrow, the men split apart as they arrived at Hermitage and Alyssa cowering in the middle of the track. Doubtless, they would surround the new arrivals and have them at their mercy. Hermitage closed his eyes and waited for the inevitable.

Then he opened them again and watched as the soldiers

carried on walking down the hill having paid them not the blindest bit of attention. In fact, they were chatting to one another amicably and one of them was eating an apple.

As he finished the fruit, the soldier turned and threw the core at Hermitage. His fellows had a good laugh at this and carried on down the hill.

Hermitage had absolutely no explanation at all, but he wasn't going to start chasing a band of Norman soldiers to find out what they were up to. He just had to assume that a monk and a child were no sort of threat and so were welcome to pass.

He looked back down to Wat and Cwen's hiding place and could see them gesturing enthusiastically for him to continue up the hill. Straight after that, they vanished behind their tree, clearly anxious to avoid the soldiers who were now heading their way.

'Come then,' Hermitage said, trying to sound as optimistic as he could. 'We are obviously of no interest to the Normans. We shall see what we can discover.'

They now reached the first of the palisades that protected the keep sitting atop its hill and the gate was firmly shut.

Taking some courage from the fact that the first soldiers had ignored them, Hermitage banged on the gate. He then banged a second time when there was no answer.

Looking around for something to make more of a noise, he picked up a rock from the side of the path and used this to hammer out a call.

'Oy,' a voice called from inside. 'It is open.'

Hermitage hadn't thought of that. He didn't know much about castles but weren't they meant to keep people out? He pushed at the gate, and it swung back on its hinges.

Inside, just to the left of the path sat a small hut, roughly built and topped with a very ineffective looking thatch. Outside of this another Norman soldier sat on a three-legged stool. He seemed to be whittling something from a small piece of wood. He looked up as they appeared.

'A monk, eh?' the man stated the obvious in a thick Norman accent. 'Is it alms, or are you trying to sell the child?' He glanced at Alyssa. 'Not that we'd get much work out of her. And anyway, Normans don't have slaves, not like you disgusting Saxons.'

'No, no,' Hermitage had to protest quickly. 'Nothing like that at all. I am a man of God.'

The Norman simply spat on the floor at this.

Hermitage knew that many Saxon men of God had slaves; the more senior the man, the more the slaves. There wouldn't be many households and certainly no estates in the land that were not worked by a good number of slaves, most of whom were Saxon themselves.

Of course, Hermitage had encountered many slaves in his time and had frowned upon their condition and the whole practice of slavery. Unfortunately, rulers spiritual and secular were quite clear on their support for the awful business, which frequently was a business. And the Bible itself had quite a lot to say about obedient slaves so Hermitage's position was in a minority, which meant he had to keep it to himself.

If the Normans really were against it, there might be some good from this conquest after all.

'We are seeking the girl's father.'

The soldier now frowned at Alyssa. 'She's a bit old to have a Norman father.'

'We think her father came here, Nigel of Lincoln?'

The soldier showed no sign of recognition. 'You'd better

ask at the keep,' he said, nodding up the hill.

'I am free to go up there?' Hermitage asked. Partly, he was doubting the security of this castle, but he also harboured a secret hope that he would be told to go away.

'Do as you please,' the soldier said. 'I don't think a monk and a girl are going to take the castle.' The soldier had a good laugh at this.

Hermitage had to ask. 'Don't you need to keep the gate closed to stop the Saxons?'

'That lot?' the soldier chortled. 'We can see them coming a mile off, and I doubt they could even take their own hats off.'

Hermitage shrugged at Alyssa, and they started to make their way up the hill towards the second gate.

This one was closed and barred as if the proper Normans stayed at the top of the hill while the lazy and useless were left at the bottom.

Hermitage hammered once more at a Norman gate and this time was answered promptly. A small window-like section of the gate opened, and a well-presented Norman soldier's face appeared.

'What do you want?' This soldier demanded in a much more military style.

Hermitage gave a short bow of the head. 'I am Brother Hermitage.'

'There's no Brother Hermitage here,' the man said.

'No, I am Brother Hermitage and this is Alyssa.'

The soldier looked down at Alyssa and seemed puzzled.

'We are seeing if her father is here.'

'Her father's a monk called Hermitage?'

Hermitage wondered if the language was causing a problem, or if this was simply a stupid Norman. He tried again, spelling it out very clearly. 'I am Brother Hermitage and this is Alyssa, and we are looking for her father, Nigel of Lincoln.'

So many names at once seemed to cause the Norman no end of trouble. 'What are they all doing here?'

'They aren't here,' Hermitage sighed. 'Is Nigel of Lincoln within?' He thought that keeping the questions simple might help. One person at a time might be best.

'Lincoln?' the man asked. 'That's miles away.'

'And we have come miles to see Nigel.'

The soldier frowned but at least he seemed to understand this short sentence.

'Giscon, what is it?' A female voice drifted over the wall.

'Saxons, my lady.' The soldier, who at least had a name, turned his head back to speak to someone and sounded quite disgusted at his own news.

'What do they want?'

'Nigel,' Hermitage repeated, hoping that the soldier would remember the name for at least a moment.

'It's a monk,' Giscon reported back. 'And a girl.'

'A girl?'

Soldier Giscon peered back at them to check. 'Quite a small one.'

'Well, open the door.'

'Open the door?' Poor Giscon sounded rather alarmed at this instruction.

Uncharitably, Hermitage thought that this might be because he didn't understand it.

'A monk and a small girl are not going to be a problem, are they?'

'I suppose not,' Giscon grumbled.

'And we don't want any unpleasantness.' The lady said this quite pointedly as if unpleasantness was a common occurrence where Giscon was concerned.

'No, my lady,' Giscon muttered. He closed the small window and the sound of bars being lifted was now heard.

The gate was heaved back, and Hermitage once more drew Alyssa close in case any threat materialised. The woman had sounded reasonable and may well be the lord's wife, but she would still be Norman.

Inside the enclosure, a very well-dressed young woman stood looking out. She was a contradiction in this rough place, wearing a fine yellow dress of no little expense and shoes that were certainly not made for walking up and down any hills.

She had a slightly haughty look about her and appeared to be looking down her nose at the new arrivals.

Hermitage's mouth could only fall open at the sight.

The haughtiness of the lady vanished as she saw Hermitage and her face pinched into a shape that would put a vindictive weasel to shame.

'You,' she almost spat.

'Aha,' Hermitage's voice quaked. 'Lady Aveline, how nice to see you again.'[7]

[7] *The Tapestry of Death;* shows that it wasn't very nice seeing Aveline the last time.

Caput XII: Old Friends-ish

'Where's the other one?' Lady Aveline demanded.

'Erm, other one?' Hermitage asked meekly.

'The weaver.' Aveline said the word as if it were akin to a dung gatherer's apprentice.

'Oh, erm, he's somewhere or other.'

'I'm not surprised he's hiding. You've got some pluck turning up here.' Lady Aveline had now put her hands on her hips, and the expensive yellow gown was looking an awful lot more threatening all of a sudden.

'We, er, that is, I didn't know you were here, my lady.'

'Don't you, "my lady" me. You, you...,' she seemed to be searching for the most insulting name. 'Monk,' she came up with. 'And you've got a new one to take from their life and then ruin, have you?' Aveline gave Alyssa a passing glance.

'Not at all,' Hermitage protested. 'We are helping Alyssa find her father.'

Alyssa was watching this exchange with great interest.

'Likely story.' Aveline dismissed the explanation. 'You watch this one child,' she warned Alyssa. 'Do you know what he did to me? Him and that weaver of his?' Aveline did not wait for an answer. 'Wrenched me from a perfectly happy existence and delivered me into servitude.'

'With your father,' Hermitage had to point out.

'Don't interrupt. My father is Gilbert, now lord of this castle, which makes me a lady. A lady can do what she likes, can't she?' Again, this seemed to be a rhetorical question. 'And I did do what I liked until a monk and a weaver had me dragged away and thrown into the castle keep.'

'Which was where you lived,' Hermitage responded. 'We only brought you back to your father at his request.'

'You interfered is what you did. And you had no business.'

Hermitage was perfectly comfortable that their actions had been entirely reasonable. They had been instructed by Gilbert, a Norman lord, after all, to go and find his daughter as he had been genuinely concerned about her. They did what they were told. Just because the daughter didn't want to be found shouldn't be his problem.

Unfortunately, he wasn't perfectly comfortable being attacked by Lady Aveline in this manner. He had little hope that Wat would see what was going on and come to his aid; he was as wary of Aveline as everyone else.

There was absolutely no question of raising the topic of where they had found Aveline and what she had been up to. Hermitage thought that abject submission was better than fighting back in the face of this yellow onslaught.

'And now look at me!' Aveline instructed.

Hermitage did so but didn't know what he was supposed to do next.

'Back in another wretched castle keep.'

'Ruling the whole of Nottingham,' Hermitage suggested.

'A gathering of lazy Saxon peasants,' Aveline summed up the town. She folded her arms now and considered Hermitage with horrible care. 'Perhaps I should get Giscon to throw you in the lock-up.'

'But, my lady…,'

'That'd show you. You deserve a punishment for what you did. And, as you say, I am Lady Aveline, ruler of Nottingham.'

Hermitage was going to have to point out that she was actually the daughter of the ruler of Nottingham, and that it was him they'd like to see. However, if she threw him in the lock-up, he wouldn't be able to point anything out. And he did not think that Aveline was open to reasonable argument.

'Well, well, well.'

Hermitage almost sank into his own habit with relief as he heard Wat's voice behind him.

'If it isn't the lovely Lady Aveline.'

The lovely Lady Aveline appeared to be lost for words. Her fists were clenched, and she had gone so stiff that she looked like a new yellow palisade.

'Weaver,' she managed to grind out through firmly clamped teeth.

'Fancy seeing you here,' Wat said brightly. 'Gone up in the world, then?' He turned to Cwen. 'Last time Hermitage and I saw Aveline she was in a dingy keep in the woods with her father, Lord Gilbert. It was her we had to get while you were having your chat with Virgil.'[8]

Cwen nodded that she had no problem recollecting those events.

'Spent a lot of her time with Briston,' Wat added. 'Isn't that right, Lady Aveline?' He emphasised the word, "lady" as if it were something very disreputable indeed.

Hermitage didn't know whether to be pleased or even more nervous as he saw Aveline's face redden.

'Oh, did she?' Cwen asked in a very knowing way. She even squinted at the lady and tipped her head on one side. 'Can't say I recognise her, and after all, I did do a lot of Briston's actual work.'

'Maybe you don't recognise the dress,' Wat suggested with a most improper leer.

'Shut up,' Lady Aveline instructed. 'I'll have you all thrown in the lock-up. Giscon,' she called.

'What's amiss, my dear?' A deeper voice replied, and Lord

---

8 *The Tapestry of Death* again; you're going to have to read it now.

Gilbert appeared from the door of the keep.

Lady Aveline turned and looked at her father. Then she glared at him. After that, she glared at everyone else before stomping off into the keep as stompily as her fine footwear would allow.

'You see,' Cwen said to Alyssa. 'You carry on and that's how you'll end up.'

Lord Gilbert, a giant of the Norman warrior race, a man ready at a moment's notice to throw his life into battle wielding no-doubt mighty weapons, sagged with resignation as he watched his daughter go. His fate this day was clearly not a happy one.

He turned back to the new arrivals. 'Aha,' he cried with some pleasure, throwing off the pall of Aveline's discontent. 'If it isn't the King's Investigator.' He stepped forward and clapped Hermitage on the shoulders. 'And the weaver, Wat.' He looked quizzically at Cwen and Alyssa.

'This is Cwen,' Wat introduced her. 'Also a weaver who got caught up in the business last time we met.'

Cwen gave a cursory nod, which carried all her disapproval of Normans, their castles and everything that went with them.

'And this is Alyssa,' Hermitage said. 'It's about her that we've come.'

Gilbert gave them a disapproving scowl. 'We Normans don't approve of slavery, you know.'

'She's not a slave,' Hermitage insisted. Honestly, did the Normans believe that everyone in England was someone else's slave?

'If you say so.'

'We do,' Wat added. 'She's the daughter of Nigel of Lincoln.'

'Ah, I see.' Gilbert nodded. 'He didn't tell me he had a child.' Gilbert said this as if Nigel was to blame for having a daughter.

'You've seen him then?' Hermitage asked. 'He is here?'

Alyssa's face brightened and she took half a step forward.

'He was,' Gilbert said. 'To be honest, I don't know where he is now.'

'Oh,' Hermitage sagged with disappointment. 'But you did see him. When was this?' He had a new puzzle now. If Raegnald's report was correct, the Normans wanted Nigel dead. Yet here was Gilbert, apparently quite happy that the man had been here. Unless Gilbert had killed him, of course, and just didn't know where the body was?

'Come inside,' Gilbert said. 'This is not the place for conversation. Come in, take some wine.'

Hermitage thought that Gilbert sounded as if he were grateful for their visit. That was a bit odd, considering he was the lord of the castle of Nottingham and had the whole place to himself. Well, him and Aveline; in the keep probably, with just one another for company. Hermitage now saw why Gilbert might be pleased to have some friendly visitors.

Gilbert led the way into the keep which was a considerable improvement on the last one they had visited together. That had been more like a combined stable and privy on top of a pile of mud. This was much more like a permanent construction and long-term home.

The doors were well made and properly fitted. The floor had stone flags at the entrance and wooden boards across the rest of the space which stretched out in front of them.

This was a single, open area with supplies stacked around the walls and a single large table in the middle. A fireplace at the back, large logs gently glowing within, had leather-covered chairs before it.

A wooden ceiling not far above their heads told of another storey above, probably Gilbert and Aveline's private chambers.

For a castle of the invaders, Hermitage thought it remarkably comfortable.

'Aveline's doing,' Gilbert said as if apologising for the neatness and order. 'She won't even have straw on the floor,' he gave a rather pained laugh and led the way to the fireplace.

Bidding them all sit, a servant appeared without instruction.

'Wine,' Gilbert said. 'You will take wine?' He asked this as a man who didn't get the opportunity very often.

'Oh, yes,' Wat confirmed as he got comfortable in his chair. 'That's interesting,' he said, pointing to the wall above the fireplace.

'One of Aveline's touches,' the lord of the castle explained.

The wooden wall above the fire had a pattern painted on it. As far as Hermitage could make out, it looked to be a shield with some flowers on it. Above that, a Norman helmet seemed to have swirls of leaves sprouting from it. Below the shield, the name "Gilbert" was written in red. The whole thing was quite disconcerting.

'She says everyone's doing them these days.' Gilbert didn't sound at all sure about this.

'Everyone?' Wat asked, standing to peer at the thing.

'So she says. I said that I didn't know anyone who did one, and apparently that's typical.'

Wat shrugged. 'Erm, what is it?'

'Arms.'

'Arms?'

'That's what she said.'

'What's the point of doing a picture of some arms? I can see there's a shield and a helmet and your name, but what are the flowers and the leaves for?'

'She likes flowers and leaves,' Gilbert's shrug said that this was entirely incomprehensible to him. 'Daughters of the other families come up with their own.'

'Do they?' Wat sounded just as confused. 'And what do they do with them?'

'They talk about them.'

'Talk about them.'

'So I'm told.'

'Really?'

'Ah,' Gilbert called with relief. 'Thank God, the wine.' He took a goblet from the servant and indulged in a deep draught.

'Now then,' he said, with a positively nervous glance at the arms above the fire. 'You were asking about Nigel.'

'That's right,' Hermitage said. 'Alyssa is his daughter, and she came to us saying that he had vanished from his home in Lincoln. She had heard some mention of him taking a position in Nottingham and so we came looking.' There was no way he was going to mention Raegnald or Father Baldice. If it was true that the Normans wanted Nigel dead, they would find out soon enough.

Gilbert gave a slight frown. 'Seems a paltry task for the King's Investigator?'

'Ah well, Alyssa sought us out.'

Alyssa nodded to confirm this.

'Something about a purse?' Wat said as nonchalantly as he could.

'What do you know about the purse?' Gilbert asked in all seriousness.

'Nothing, nothing at all,' Wat held up his hands. 'It's only something Alyssa heard her father mention.'

'You shouldn't know about the purse.'

'We don't. It was only a word.'

It was obvious that this purse was a touchy subject. Perhaps Nigel had stolen it?

'You said that Nigel had been here?' Hermitage moved the subject away from the purse.

'That's right.' Gilbert still didn't sound very happy.

'But has gone now?'

'So it seems.'

'Were you expecting him to go?'

Gilbert didn't reply immediately and seemed to be thinking carefully about what he should say. 'You are still the King's Investigator?' he asked.

'Yes,' Hermitage confirmed.

'Bound by oath to the king?'

'Well...,' Hermitage had never sworn an oath to the king, but then he'd never wanted to be King's Investigator in the first place. 'There's never been any formal ceremony. The king and Lord Le Pedvin just seem to summon me when the need arises.'

Gilbert was obviously considering whether to share the information he had. Hermitage was nervous that this might be the fact that Nigel was dead. He gave Alyssa a sympathetic glance.

'Alyssa already knows of the purse,' he said, hoping that this was Gilbert's main concern. 'As you know, Wat and I have been in service of the king for some time now, Cwen as well.'

Cwen gave a little growl that she did not like the description of being in service of the king.

'Hm,' Gilbert seemed to reach a conclusion. 'Nigel was here.'

Alyssa gasped with relief. Hermitage nodded encouragingly, but even if Nigel had been here, he wasn't now and might have come to a sorry end.

'About the purse?' Wat asked.

Gilbert nodded. 'It was the king's idea.'

'The king?' Hermitage always thought of William with fear and trepidation and hadn't expected him to have anything to do with this business.

'A Saxon responsible for the purse,' Gilbert said with resignation.

'Why would the king want that?' Wat asked.

Gilbert could only shrug.

Hermitage could see that there might be some reason in it. 'It could be simply that Nigel had the skills and the reputation.'

'But a Saxon?' Gilbert asked rather plaintively.

'Mayhap the king seeks to involve Saxons in the business of the kingdom. Trustworthy ones, of course. It would show that the life of the country is returning to normal and that if the Saxons cooperate, they have no need to fear.'

Gilbert grumbled at this suggestion. He'd obviously rather they did have something to fear.

'Nigel came here to discuss the purse?' Cwen now asked.

'That's right. He arrived only a day or two ago.'

'Why didn't he tell me where he was going?' Alyssa complained. 'Why just vanish without word?'

'It is a significant step,' Hermitage said. 'King William asking a Saxon to take on a position of responsibility. There could be those who are against the idea, on both sides.'

The rumbles from Cwen and Gilbert said that two of these

were in the room.

'And where is Nigel now?' Hermitage asked.

'Gone.'

'Gone back to Lincoln? Or gone to collect his belongings and return here?'

'Just gone. Vanished,' Gilbert said.

'Not again?' Cwen complained. 'The man's got a habit of vanishing.'

'You didn't expect him to go?' Hermitage checked.

'No. He came here and we discussed the business. The next morning he was gone.'

'Perhaps he didn't fancy the job?' Wat suggested. 'Norman lords who ask you to do something being hard to turn down.'

Alyssa sagged in her chair.

'Don't worry,' Hermitage reassured her. 'We know your father was here.'

'He left no word?' Cwen asked.

'None.'

'And no sign of him being taken?'

'From inside the keep of a Norman castle?' Gilbert asked.

'He left of his own accord, then,' Wat said.

'Or was taken by a Norman,' Cwen suggested.

Gilbert shook his head. 'He was here at the king's behest and under my protection.'

'Of course,' Cwen agreed. 'All Normans agree with one another about every little thing and wouldn't dream of defying their duke.'

Gilbert's face revealed his own doubt about that sentence.

'Well,' Wat said, 'if he's gone, he's gone. He obviously doesn't want to be found. As soon as anyone knows where he is, he leaves. Seems to be quite capable of looking after himself. We'll just have to take Alyssa to her nearest relative where she can wait.'

Hermitage was about to say that this was out of the question when he saw that Gilbert's head was shaking.

'You must find him,' the Norman said. 'It is actually most fortuitous that the investigator should arrive just now. William asked me to deal with Nigel and he has gone. He must be recovered before any word gets to the king.'

'Oh, marvellous,' Wat complained. 'Remind me not to visit the next castle you have. Goodness knows who'll go missing from that one.'

Gilbert leaned over in Wat's direction and had a smug and confident look on his face. 'There is one person you can question about events,' he said.

'Oh yes?'

'The one who deals with all important guests: Aveline.'

Caput XIII: Cave Life

Not very far away at all, a lone figure huddled in darkness and tried to make sense of events. If those worrying for him knew that Nigel of Lincoln was only a few hundred feet away from the castle, they might rest a little more easily.

Unfortunately, there was little chance of them stumbling upon him by mistake; the few hundred feet from the castle were straight down.

Nigel's thoughts were going round and round in circles and so completely failing to make any useful progress at all. He was in a cave, that was his first conundrum, and he tried to understand why he was in a cave.

Well, he knew why he was in a cave, he had come in here to hide, and it had proved a successful strategy. But why had he needed to hide in the first place? A man of his stature and position should not be hiding in a cave. He shouldn't even go in a cave; they were places for stores and the like, things that servants and slaves dealt with.

He had a lovely home in Lincoln and had been very content. Several worthy positions had fallen his way. Others he had sought and they had made him a person of some significance; just the right amount of significance.

With the arrival of the Normans, he had learned that being a rather minor Saxon functionary was the best sort. The major Saxon functionaries had a habit of vanishing in the middle of the night, only to be replaced by a Norman.

Then his mind came back to the cave once more, having still reached no useful conclusion.

How did a minor Saxon functionary end up hiding in a cave? Had his significance reached some sort of tipping point such that he was in the way of a Norman who wanted his roles? They only had to ask, he would step aside without a moment's hesitation. He knew some who resisted the oppression of the invaders, but he soon noticed that they got oppressed to death. He quickly decided not to do resistance.

But the Normans tended not to do asking, they just did.

Were they working their way down the Saxon order? First the king and the nobles, then the landowners and the wealthy merchants, next the minor functionaries?

Even that made no sense.

He had been summoned here at the command of the lord of the castle, Gilbert, and the man seemed to be a little confused, but welcoming when they met.

He was sure that it was the summoning that had been the first step on the road to his cave.

As soon as the word had been received, the local Normans started grumbling at him and about him. And they'd asked such peculiar questions; when was he taking up his new role? Where would he be when he began work? Was there anyone who would miss him? Did he own a sword?

It was no surprise that they knew about his appointment. A role of this significance would not be the whim of an individual, it would be common knowledge. At first, he had thought that they might be his new assistants, but they seemed too keen to know exactly what his plans were, and they carried too many knives and swords for assistants to a purse-holder.

He quickly concluded that leaving Lincoln without these people knowing might be for the best. After all, they hadn't actually told him to wait for them.

This had been a worrying start, but he was used to jealousy. He didn't become almsman to the chapter of canons without some stiff opposition and subsequent resentment.

But his main rival for that position had been the under-dean's mace bearer, who was a lot less well-armed than the Normans - apart from the mace, obviously.

He wasn't so naive to miss the fact that he was a Saxon being appointed to a Norman role, and a jealous Norman would doubtless be a handful. Once he was in the protection of his lord, though, the troubles would disappear.

A hasty departure, without even telling Alyssa, had led to the welcome of Gilbert; and he had been welcoming, which was a huge relief. Nigel put the whole situation down to competition for his position and so once he was settled, everything would calm down.

People would simply have to get used to the idea that he was the keeper of the purse.

But someone had carried their dissatisfaction with them.

Arrival in the cave was obviously connected to the purse. No one had ever chased him into a cave because he kept the Shire Reeve's wardrobe. But the purse was just a piece of routine business. He knew that he had a reputation for sound management and that this must have come to the ears of the Normans. It was an honour. Why was a man with an honour running away from assistants with knives and hiding in a cave?

He tried once more to order the events that had led to his cave in the hope that something would become clear. Such was his confusion and distress that the order kept changing.

Minor functionary in Lincoln; summoned by Norman noble; approached by strangers with too many questions; leave for Nottingham without notice; welcomed by Gilbert. And then the mysterious warnings that he was earmarked for a horrible fate, followed by hiding in a cave.

It made perfect sense. It was all completely reasonable. If

anyone issued mysterious warnings these days, it was wise to take them seriously. And Nigel had not acquired all his positions by being a difficult fellow. Cooperation, that was his skill. Keep everyone happy, even if they were diametrically opposed. He had the ability to say the right thing to the right people, without ever being held to account for saying anything of significance at all.

Everyone thought of Nigel as a reliable and safe fellow. He wouldn't cause trouble.

Obviously, the issuer of mysterious warnings hadn't heard about this. A voice in the dark night of the castle had driven him from his bed. And they didn't even give him the chance to give any excuses; whatever they might be.

Yes, he could have sought out Lord Gilbert for aid, and in hindsight, that would have been a good idea; a much better idea than running away and hiding in a cave, but threats in the night seemed much more vivid and, well, threatening somehow.

And so, with nothing but his clothes, he had left the castle. And that had been no easy feat.

Being a castle of the invaders, the place was quite secure. Bolted doors all over the place and patrolling Normans looking out for any threat. Fortunately, they were looking out. It was probably quite sensible to assume that any trouble would come from outside the castle, not from within.

The construction of the place also helped him. Rough timbers, quickly thrown together provided enough hand and footholds to make climbing them easy. Well, easy for someone who was used to climbing walls, perhaps. None of Nigel's worthy positions had prepared him for anything like this.

His duties as doorkeeper to the Dean only expected him to

open the thing and get it repaired; he wasn't required to go up it. And if he had been, he'd never have taken the job. And it had come with a fine sash, which was not at all suitable for door climbing.

Nonetheless, the prospect of someone coming to him in the night and making sure he never saw the morning, was enough to discover hitherto unknown abilities. He didn't even care that his fine clothes suffered the attention of numerous splinters and snags.

And once over the wall, the Saxon village was still some way off. Would he be able to make it across the open ground without being spotted? It was dark, but people could be after him and he wouldn't know it.

He knew of Nottingham's reputation as a place of caves. After all, the original name in the old tongue, was Tigguo Cobauc, the Place of the Caves. Which, even in his current state, Nigel realised probably meant that there were some caves.

And he had never known that his knowledge of the old language would come in handy. Perhaps he would hide in his cave and pretend to be a Celt who didn't even know the Saxons had arrived, let alone the Normans.

He was getting carried away. He needed to be practical.

His flight from the castle completed, he had spent a fitful night, alternating between fretting, worrying and dozing. Dawn had come with no hint of discovery, but he rapidly concluded that he could not spend the rest of his life in this cave, despite the attraction that it had no one in it who wanted to kill him.

His various attempts to work out what on earth had happened had taken most of the morning, and hunger was starting to bother him. He had to move. But where?

Someone wanted him not to be the purse holder and the best way of achieving that was to make sure he wasn't anything anymore. Emerging from the cave was the surest way to make something horrible happen.

Would they really kill him, though? He had been offered an official appointment. Surely, even the Normans didn't go round killing the duly appointed?

He recalled that King Harold had been duly appointed by God, and it hadn't helped him.

Perhaps it would be enough if he simply went away. If no one saw him ever again they couldn't kill him, could they? He would sneak out to the Saxon town, perhaps hide there, change his clothes and then head off into the country.

But then he thought of Alyssa. The poor child, although comprehensively irritating most of the time, and with a very weak grasp of the intricacies of civil administration, was his only issue. Her mother had not survived her birth and her upbringing had been entirely his responsibility; he had personally selected the staff to do it.

She must be worried about him, if not in actual danger herself. At least she was still young enough to pass unnoticed as an insignificant child and not be seen as a threat; he hoped.

Making sure Alyssa was safe would definitely require leaving the cave. Leaving the cave would mean discovery. He wouldn't be able to help Alyssa if he was taken. And he couldn't help her sitting in a cave.

A dilemma. But he dealt with dilemmas, he told himself. And the fact that he had been in this cave for some time now, reassured him that pursuit was not on his heels.

He cast his mind back to the various encounters he had with the great and the good of Lincoln to see if there was anything that would help in a situation like this. He tried to ignore the fact that he had never even heard of a situation like this, let alone been in one.

There had been that one time when he was scribing for the wapentake court. The man brought before them had been accused of murdering his neighbour's chicken. The court quickly ruled that a chicken could not be murdered, not having a soul, it could only be killed. The charge had then changed to killing a chicken, which hardly seemed worth the court's time.

The point had been that the chicken killer, who denied the crime, said that he dared not leave the court as he would be set upon by an angry mob.

Nevertheless, he had to leave as he had a chicken that needed preparing for the pot and it might be stolen as there were a lot of disreputable people about.

And what had he done? He had sent for help. Word was taken to his brother who came to the court to take him home.

Well, that was no help. Who could Nigel send to? Gilbert seemed friendly but he could hardly ask someone passing by to see if the lord of the castle would mind popping down to a cave.

And who was going to pass by a cave anyway?

There was no way he could cry for help. The wrong sort of help might come and very effectively stop him crying.

Should he wait until nightfall and then head back to the castle and Gilbert? Would the threatening voice be waiting for him? Or was it watching out for any sign?

From sitting disconsolately at the back of his cave, Nigel stood, to see if pacing up and down might help his thoughts.

He was careful not to pace too close to the cave entrance, in case anyone was searching for him. He had been fortunate to find the place as he scrambled down the castle hill, and was confident that it was well-hidden.

Trees and bushes had grown around the entrance, and he hadn't even known the cave was there until he almost fell into it.

His pacing led him farther and farther into the cave, which seemed to extend for some distance. Naturally, it was very dark and so his pacing was slow and cautious. He went so far from the cave entrance that he couldn't even see his feet, let alone what they might be treading on.

He suddenly considered the possibility of some mighty drop right in front of him, which would carry him to his death in the bowels of the earth.

He stopped pacing and felt about him for his flint and striker. Another dilemma of whether to make light or not was too much. He was well away from the entrance to the cave and he had to see where he was. Perhaps there was some other way out of this place.

He slowly approached the opening of the cave, crawling on his stomach, for goodness' sake, ruining a very fine surcoat, and scrabbled about for some kindling and larger pieces that would burn.

With a handful of dry twigs, he peeled the bark away and shredded it in his fingers to create a fuel that would take his spark. He reflected that he hadn't done this for himself for many a year. He only carried flint and striker as an affectation, as most of the great men of Lincoln did. They weren't actually expected to start their own fires.

He took his harvest as far back in the cave as he dared, and unable to see what he was doing, had to guess roughly where he had put the small pile of bark, and strike his flint in that direction.

As the sparks leapt, he saw that he was trying to ignite his own shoe, so he adjusted accordingly.

At least there was no wind in this cave and so the sparks hit their target. It took several goes, all of which alarmed him with their noise before the faintest whiff of smoke rose from the kindling.

Bending down, he could only tell where the smoke was by smell. He blew very gently in that direction.

His chest swelled with pride as he saw a small red glow develop. Here he was, a man running from attack who had hidden in a cave and started his own fire.

He suddenly wondered if starting a fire in a cave was a good idea after all. Never mind, he could always stamp it out again if it got out of hand.

Leaning over, blowing and adding progressively larger pieces of kindling, it wasn't long before he had his first flame.

Adding to this, he soon got a reasonable fire underway. Taking his larger piece of wood, he laid this in the fire until it too caught. He knew that it would really need some oil or other fuel to act as a torch, but this cave was not well provided, he would just have to manage. He held his timber up and dipped it to allow the flames to take a better hold.

Holding it out in front of him he saw that there was no danger of plummeting into the abyss. In fact, the cave continued flat and open, farther into the side of the hill.

Picking up a second log to take over when this one expired, he moved ahead. He took encouragement from the fact that the flames and smoke were drawn farther into the cave, indicating that the draft had to be getting out somewhere ahead.

The cave entrance was now long gone, and the path bent around an outcrop of rock, taking Nigel away from the outside world and its threats and comforts.

Suspecting that he would come to an end at any moment, he pressed on and rounded one more slight corner.

He considered the scene his torch revealed and froze. Without releasing the breath he had trapped in his mouth, he took a very cautious and careful step backwards. But that one step was too much.

'Here,' the Norman in front of him demanded. 'What the devil do you think you're doing?'

Caput XIV: Division of Labour

With a hearty chuckle at their fate, Gilbert left Hermitage, Wat, Cwen and Alyssa by the fireside, saying that he had other business to attend to and that he looked forward to hearing what had happened to Nigel.

'Well,' Cwen said with some satisfaction. 'There's no point either of you going to talk to Aveline, is there?'

Hermitage and Wat exchanged glances that said they were perfectly happy with this conclusion. 'Whatever you did to her has made her very angry. And she seems a strong young lady.'

'She is that,' Wat agreed.

'Strong enough to carry a very heavy grudge for years.'

'We didn't do anything to her,' Hermitage had to dispel that idea. 'Her father was worried because she had run away. He was quite right. A young Norman woman alone in hostile country.'

'Except she wasn't alone,' Wat said. 'She'd taken up with Briston and thought he was going to show her a life of adventure.'

Cwen snorted. 'I can imagine what sort of thing Briston had in mind to show her. Or more accurately, for her to show him.'

'Exactly. And Lady Aveline got straight down to business. She took the opportunity to do all sorts of things that her father wouldn't approve of. In fact, she threw herself into them, you might say. Now, of course, she would prefer it if the details of her excursion with Briston were not made known to her father.'

'Aha,' Cwen smiled and nodded. 'Got her then.'

'And she is a strong young lady who doesn't like being got.'

'Right,' Cwen rubbed her hands. 'Leave her to us. Come on Alyssa, let's go and have a talk with Aveline. There's nothing like a friendly female face to lull her into a false sense of security.'

Hermitage watched them go and could only recall a peculiar concept he had heard from a widely travelled pilgrim. It involved a spear that could pierce any shield and a shield that could protect against any spear. If he followed Cwen he thought that he might discover what happened when an invincible spear struck an impregnable shield. He decided he'd rather stay by the fire.

'I'm confused,' he said. Wat had no comment to offer.

With Alyssa gone, at least they could talk about the whole Nigel situation. 'If Raegnald was right, the Normans want Nigel dead.'

'If Raegnald was right,' Wat cautioned.

'Quite so. Here we are with Gilbert who says the king has instructed Nigel be given an important appointment. They can't both be right.'

'Could still be disputing Normans. If the king favours Nigel, a Saxon, some of the Normans might want him removed. They're the ones that Raegnald has been listening to.'

Hermitage thought it was bad enough that the country was arranged Normans against Saxons. If the Normans were against one another as well, what was to become of the place?

'Gilbert is clearly not one of them.'

Wat nodded. 'For all his importance to Nottingham, he seems like a simple fighting man. One who'd rather be out fighting the enemy than dealing with his family.'

'He doesn't strike me as a dishonest man.'

'Most people don't, Hermitage. Even the proven killers.'

Hermitage knew that this was a failing, one of his many. And a pretty major hindrance to being an investigator of murder; or of anything at all, come to that.

'I mean that I don't think he killed Nigel and is deceiving us by saying that he's gone.'

Wat nodded his head in agreement. 'I don't think he'd ask us to find him if that were the case. Unless it was some clever ruse within a ruse, and I don't think he's up to that sort of thing.'

'And playing ruses on the king must be a dangerous thing to try.'

'We've heard of Normans trying it,' Wat said. 'His own people have been trying to kill him since he became duke.'

Hermitage nodded. 'And we mustn't forget Father Baldice, of course.'

'Who could?'

'The Normans want Nigel dead, or some Normans do, and Baldice doesn't want it investigated.'

'They're in it together?' Wat suggested.

Hermitage considered this possibility very carefully before coming to his conclusion. 'I have absolutely no idea.'

Wat sighed.

'How did we end up in the middle of all this?' Hermitage fretted.

'I beg your pardon?' Wat sounded quite irritated. 'We ended up in the middle of this because you insisted on helping Nigel. All Raegnald wanted to do was have him killed. We said no and that was that. But oh no, the King's Investigator has to investigate.'

Hermitage thought that was unfair. 'Alyssa came to us for aid, we couldn't turn her down.'

Wat muttered something about "he could" but said no

more, instead staring at the fire.

'I wonder if there is something peculiar,' Hermitage pondered aloud.

'I'm sure of it,' Wat grumbled.

'I mean, peculiar about this role of Nigel's. Is this all simple Norman anger at a Saxon appointment, or is there something more?'

Wat gave a shrug. 'The Normans do tend to kill people for the slightest little thing.'

'That's true, but perhaps we need more information from Gilbert. All he's told us so far is that the king wanted the appointment made.'

'And he didn't seem too keen on the idea himself. If he didn't do for Nigel, he might have made it clear that someone should,'

'We need to ask,' Hermitage stood from his chair. 'Lord Gilbert wants us to find Nigel, the least he can do is help.'

Wat didn't look hopeful as he rose to follow Hermitage. 'We don't even know where he's gone.'

'It's not a big place, I'm sure we'll find him.'

As a first step, Hermitage returned to the main door of the keep and looked out. From this high vantage point, the land around spread out like land at the bottom of a hill. The great River Trent snaked its way across the fields to the south while the Saxon dwellings huddled in surrender to the east.

It was a wide vista and Hermitage realised that he wasn't going to spot Gilbert if the man had left the castle.

Just outside the door, a Norman soldier loitered, not doing anything at all, by the look of him. At least this wasn't Giscon, who Hermitage suspected wouldn't be able to help them find his own nose.

'Ah,' Hermitage began as he stepped over.

'Ah,' the soldier replied in some surprise. 'Don't do that,' he said when he had recovered. 'Sneaking up on people.'

'You are a Norman guard,' Wat pointed out. 'I'd have thought it was what you were here for, people sneaking.'

'Don't remind me,' the soldier complained, which seemed an odd thing for a soldier to say.

'Erm, right.' Hermitage didn't like to start conversations this confused. The confusion usually came later. 'Have you seen Lord Gilbert?'

'Have I seen him?' the soldier asked with surprise. 'Of course, I've seen him. You don't guard a man's castle without seeing him.'

Hermitage was already wishing he'd asked someone else, not that there was anyone else to ask. 'I mean have you seen him recently, just now in fact? Has he left the keep?'

'How should I know?' the soldier complained.

'Aren't you guarding the door?' Wat enquired.

'Yes,' the soldier replied sharply. 'From people getting in. If anyone wants to come out that's up to them, isn't it? And if it's Lord Gilbert? Well, it's his keep isn't it, he can come and go as he likes.'

'Erm.'

'If you want to guard against people coming out as well as going in, you need more guards. I've only got one pair of eyes.'

'Well, of course.'

'But if he came out,' Wat explained, 'you'd have seen the back of him. On its way out, as it were.'

'Clever little Saxon, aren't you?' The soldier did not sound happy about clever little Saxons.

'And the guest of Lord Gilbert,' Wat added equitably. 'Given a mission by him, in fact.'

'Oh, very nice, I must say,' the soldier's sarcasm stood to

attention. 'A mission from the lord of the castle for a couple of Saxons while the rest of us have to stand on a hill looking at nothing all day.'

'You can help, if you like,' Wat offered. 'You might know where to look for him.'

This seemed to pique the soldier's interest. He looked around as if checking that no one else was about to interrupt this exciting prospect. 'What are you doing, then?'

'We're looking for Gilbert,' Hermitage said. He knew he had said this already but thought it best to start again.

The soldier shook his head. 'I haven't seen him.'

Hermitage resisted the urge to sigh very heavily.

'You could help us look,' Wat offered brightly. 'After all, you know the place.'

The soldier considered this very carefully. 'I'm not sure,' he eventually concluded very slowly. 'I'm supposed to be guarding the door.'

'This door here.' Wat checked.

'No, the door to the Tower of London,' the soldier sneered.

'There's another door down there.' Wat gestured down the hill to the outer palisade. 'A much bigger one with more guards on it. Anyone who wanted to get in this door would have to get through that one first.'

'You think I don't know that?'

'So, it won't do any harm to come with us. We are Gilbert's guests after all. You could blame us if someone complains.'

'If someone complains?' The soldier sounded shocked at this suggestion, but it was clearly mock shock. 'Oh, heaven forfend that anyone in this place should complain about anything. Let alone whether a guard is standing at the right door. Or whether his sword is properly maintained or his helmet's on straight. That would never do.'

Hermitage quickly concluded that they would go and look for Gilbert on their own.

'I only came for the conquest, you know,' the soldier moaned.

'Really?' Wat asked with a mischievous glint in his eye.

'And by the time I arrived, it was all over. There was only guarding, they said.'

'Did they?'

'They did. Conquest is all over, friend, you're too late. Tell you what you can do, you can guard what's been conquered.'

'That's nice.'

The soldier ignored Wat. 'Here I am on top of a wet hill in a horrible country full of horrible people. Call this guarding a conquest? I've got a perfectly good home in Brittany, you know.'

'Is that right?'

'I should have stayed there. Mother was right. Oh, no, my Uncle Antric said, you go with William, there'll be conquest and land and treasure for all.'

'Except it had all gone by the time you arrived.'

'Too right it had. And I wasn't just a bit late, you know.'

'Really?' Hermitage felt it would be rude to simply walk away from this guard, but that was what he really wanted to do.

'Oh, yes. I wasn't on the boat after the one that landed first. I didn't arrive just after the battle had started, or even soon after it finished.'

'You don't say.'

'Two bloody years!' The soldier looked on the verge of throwing down his helmet and sword. 'What sort of uncle sends their nephew to a conquest that finished two years ago?'

'I wouldn't know,' Hermitage said. His only uncle had long since disappeared in a mysterious fishing accident; the mystery being that he hadn't gone fishing.

'And they don't let you go home, you know.'

'Do they not?'

'You're a guard now, you guard, no choice. Never mind that the conquest is over.'

'I can see it must all be a disappointment.'

'Disappointment!' The soldier considered this to be a mighty understatement.

'There could be some more conquering to do,' Wat suggested.

'Oh, yes? And where would that be, exactly?'

'All sorts of places. There's the north? We've heard William isn't happy with the north. Or there's Wales, he's not done Wales yet.'

'And Ireland,' Hermitage added.

'Oh, yes, Ireland. Big place, Ireland.' Wat nodded encouragement.

The soldier appeared to be considering this with some scepticism. 'I'm not going near any Druids.'

'I'm sure you wouldn't have to.'

The soldier looked thoughtful for a moment, but then seemed to conclude that such good fortune would not come his way. 'They'd only have me guarding it again.'

'Look,' Wat tried to sound encouraging. 'You come with us and help find Lord Gilbert. I'm sure he'll be pleased about that and he might give you a better job.'

'Or let you go home,' Hermitage added.

'No chance of that,' the soldier grumbled. 'But come on

then,' he sighed. 'It's got to be better than just standing here all day. Lord Gilbert could be in the store. We're supposed to have had some more supplies.'

'That's very kind,' Hermitage said as they wandered on.

The soldier grumbled as if being kind was the one drawback of this whole business.

He led the way, disconsolately and with continuing complaints about the state of the ground up here, the direction the wind came from and the awful weather.

Hermitage and Wat exchanged looks of hopeless despair as they followed.

Round the corner of the keep they went, although Wat and Hermitage had stopped listening to the complaints. They had probably moved on to how the keep was too big and it took an age to walk around.

At the back, they came to an entrance which was a complete surprise; mainly because it was in the ground.

'Erm?' Hermitage asked, not sure whether he wanted to go into a hole in the ground with a disturbing Norman.

'The whole place is full of caves,' the Norman complained that decent countries weren't full of caves. 'I suppose they have their uses.'

'As a store.' Wat saw the sense of this. 'Nice and cool, keep things fresh.

'And we can bar them to keep the rats out,' the soldier added.

The entrance to this cave was set in the slope of the hill and had a wooden door fitted across it. The three of them climbed down some steps set into the ground and the soldier pulled the door open.

Inside, it was remarkably well-ordered for a cave. Hermitage's ideas included bats and dragons and utter darkness. This cave had torches at the entrance and oil lamps along the way set into shelves on the walls. The floor was strewn with straw and looked quite habitable.

From further on, voices could be heard, the drone of conversation bouncing from the rock. There were no raised voices as people scrabbled to get away from the bats and the dragons, so Hermitage relaxed a little.

He even thought that this might make a nice cave for a Hermitage. One that he would happily occupy if the door could be firmly bolted from the inside. Of course, they would probably still knock to have their murders investigated.

'Sounds like he's in,' their soldier reported.

He led the way, and within a few paces, they entered a large chamber, neatly organised with boxes and piles of supplies for men and animals. Straw for the horses, meats for the men to eat, and weapons for them to kill with were stored in this place.

Lord Gilbert was in the middle of the room talking to another man who held a slate in his hand, doubtless the victualler. He turned at the new arrivals.

'These men say they're your guests, my lord,' the soldier said.

'Ah, yes, erm, that's right.'

The soldier muttered at Wat and Hermitage. 'Doesn't even know my name!'

Hermitage and Wat half-bowed, half-nodded to Gilbert.

'We wanted to ask some more about Nigel and his appointment, my lord,' Hermitage said. 'The circumstances and so forth.'

'And we left Cwen to talk to Aveline,' Wat explained.

'Hm,' Gilbert grunted. 'That was probably wise.' He turned back to the man with the slate, and they carried on discussing the business of supply.

Hermitage looked around the space with interest, noting the very large volume of material there seemed to be. Still, a lot of Normans ate a lot of food, he supposed. He wandered over to one heap of rather dirty sacks, curious to see what might be in them.

With hands behind his back, he leaned forward and examined the pile with interest. There was nothing in the smell or appearance to reveal what they contained, and so he reached out and gave one a poke.

It was soft and giving, so probably a meat of some sort. Perhaps a sack of chickens waiting for the butcher.

The scream he released drew everyone's attention as the next sack he poked moved.

'What the devil?' the victualler complained. 'If that slaughterman hasn't finished them all off, I'll have his guts instead.' He strode purposefully over to the offending sack and dragged it into the middle of the room. Even he seemed surprised at the weight.

He undid the twine at top of the sack cautiously and peered within. He then uttered a cry and jumped back, which made Hermitage feel a bit better.

'Ah,' Lord Gilbert said as the sack fell down and the contents were revealed. He nodded towards Hermitage and Wat. 'You found Nigel already, that was quick.' He then frowned. 'Why's he in a sack?'

Caput XV: There He Is

'This is Nigel of Lincoln?' Hermitage asked. He couldn't really take the idea in. If people went missing and were searched for as part of a wider investigation, you didn't find them in a sack in a cave. Much less did you poke them. There should be days of speculation and searching before coming to discovery slowly and with painstaking care. A poke in the sack was simply ridiculous.

'It is,' Gilbert confirmed. 'Have you been here all the time?' he demanded of the man who sat forlornly in the middle of the cave.

Nigel himself was looking round with obvious shock and fear.

Hermitage thought that getting in the sack in the first place must have been an experience for Nigel. He couldn't imagine that any of the man's largely minor titles required time in a dirty sack.

'We mean you no harm,' Hermitage said gently. He concluded that coming to harm was probably one of the major motivations for climbing into the sack in the first place.

Nigel's wild eyes seemed to recognise Gilbert and he relaxed a little. He then noticed that Hermitage was a monk and started to look worried again.

'We have been looking for you,' Hermitage explained. 'Your daughter, Alyssa..,'

'You know Alyssa?' Nigel croaked out.

'We do. In fact, she's up in the keep at this very moment. Also looking for you.'

Nigel sagged with relief at this news and started to untangle himself from the sack.

'How did you get in there?' the victualler demanded.

'I just climbed in,' Nigel explained rather sheepishly.

'I mean how did you get in there, in here.' The victualler indicated the cavern in general.

Nigel worked his way out of the sack and up to his feet. 'I came in through a cave in the hillside.' He waved back in the direction he had come, behind most of the boxes and stores.

The victualler gave a fearsome scowl. 'And who helped you get in the sack?'

'Oh, no one,' Nigel said nonchalantly.

'Really?' The victualler was sceptical. 'You managed to get in a sack and then tie it from the outside, eh?'

Hermitage was impressed by that reasoning and thought it was probably the sort of thing an investigator should have noticed.

'Someone helped you,' the victualler accused. 'And I think I know who. Ingolf!' He called a man's name. 'Where are you? I want a word with you. Letting people into my stores and putting them in sacks. It's not right.'

He turned to the soldier who had accompanied Hermitage and Wat and who appeared to be making the best of not being noticed and had stopped doing anything. 'Come with me,' the victualler ordered. 'If Ingolf is up to his usual, I may need a man with a sword.'

Lord Gilbert watched them go and then turned to Nigel. He clearly thought the practicalities were less important than the motivation. 'What are you doing here?' he asked.

'Hiding,' Nigel confirmed.

'Hiding? Hiding from what?'

'Not a what, a who.

'All right, who?'

'I don't know.'

'All makes perfect sense,' Wat shook his head looking

amused by the whole scene.

'You don't know who you're hiding from?' Gilbert asked, clearly thinking that Nigel might be an idiot of some sort. 'What are you doing hiding from anyone? I just gave you the king's appointment. King's appointees don't hide. Particularly not in sacks.'

'I was threatened.' Nigel appeared to be realising that he might look a bit foolish.

'We're all threatened,' Gilbert dismissed this weak and woolly excuse. 'The king's appointees do not run away and climb into sacks.'

'Someone said they'd kill me.' Nigel glanced at them all again, in case one of them was about to do it.

'Who said they'd kill you?' Hermitage asked. He longed to find out it was Raegnald but thought that dropping the name in might give too much away.

'I don't know,' Nigel wailed. He moved over to the side of the cave and sat on another sack. No one climbed out of this one.

'Perhaps an explanation would help?' Wat got in before the whole series of questions went round in another circle.

Gilbert folded his arms in a manner that said he was expecting this explanation to be thorough and believable. He also had the look of a man who did not get into a sack at the first threat of death.

'I was in my cot,' Nigel began. 'Lord Gilbert had told me about the role, and we agreed that we would discuss details in the morning.'

Gilbert nodded that this was true so far.

'Then, when it was dark, I heard a voice calling from outside.'

'So you hid in a cave?' Gilbert snorted.

'The voice said it was going to kill me.' Nigel clearly thought hiding in a cave was the natural response.

'What did it say, exactly?' Hermitage asked. 'What were the words?'

Nigel shivered as he repeated them. 'Nigel of Lincoln,' it said. 'It is now your time to die.'

'It is now your time to die?' Wat didn't sound convinced.

'That's what it said.'

'What's wrong with, "I'm going to kill you", or "you're going to die"?'

'I wasn't particularly worried about the actual words,' Nigel complained.

'It's a bit odd though, isn't it?' Wat asked. 'It is now your time to die? What's so special about now?' He raised his eyebrows at Hermitage who nodded in reply.

Raegnald had come and asked for Nigel to be murdered days ago, why did this mysterious voice say that now was the time?

'Maybe it didn't mean now, specifically,' Hermitage suggested. 'The voice just wanted to indicate that the dying was going to happen very soon, rather than at some point in the future. After all, we're all going to die at some time in the future, so that wouldn't be much of a threat.' Hermitage's words trailed off as he noticed that the others were looking at him in a rather odd way. 'I'm just saying.'

'Yes,' Wat agreed, 'very helpful. The voice said, "now", as if it hadn't been your time to die until now.'

Gilbert grumbled. 'I think we're getting carried away over one word, for goodness' sake. I've had hordes of Saxons outside my wall threatening to kill me and it didn't stop me getting a good night's sleep, never mind running off to a sack in a cave.'

'But then, you are used to that sort of thing, I expect?' Hermitage suggested.

Gilbert shrugged that this was probably true.

'And who would be in your castle threatening your guests at night?'

'It wasn't in the castle,' Nigel said. 'It was coming from outside the walls.'

Gilbert snorted. 'What the devil are you worried about, then? The whole point of a castle is to stop the people outside from killing those on the inside.'

Wat ran a hand over his face. 'Hermitage, I think it's time we shared our tale thus far, don't you? All of it?'

Nigel and Gilbert both looked at them expectantly, and with a little surprise.

'It doesn't seem that Lord Gilbert wants Nigel dead, after all.'

'What?' Gilbert and Nigel were both surprised at this suggestion.

'Perhaps we should return to the keep?' Wat suggested. 'Sit down with a goblet or two and we'll explain.'

Gilbert had a suspicious cast to his face but clearly wanted to find out what was going on. He nodded and they started towards the cave exit.

As they got there, there was a loud shriek from above; a female one.

'Aveline,' Gilbert said with more resignation than concern.

'Cwen and Alyssa are with her,' Wat said. 'Or they were.'

Gilbert hesitated for just a moment before concluding that he was going to have to go up there and find out what was happening.

The next sound that emerged from the keep rooted all four men to the spot.

'Good God,' Gilbert breathed, an expression both stunned and puzzled on his face. 'She's...,' he had trouble finding the word. 'She's laughing.'

A second and third voice joined in the piercing sound.

'They're all laughing,' Wat said very carefully. He looked to the others, none of whom had moved. 'Perhaps we'll stay in the cave, eh?'

Gilbert quickly nodded assent. 'There's plenty of wine.'

Nigel glanced up at the keep and smiled at the sound of his daughter's happy voice. He seemed content to leave her undisturbed as he took his sorrows back underground.

Gilbert even closed the door behind him as they returned to the store and settled themselves. The victualler and his armed assistant were nowhere to be seen, so Wat quickly searched and found the wine as if he knew where it was. It was still in skins, so he simply handed one each to everyone. Hermitage put his down on the ground.

Gilbert un-stoppered his and took a warrior-like swig. Wat took a good mouthful, swilled it around and swallowed happily, Nigel sniffed the contents and turned up his nose slightly, but took a small mouthful. He did not find the result to his taste and so put the skin down.

'Now then,' Wat began. 'Why does everyone want Nigel dead, eh? That's the question.'

'Everyone?' Nigel bleated. 'What do you mean, everyone?'

'Oh, there are people queuing up to have you dead.'

'Are there?' Nigel's voice trembled.

'What's this?' Gilbert asked.

'Raegnald,' Wat said. 'Either of you ever heard of him?'

Both men shook their heads.

'Very well. Raegnald turned up at my workshop a few days ago asking if Hermitage would mind killing Nigel for him.'

Nigel's mouth simply hung open. If a voice in the night made him climb into a sack, being given the name of his killer was more than he could cope with.

'Him having got completely the wrong idea about what investigation of murder meant,' Wat explained. 'And Raegnald said that the Normans wanted you dead.'

'What Normans?' Gilbert demanded.

'Well, de Sauveloy and Le Pedvin were mentioned.'

Gilbert seemed to sag at those names.

'But of course, Raegnald could be a liar, in fact, he probably is, among other things. Nevertheless, he wanted a murder done and seemed pretty sure that this would make the Normans happy.'

'Nigel is the king's appointment,' Gilbert insisted.

'Indeed he is,' Wat agreed. 'Which might be enough of a death sentence on its own. Then we have Father Baldice,' he went on before any questions could be raised.

'Father Baldice?' Nigel enquired with horror.

'You know him?' Hermitage asked.

'No, but a priest wants me dead as well?'

'Not exactly,' Wat reassured him.

Nigel sighed.

'He just wants us not to bother investigating when you are murdered.'

'What have I done?' Nigel wailed.

'Another good question,' Wat smiled. 'We are coming up with them, aren't we?'

'Who's this Father Baldice?' Gilbert asked.

'You've never heard the name?' Hermitage enquired.

Gilbert shook his head. 'But then I don't get on with priests.'

'He seemed a pretty important priest, according to

Hermitage.'

Hermitage nodded. 'Very well presented and educated. Always talked around a subject instead of coming to the point.'

'I know the type,' Gilbert complained.

'We also have people knocking on Nigel's own door asking questions,' Wat continued. 'And they didn't stop after Nigel had left.'

'They didn't?' Nigel asked with some concern. 'I thought that if I went, they'd leave Alyssa be.'

'I'm afraid not. They came asking where you were and she thought they were threatening her, so she left.'

'She left? On her own?'

'She seems a very capable young lady,' Hermitage said.

'Aye, that she is.'

'She heard about Hermitage and came asking for our aid.'

'That was kind of you,' Nigel said.

Hermitage didn't like to point out that Wat had wanted not to be very kind at all.

'And,' Wat said with some significance. 'I assume that none of these people wanted Nigel dead before he got his appointment.'

'Certainly not,' Nigel protested. 'The world has gone mad. I should have stayed where I was and turned the work down.'

'It's not easy to turn down King William,' Wat pointed out. 'Not unless you've got a large army at your back. And even then there are no guarantees. Ask Harold.'

Gilbert nodded at the truth of this.

'I thought I'd be safe once I got here,' Nigel complained. 'After all, I was told to report to Lord Gilbert. But what do I find? Even someone here wants me dead.'

'It's not on my order,' Gilbert said.

'Then whose?' Wat asked. 'Interest in a dead Nigel is remarkably high. It must be to do with the appointment. There must be Normans who do not want a Saxon to have this position. If that Saxon becomes a dead Saxon, someone more suitable might replace him.'

'There is always scheming,' Gilbert mused.

'Scheming!' Nigel despaired as if being killed by scheme made things even worse.

'But what can we do about it?' Hermitage asked. 'Does Nigel simply have to live like this? Under the constant threat of death?'

Nigel did not look at all keen on that idea.

Gilbert simply shrugged that living under the constant threat of death was not that difficult.

'I'll give it up,' Nigel said. 'Some people would rather I was dead, I would rather I was alive. I don't want this role anymore.'

'William?' Wat prompted. 'The king? Remember him?'

Hermitage thought that this whole situation was a bit extreme, to say the least. Threatening people with death just because of what they'd been asked to do was outrageous. And it wasn't even that important a job, for goodness' sake. He supposed that Nigel was paying the price for being Saxon in a Norman land.

'All this over the purse of Nottingham,' he thought aloud. 'It is all so unnecessary.

'The what?' Gilbert asked.

'The purse of Nottingham,' Hermitage repeated. 'Poor Nigel is asked to manage the purse of Nottingham castle, and you'd think he'd been given the keys to the kingdom.'

'What?' Nigel asked in surprise. 'I have to manage the purse of Nottingham?'

'Erm, yes?' Hermitage's sinking feeling returned, the one he got when he saw that all his conclusions about the world and how it worked were about to fall to pieces.

'What are you talking about?' Gilbert asked.

'The position?' Hermitage asked cautiously. 'The appointment. The purse? Nottingham?'

'The appointment and the purse, yes,' Gilbert agreed. 'But not Nottingham. Is that what you've been thinking all this time?'

'Ah.' Hermitage didn't like to say yes, even though it was obviously the right answer.

'Why would anyone be killed over the purse of Nottingham?' Gilbert sounded very confused. 'And my victualler manages the purse anyway. No one wants to kill him. Well, not that I know of.'

'So which purse is it?' Wat asked plainly.

'Peter's,' Nigel said.

'And who, exactly, is Peter?'

'Who is Peter?' Nigel sounded as if he didn't understand the question.

'Yes, that's right.' Wat did not like people treating him as an idiot.

'Well, he's a saint, isn't he?'

'A saint?'

'Saint Peter?' Nigel was looking worried that Wat had never heard of Saint Peter.

'What?' Wat asked, 'the Saint Peter.

'That's the one.'

'Oh, good Lord,' Hermitage breathed. 'You've been asked to manage Peter's Purse?'

'Yes.' Nigel sounded quite annoyed that they were only now getting this.

Hermitage shook his head. 'It's no wonder people want you dead.'

Caput XVI: All This For A Purse?

'Saint Peter's Purse obviously means a lot to everyone else,' Wat complained. 'Personally, I'd have thought his purse is long gone by now. And what's it doing in England anyway?'

'It's not a real purse,' Hermitage explained.

'Well, that's good.'

Hermitage was about to explain as much as he knew when he thought that repeating it all for Cwen might be a waste of time. 'Let's find the others and we can go over this just the once.'

'What others?' Wat asked.

'Cwen and Aveline and Alyssa.'

Gilbert didn't look too keen on this option. 'I'm not sure Aveline will be interested.'

'We need to tell Cwen.'

'It sounded like they were enjoying themselves, it seems a shame to disturb them.'

'When Nigel's life is in danger?' Hermitage thought this took precedence.

Gilbert sighed. 'I suppose so.' He stood as if a great weight was upon his shoulders and led the way out of the cave and back round to the keep.

The evening was fast approaching and the sun, dropping towards the horizon, cast a warm glow across both sky and landscape. Hermitage felt anything but a warm glow as he trudged along. He could now see what the Norman interest in all this was, and that of Father Baldice.

He couldn't think what on earth had possessed Nigel to take this responsibility on. Perhaps he didn't know what he was doing. Or he had no choice. Probably both. Hermitage had led a humble life, he knew that. He had little understanding of the intricacies of church business; and no desire to understand any more than that little. Nevertheless, even he had heard of Peter's Purse and knew that it was something to be avoided.

Arrival back in the keep was disturbing. More disturbing than if a troop of Norman soldiers had been standing there with weapons drawn.

When the men pushed through the door, Cwen, Aveline and Alyssa were lined up with arms folded.

Then they burst out laughing.

Alyssa ran forward and threw her arms around Nigel, who gave his daughter a warm embrace. The daughter then took a step back and looked at Nigel. The laughter stopped.

'What do you think you are doing?' she demanded. 'Running off without a word? Not even a message. Nothing. You could have been dead for all I knew. And then those horrible men come asking for you. What sort of thing was that to do to your only child?'

Nigel could only try and look apologetic.

Unfortunately, Alyssa's stare was backed up by reinforcements from Cwen and Aveline.

'And why are we pulling this man from his family?' Aveline interrogated Gilbert. 'Leaving a poor child on her own, defenceless.'

'Her?' Wat asked with incredulity. 'Defenceless?'

'And you can shut up,' Cwen instructed. 'Wanting to throw her out to fend for herself amongst the rogues and robbers.'

'You're right,' Wat said. 'I should have warned the rogues and robbers and then thrown her out.'

'Everyone,' Hermitage tried to calm the engagement. 'We are where we are.'

'And that's not much help,' Cwen said.

Hermitage knew that it was a largely useless statement, but it worked in so many different situations; situations where you wouldn't have ended up where you are if you'd taken more care in the first place.

'Nigel is alive and well,' Hermitage said. 'He thought he was protecting Alyssa by leaving Lincoln quietly. He hoped to draw the danger away, or at least to reach Lord Gilbert's protection before anything untoward happened.'

This very reasonable explanation got nothing but hard stares from the women.

'And Lord Gilbert is only following the king's instruction. What else can he do?'

'Hm,' Aveline was obviously not satisfied with that pathetic excuse.

'We need to think what to do next.'

'Do next?' Wat asked, not understanding why there was a question. 'Nigel is alive, he's reunited with his daughter, none of which was any of our business in the first place, and so now we go home.'

'We cannot,' Hermitage was serious and sombre.

'I think you'll find we can.'

'Nigel is still in danger.'

'He's got Lord Gilbert and a keep full of Normans to look after him now. I'm sure Alyssa and Aveline can play together nicely and we can get back to what we're supposed to do.'

'What's that?' Hermitage asked, not thinking that they had anything pressing.

'Weaving? Remember? Wat the Weaver? Weaver's workshop.'

'Ah, yes.'

'I know it feels more like an investigator's workshop at

times, but some weaving does still get done.'

'Not by you, it doesn't,' Cwen said. 'You just sit around all day drinking ale and counting your money.'

'Which shows just how successful the weaving is. And it won't stay that way if we keep interfering in other people's problems.'

'Hermitage is the King's Investigator,' Cwen pointed out.

'Who has not been asked to investigate anything,' Wat replied. 'In fact, he has been positively asked not to.'

'Look...,' Cwen began.

'Silence.' Gilbert ordered loudly

Hermitage had quite forgotten there was a large Norman warrior in the room. Gilbert got his silence.

'I want to know just what the devil is going on,' he told the room. 'I make a simple appointment on the king's instruction and then the world falls apart. I want to know why, and who is responsible. And if you have to stay in my dungeon while you explain it, then that is what you will do.'

'You haven't got a dungeon,' Aveline pointed out.

'I've got a lot of caves,' Gilbert said with some menace. 'I'm sure one of them will make a nice dungeon. For everyone.' He clearly included his own daughter in this, and she did not look at all happy.

'Back to the fire and everyone sit,' Gilbert instructed. 'And no one leaves until I'm satisfied.'

The lord of Nottingham had taken on his full Norman might and it was irresistible. Even Aveline and Cwen succumbed to it and wandered over to the seats by the fire, albeit they mumbled and complained on the way.

The available seats were taken and Gilbert dragged a bench over from the large table, indicating with a very curt gesture that everyone should find a space and stay in it.

Wat had taken the large chair by the fire until Gilbert came and stood over him, indicating that this was his place.

Wat graciously moved, revealing that he had managed to bring a skin of wine with him from the cave.

'Now,' Gilbert instructed. 'Explain.' This was clearly directed at Hermitage.

'Well,' Hermitage began with a clearing of the throat. 'I will tell as much as I can but there may be gaps. We need to start with history.'

'We always do,' Cwen complained.

'Shut up,' Gilbert instructed, much to Cwen's annoyance, although she did comply.

'Yes, Cwen, shut up,' Wat confirmed. He got a pointing finger that indicated some punishment to come.

'King Offa,' Hermitage began.

'Where's he king of?' Gilbert demanded.

'Nowhere, he's dead.'

'That's good. Carry on.'

'Erm, right, yes. King Offa, or rather his wife, committed a terrible sin.'

'What did she do?' Wat asked with a leering interest.

'She killed King Ethelbert to get his money.'

'Ha,' Cwen crowed, clearly thinking this sounded like quite a good idea.

'So, King Offa,' Hermitage pressed on, 'to make penance, built Saint Alban's abbey. He also gave away a portion of his wealth to the poor and made a pilgrimage to Rome.

'When he was there, he gave Pope Adrian a penny for every household in his kingdom.'

'Very generous.' Wat plainly thought such generosity was unwarranted, even for killing a king, which he hadn't even done himself.

'There are tales of King Ine making a similar donation a hundred years earlier, but the records are unclear.'

'What does this have to do with Nigel?' Gilbert asked. Nigel nodded that he'd like to know this as well.

'Well,' Hermitage continued, 'once Offa had made his donation, it became a sort of tradition.'

'Tradition?' Gilbert asked. 'Sounds more like a tax to me.'

'Precisely,' Hermitage agreed. 'Which is where the trouble begins. We do have records from King Cnut, who wrote to the clergy, saying that every household was to pay a penny. I've even seen the letter,' Hermitage said proudly. 'It's very fine.'

'How lovely,' Wat said. 'I've never been asked to pay a penny.'

'Not that you would anyway,' Cwen put in.

'Households who paid less than thirty pence rent a year were exempt.'

'Which explains it,' Cwen said. 'You not paying any rent at all.'

'I own my workshop,' Wat said proudly.

'At least that's what you told the Saxon rent collector.'

Gilbert snorted. 'If you two want to carry on talking, you can do it in my dungeon.' He glared at them both and then nodded to Hermitage. 'Continue.'

'Ah, yes. So, King Cnut was paying the penny to Rome and by this time it was known as Peter's Pence. Hence Peter's Purse.'

'Why Peter?' Wat asked.

'Why Peter?' Hermitage didn't understand the question. 'The pope.'

Wat looked confused.

'Saint Peter was the first pope.'

'Was he?' Wat sounded quite interested in this.

'Oh, heaven's above,' Hermitage sighed.

Everyone else tutted at Wat's ignorance and Gilbert gave a grunt that said Hermitage had better get on with it.

'Now, I have heard rumour that King Edward was not convinced that giving all these pennies to Rome was such a good idea and so the payments reduced and then stopped completely.'

'Which can't have left Pope Adrian very happy,' Cwen said.

'Pope Adrian?' Hermitage asked. Hadn't she been following?

'Yes, the one who wanted the pence.'

'That was in the time of King Offa,' Hermitage explained with some surprise.

'Which was when, exactly?'

'Oh, Offa would have been about the year seven hundred and ninety, or thereabouts.'

'What?' Cwen was astonished. 'That's nearly three hundred years ago.'

'That's right.' Hermitage couldn't see the problem.

'Three hundred years is a lot of pence.'

'Which is perhaps why Edward sought to stop the practice. After all, there were a lot more households under his rule than had been the case for Offa.'

Wat was thoughtful. 'Now, King William has appointed someone to manage Peter's Purse again.'

'Quite so. One can only speculate why.' Hermitage understood money, of course he did, but he couldn't see what all the fuss was about. Having it only seemed to make people less content, rather than more. He had to leave such matters to others.

Aveline was nodding and leant forward in her chair. 'The

king and the pope,' she said.

Everyone looked to her, including Gilbert.

'William submitted his claim to the English throne to the pope,' she said. 'And secured Alexander's support for the invasion.'

'Who's Alexander?' Cwen asked.

"The pope,' Aveline sighed at the ignorance.

Cwen stuck her tongue out behind Aveline's back.

'So, in seeking permission, William was tacitly accepting the pope's authority.'

'How do you know this?' Gilbert asked, sounding quite confused.

'It's called paying attention,' his daughter replied. 'Now, Pope Alexander, in order to secure his authority over William, might have said that he expects the payment of Peter's Pence to resume.'

'Hence the appointment,' Hermitage concluded.

'Exactly.'

'So, why the trouble?' Wat asked. 'And why appoint a Saxon?'

Aveline looked quite disappointed that she was in the company of such stupid people. 'Obviously, William does not want to pay the pope. What's the point of conquering a country and taking all its riches if you have to give it away to someone who didn't even raise a sword?'

'But it is the pope,' Hermitage pointed out.

'And it is William,' Aveline responded. 'Doubtless, he has to make indications that he's going to pay. He even promises to appoint someone to manage the whole business.'

'A Saxon,' Hermitage could see the awful scheming.

'A nice, expendable Saxon,' Aveline confirmed.

'Do you mind?' Nigel complained.

'What could William do?' Aveline asked as if playing the part of the king. 'He's tried his best to get this money collected and sent to Rome. What can he do if someone's murdered his tax collector?'

'Even if he was the one who had the murder committed,' Wat nodded at the very neat conclusion.

'What a shocking suggestion,' Aveline said, obviously not shocked in the least.

'Which explains Raegnald,' Hermitage said.

'Who's Raegnald?' Alyssa asked. The poor girl was looking very confused as she followed all this. Confused and worried for her father.

'He came to us asking if we'd mind killing your father for him,' Wat said. 'Said the Normans wanted it done.'

'What? You didn't mention this,' Alyssa accused.

'Not the sort of thing you bring up,' Wat said. '"Oh, you're Nigel's daughter, are you? That's funny, we had a man wanting to kill him here this morning."'

'And Father Baldice,' Hermitage added.

'A priest wants him dead as well?' Alyssa asked with some shock.

'That's what I said,' Nigel moaned.

'Not exactly,' Hermitage said. 'But we don't know whose side Baldice is on. Is he supporting William in seeing that Nigel simply gets on with being murdered as soon as possible?'

'Must be,' Cwen said. 'If he was with the pope, he'd want the money collected and delivered.'

'Don't you understand anything?' Aveline asked with a sigh.

'Do tell,' Cwen sneered.

'The pope might want the tax collector murdered as well.

That way, he can blame William for it and make even more demands.'

'What an awful suggestion,' Hermitage said.

Aveline shrugged.

'I really don't follow this,' Gilbert complained.

'Father,' Aveline said, 'you seldom do. If it doesn't have a sword in its hand or is sitting on a horse, you get confused.'

Gilbert seemed quite happy with the assessment.

'Of course,' Aveline speculated further. 'It could be that William knows that the pope is trying to have the tax man killed and that's why he appointed a Saxon.' She nodded to herself. 'He could let it happen and then blame Alexander. Unless the pope knows that William knows that he wants him killed, in which case...,'

'Can you stop talking now,' Cwen said. 'The point seems to be that everyone wants Nigel dead.'

All those in the room seemed content that this was the case; except Nigel, naturally.

'Not Nigel, necessarily,' Wat said. 'The Collector of Peter's Pence.'

'Who happens to be Nigel,' Hermitage said.

'That's true.' Wat looked at Nigel with some sympathy. 'Sorry,' he shrugged. 'Sounds like there's not much hope, particularly if the king and the pope want you dead.' He gave a little smile. 'We can wait until you are murdered and then investigate for you if you like. You know, find out who did it in the end.'

Caput XVII: A Queue Of Killers

Nigel did not look in any state to deal with anything at that moment. 'I only want to help,' he whimpered. 'Just take on roles as they turn up. No one told me the pope would want me dead.'

Alyssa took his hand. 'Just give it up then. You know that as soon as someone suggests a task that needs doing you say yes. You love a ceremonial robe and a bit of parading through town, and most of the time it's harmless. Mingling with the well-to-do of Lincoln is one thing, dipping your toes in the water with the pope and the king is a step too far. Just say no.'

'It's a bit late for that,' Wat said. 'Kings and popes probably don't take kindly to people turning them down. Or trying to.'

'They can just find someone new,' Alyssa insisted.

'I'm sure they could, as long as the old one was dead.'

'Wat,' Hermitage reprimanded, 'you are not helping. The question is, what do we do about all this?'

'Do about it?' Wat asked in surprise. 'What do we do about getting between the king and the pope and the man they both want murdered?'

'Yes,' Hermitage couldn't see this was a problem. Murder was the worst sin of all, and it must be prevented. Murder of an innocent such as Nigel was unthinkable. The poor man had been singled out for a role precisely so he could be killed for doing it. This could not stand. And the king and the pope should know better, for goodness' sake.

'We don't,' Wat said.

'We don't what?'

'We don't get between the king and the pope and the man they both want murdered. That's what we don't do.'

'You can't,' Alyssa complained. 'You can't just leave him.'

'We are in Lord Gilbert's protection now, Alyssa,' Nigel reassured his daughter. 'It may well be that circumstances are as described, but now that we know, we can take measures and be careful.'

'Ha!' Aveline's laugh was completely heartless. 'Good fortune with that.'

'She's right,' Cwen reluctantly admitted. 'If the king and the pope really are using Nigel as a bargaining tool, what chance do any of us stand of influencing events? Gilbert included.'

Gilbert stood and stepped to stand in front of the fire. 'I will not believe this,' he said in a firm tone.

'Which bit?' Wat asked.

'All of it. It is simply ridiculous that King William would think to behave in such a manner. And the pope! Do you know who you are talking about?'

'Of course we do, father,' Aveline said. 'That's why it's all perfectly believable.'

'Nonsense.' Gilbert dismissed the notion. 'Absolute nonsense. The king is a great man who would not stoop to such underhand dealings. These are all lies.'

'Lies?' Aveline asked. 'Who's lying?'

'Well, stories, then. You are all simply making things up with no justification.'

'How do you explain Raegnald, who came asking for a murder, and Father Baldice, who wanted it not investigated if there was one?' Cwen asked.

'It's just a misunderstanding,' Gilbert waved the inconveniences away. 'King William simply wants a man appointed to collect Peter's Pence.'

'A Saxon man,' Wat specified. 'Which is a bit odd for a

Norman king who has spent much of his time thus far killing Saxons.'

'The king consolidates his rule,' Gilbert said plainly. 'And is doing a good job of it.' He narrowed his eyes at them. 'Or do we have traitors in our midst?'

'Traitors?' Aveline was mightily offended. 'Father, I have told you about this before. You have got to stop believing every little thing the king says. He's right on some matters and wrong on others. Pointing that out does not make anyone a traitor.'

'Sounds like treason to me,' Gilbert replied. 'Saying the king is wrong is what treason is.'

'Plotting against him is treason. Attacking him is treason. Questioning some of his decisions is advising him. The king is not infallible, you know.' Aveline insisted.

'The pope is,' Hermitage said, unhelpfully.

'Is he always this loyal?' Wat enquired with a nod to Gilbert.

'Oh, yes,' Aveline sighed. 'Even when William was only a duke he could do no wrong.'

Gilbert looked very proud of his unswerving faith.

'Which is the reason he's in trouble now,' Aveline continued. 'And the reason you are going to sort it all out.'

'Eh, what?' Wat looked worried.

'What trouble?' Gilbert asked.

Aveline sighed. 'Look, father, the king and the pope are playing games with this Peter's Pence business. It's nothing to do with the actual money, it's all to do with who is in charge. And neither of those two is going to back down. And it was William who instructed you to appoint Nigel to the role, yes?'

'Yes,' Gilbert confirmed with pride.

'Nigel, specifically?'

'He'd had word from Lincoln of a man who was suitable.'

'Hm,' Aveline mused. 'That's suspicious enough in its own right, but we'll leave it for now. The king did not appoint Nigel himself, he got you to do it for him.'

'He did,' Gilbert's chest swelled.

'Oh dear,' Wat said.

The chest sunk a bit.' What do you mean, oh dear?'

'He understands,' Aveline waved towards Wat. 'The king is covering his back.'

'Covering his back?'

'You know, when the king or the duke or whoever is in a battle, he has some unimportant people behind him so that they can get shot instead of him.'

'That's outrageous.'

Aveline shook her head sadly. 'When all this goes wrong, which it surely will, the king might need someone to blame. That would be you.'

'Me?'

'You appointed Nigel.'

'At the king's instruction,' Gilbert insisted.

'I don't think he'll see it that way. When Nigel is murdered and the pope gets very cross that his tax collector has been killed, he'll blame William. He might even blame him so much that he'll ask a friendly army to come over here and replace all the Normans.

'However, good King William will say, "oh, no, Your Holiness, it was that stupid Gilbert who appointed the man. This is all his fault. Rest assured, I'll have him dealt with."'

'Can we stop talking about Nigel being murdered?' Nigel asked.

'Would it be better if we talked about the holder of Peter's

Purse being murdered?' Cwen asked.

'Not much,' Nigel muttered as his head sank.

'The king would not do that,' Gilbert said, although there was a shiver of doubt in his voice.

'It must have been your fault,' Aveline said calmly. 'After all, you appointed him, he's in your castle. You haven't been looking after him properly.'

'And,' Wat added merrily. 'If the pope has it done and makes it look like William, you get the blame as well.'

Gilbert was looking a little less the fearsome warrior now. 'This is all ridiculous.'

'Father.' Aveline went over to Gilbert and placed a consoling hand on his arm. 'When William was a conqueror, he needed bold and brave fighting men who could carry the field before them.'

Gilbert's chin seemed to broaden at this idea.

'And you were perfect for the job. Next, he needed people who could go out into his new kingdom and subdue the locals.'

Gilbert nodded that subduing was what he did best.

'But now he is a king, he doesn't need all that. Now he needs scheming, deceitful, weasels who will lie from the moment they wake up in the morning.'

'Ranulph de Sauveloy,' Hermitage couldn't help but let the name of that awful Norman tumble from his lips.

'Exactly,' Aveline agreed.

Gilbert shivered. 'He's a terrible man.'

'That he is. And that's what William needs now, terrible men. You're terrible, father, of course you are,' Aveline said, seeing the disappointment on Gilbert's face. 'But you're terrible in a different way. Mighty and terrible. Now, the king wants sneaky and terrible.'

'And the terrible men of his past could be a bit of a problem,' Wat put in. 'The last thing a new king wants is a band of fighting men hanging around with no one to fight. They might turn on him.'

Gilbert shifted on his feet.

'Ah, it's started already then,' Wat concluded. 'Bit of discontent in the ranks? One or two of the old knights suggesting that the king's gone soft?'

'Not at all,' Gilbert protested a bit too quickly.

'I expect William has come up with a few tasks like this. Sent some leading men up to the north perhaps, or Wales, even?'

Gilbert cleared his throat. 'Some of the nobles have gone to take the king's word to the outer reaches.'

'What a surprise. I wonder how many will come back.'

Gilbert made an effort to recover his poise. 'The king knows that I am loyal. He has awarded me Nottingham, after all.'

'Some reward,' Aveline coughed.

'And he's given you Nigel,' Cwen added. 'The purse-holder everyone wants dead.'

'They certainly do.' Wat rubbed his hands in horrible glee. 'Just the sort of thing to keep a pope and a king amused.'

'I find this hard to believe as well,' Hermitage added his voice to Gilbert's. 'To suggest that the pope would use the life of a man in this manner. It's all so, I don't know, small.'

'Petty,' Aveline said.

'Beg pardon?'

'It's what we say in Normandy when something small is taken to extremes.'

'Petty,' Hermitage repeated. 'Very well, it's all so petty.'

'But the rule of the country is at stake,' Aveline said. 'Is

William beholden to Alexander or not? The great affairs of the world all come down to Nigel.'

Nigel clearly did not want anything coming down to him.

'Which,' Aveline continued, 'brings us back to you having to sort this out.'

'Us?' Wat was incredulous. 'What can we do about it?'

'I have no idea,' Aveline said happily. 'So, you'd better have a good think and come up with something.'

'Why us?' Cwen asked.

'King's Investigator,' Aveline reminded them. 'Who better to deal with a murder?'

'It was you I came to in the first place,' Alyssa put in.

'Yes,' Wat admitted. 'But that was before we knew such important people wanted your father dead.'

Nigel simply let out a groan.

'There's hasn't actually been a murder,' Hermitage said.

'Then this is the chance for you to get in early. Must be better to stop a murder than sort one out afterwards, surely?'

Hermitage could only agree with that, but it still didn't mean he wanted to do this one. The king on his own was always bad enough, for the pope to be involved as well was unthinkable.

Wat counted the issues on his fingers. 'You want us to prevent Nigel's murder while avoiding any taint falling upon your father. You want us to stop the king and the pope getting what they want without raising their anger or risking punishment. And you want three Saxons to do it.'

'That's about it, yes,' Aveline confirmed. 'You can sleep on it and if I think of anything else, I'll let you know in the morning.'

'Very kind, I'm sure. And if we decide that we'll simply go home and hear how this all turns out when the bards come round singing the song about it?'

'You could try,' Aveline said amicably. 'But I don't think you'd make it as far as the bottom gate. Then, when you're all dead, we can blame you for everything.'

Wat gaped at Aveline.

'This girl is going to go far,' Cwen commented.

Gilbert was still not happy. 'If the king wanted this Nigel dead, all he had to do was ask. I'd do it for him.'

'I say,' Nigel complained.

'But he can't be seen to want him dead,' Aveline explained rather impatiently. 'It just has to happen.'

Gilbert just shook his head and ambled back to his chair as if the cares of the world were simply too much for him.

'So.' Aveline clapped her hands and gave everyone a broad smile. 'The evening draws on and you can all make yourselves comfortable down here for the night. Father and I will be just upstairs if anything occurs to you.'

'How kind,' Cwen grumbled.

'And you don't need to worry about anyone getting in,' Aveline assured them. 'The guards will attend to that.'

'Or anyone getting out,' Wat added.

'Yes, that too. Come, father.'

Gilbert looked over at his daughter. 'I think I'll just check the stores before bed. Make sure the victualler has blocked off the cave properly.'

'Hm.' Aveline didn't look convinced but didn't object.

Wat leaned over as Gilbert went by. 'Couldn't bring a skin or two back with you?'

Aveline disappeared up the simple staircase in the corner of the chamber and could be heard singing happily as she went about her evening routine.

Gilbert gave Wat a nod of the head, indicating that he

should follow.

'I'm, erm, just going to help the Lord of the castle with his cave,' Wat said to the others.

'Of course, you are,' Cwen sighed. 'We'll stay here and do something useful instead, shall we. Like, try to think of a way out of this?'

'That would be good,' Wat said as he followed Gilbert.

Cwen shook her head as they went. 'If he's capable of climbing out of a cave in an hour's time, I'll be very surprised.'

Hermitage gave Wat a departing scowl. He thought that addressing their current problem was rather more important than consuming any more of Lord Gilbert's wine.

'He'd probably only sit here making stupid remarks,' Cwen said, which Hermitage had to agree was probably true.

'Now,' she said. 'How do we get out of this one?'

The conversation that followed was very disappointing in that it mainly followed all the conversations that had already passed by. They went over and over the situation and the people involved and moved from disbelief to resignation and back again, several times over.

Questions about what they could do to the pope or the king were quickly dismissed.

Hermitage's own suggestion of running away and hiding was given quite a period of serious consideration. Reluctantly, they accepted that as the pope was involved, any hiding would require leaving Christendom altogether.

Actually collecting Peter's Pence and handing them over to the pope was recognised as a death sentence from the king.

Not collecting the pence at all was a death sentence from the pope.

Even not doing anything seemed to involve a death sentence from someone or other, and it was all the death sentences that were at the nub of the problem.

Eventually, a silence descended with the dark of the night, and no one had anything useful left to suggest. Not that they'd come up with anything useful anyway.

'I suggest we do sleep if we can,' Nigel said. 'Perhaps something will occur to us in the morning.'

'Which is probably not that far away,' Hermitage said miserably.

As they all tried to find a comfortable spot to get what sleep was possible, a mighty crashing at the main door startled everyone.

'An attack?' Hermitage asked nervously.

'A drunken weaver,' Cwen replied.

There was more banging on the door and rattling of the fittings as someone on the outside tried to work out how to open the thing.

'Push, it,' Gilbert's slurred voice instructed.

'Oh, push it,' Wat's similarly blurred words replied.

The door did now open and sure enough, Wat the Weaver stumbled through. He was followed by Lord Gilbert of Nottingham and they both looked as if there was no wine left in the caves.

They stood still by the entrance but did so because movement would probably make them fall over.

'Very helpful,' Cwen commented with folded arms.

'Ah, hello Cwen, my lovely.' Wat waved at her but suddenly stopped as it was upsetting his delicate balance.

'Don't you lovely me,' Cwen instructed.

'We have been very helpful, actually.' He nodded and smiled as his words tumbled over themselves. Then he discovered that he couldn't stop himself nodding and grasped his head with both hands.

'Getting rid of all the wine is part of the plan, eh?'

'No, no, no,' Wat swayed about. 'Getting rid of all the wine is what gave us the answer.'

'The answer?' Hermitage asked hopefully.

'Absolumely, luterly. Yes.' Wat took this moment to sit on the floor.

'And what is this answer you've come up with?' Cwen asked.

'It's simple. I don't know why we didn't think of it before.'

'Go on.'

Wat held his arms wide. 'We kill Nigel.'

Caput XVIII: It's Murder, Is Murder

Before Cwen could deliver what was clearly going to be a withering assessment of Wat's condition and general uselessness, the weaver discovered that it was only a short distance from sitting on the floor to laying on it. And laying on the floor meant sleep, which he got straight on with.

'Idiot,' was all Cwen said. She gave her glare to Gilbert, who at least was still standing.

The Lord of Nottingham nodded once as if murdering Nigel was now the agreed plan and staggered over to the stairs in the corner. After three attempts to successfully scale the first step, he decided that he would spend the night curled up at the bottom.

Cwen stomped around and took simple blankets from the fireside, which she threw over the recumbent men, not bothering to see whether she covered them or not.

'They're not going to kill me,' Nigel half asked.

'No, of course not. He's drunk. They're both drunk.'

Hermitage could only agree that the idea of killing Nigel was ridiculous. It must have been the wine talking. Of course, Nigel being killed was what everyone outside of this room seemed to want, but there was no question of them even contemplating the act.

And there should be no question of Wat contemplating it either, even if he was drunk.

'We all get some sleep,' Cwen instructed. 'Then, in the morning, when Wat's head is really sore, I'll shout at him.'

They returned to their chosen sleeping spaces, but Nigel did look even more worried than normal. Hermitage could understand that and thought that he was going to get little sleep himself as his mind went over and over the problem before them.

At least Gilbert and Wat were so incapacitated that they wouldn't be able to do anything about their awful suggestion.

As he tried to get comfortable in one of the chairs, he noticed Cwen walk over to check on Gilbert and Wat. That was kind of her. Their behaviour had got them in such a state that they might harm themselves in the night or choke themselves to death.

He started to close his eyes, hoping that sleep would come and thought he saw a swift movement from Cwen as she stood over Wat. She hadn't just kicked him, surely?

. . .

Despite the circling worries, Hermitage did sleep and was woken in the morning by light streaming in through a small window cut into the wall. Just for a moment, he thought he might be in a monastery cell, waking just too late for Lauds, after which he would be punished.

He heaved a sigh of relief that he was actually in a Norman castle; then he realised that relief at being in a Norman castle was ridiculous. And now that the dawn had arrived, they were going to have to address the problem of Nigel. He certainly had no new ideas in his head following his sleep; well, he did, but they were no help at all, being mainly about Moses's mother.

Blinking the sleep from his eyes he looked about the hearth and saw Cwen in the chair opposite.

'Ah good,' she said. 'You're awake.'

Hermitage nodded. He looked farther and saw Nigel and Alyssa stirring from their night, Nigel putting on his worry as soon as he saw the day.

'I didn't want to disturb you,' Cwen said with a smile.

She stood, stretched herself and wandered over to the door where, presumably, Wat still slept. She stood looking down on him as a mother might on her sleeping baby. Leaning over his slumbering form, she brought him news of the new day by screaming in his ear. 'Wake up!'

'Ahh.' Wat's cry expressed many things at once. Surprise, obviously, shock and some anger, even a touch of fear, but underlying them all a very real pain that the loud sound had sent coursing through his head.

He followed his, "ahh" with an, "ohh". This was an, "ohh" of realisation; realisation that pain was going to be his companion for the rest of the day. And it would have Cwen for company, urging it on.

'What did you do that for?' Wat said although the words rasped out of his mouth like dry sand, and he groaned with the effort.

'Oh, I've only just started,' Cwen informed him, still very loudly. 'Our lives are in danger from the Normans so you decide to go off and get drunk with one.'

Wat had no reply, or couldn't bear to utter it.

At the back of the room, footsteps on the stairs said that Lady Aveline was coming to join them, doubtless disturbed by all the noise.

Hermitage watched her descend until she reached the bottom step and came across the figure of her father, still slumped in sleep, deaf to Cwen's raucous call.

She considered him with a neutral expression before moving forwards, planting her foot firmly on his stomach and using him as a stepping-stone to the floor.

Now he groaned.

Wat groaned back, like some peculiar bird responding to

the distress call of its fellow.

Unfortunately, Lord Gilbert's groan took on an even deeper tone accompanied by a very unhealthy rumbling sound. With remarkable agility for a large warrior who had only just woken, he leapt to his feet, clamped a hand across his mouth and bulging cheeks, and ran for the door.

Throwing it wide, the Lord of Nottingham rushed outside and made some noises that were unmistakable.

Cwen tutted. 'All that trouble just to move the wine from the cave to the ground outside the door.' She watched in high condescension as Wat got to his feet and followed Gilbert's lead.

Cwen closed the door on the sound of two grown men who had given their stomachs so much wine last night that the stomachs were now returning the compliment.

She strode over and took a chair by the fire, while Aveline occupied one opposite. The two women sat like ladies in waiting, and if the men knew what was good for them, they wouldn't be kept waiting long.

Nigel and Alyssa, who had watched all this with interest, perhaps as a diversion from their real problems, sat as well, and Hermitage propped himself on the edge of one of the benches.

After several moments, the door to the keep creaked open again and the lord and the weaver returned. From the pale faces and the soft moans, Hermitage could tell that most of the men's concerns were coming from the inside. Cwen and Aveline might be more than they could cope with.

Wat had always been fond of ale and wine, but then he had never had access to a Norman cave full of the stuff, none of which he was paying for.

The two men made their way to the fire and looked at the

chairs, disappointed to find they were currently occupied.

'Right then.' Aveline's voice was remarkable. It wasn't loud or piercing but seemed perfectly pitched to drive through the heads of the men and rattle their ears on the way in and out. Even Hermitage felt a mild discomfort and he was completely sober.

Wat and Gilbert winced at the onslaught.

'Let's hear it.' Cwen's tones were more in the nature of a frontal assault.

The victims wobbled on their feet and looked desperately for somewhere to sit, the risk of them simply collapsing being quite real.

The large and uncomfortable pile of logs by the fire seemed to be the best they were going to get, and they lowered themselves gently. It was clear that getting up again was completely out of the question.

'Well?' Aveline pressed.

Lord Gilbert held up a hand to indicate that he would be with them in a moment. His face said that he was more worried about what his stomach was getting up to and his cheeks bulged once more.

'Don't you dare,' Aveline instructed.

Lord Gilbert swallowed.

'Now,' Cwen said, making it quite clear that the men had had all the time they were going to get. 'What's this nonsense?'

'Nonsense?' Wat croaked very carefully.

'Your answer to our problem. Kill Nigel?'

'Oh, that.' Wat nodded at the recollection and then decided that nodding was something to be avoided. 'Just the wine talking.'

'I should think so,' Cwen agreed.

Nigel heaved a sigh of relief and Alyssa reached out and took his hand once more.

'And your sensible idea is what?' Cwen asked.

Gilbert and Wat looked at one another as if they'd just walked into a trap.

'Sensible idea?' Gilbert asked timidly.

'Yes,' Aveline confirmed. 'You're the ones who went off and drank the wine instead of staying here and being helpful. We naturally assume you have used the time sensibly and come up with how we're going to get out of this.'

'Ah, is that what you assume?' Wat enquired.

'We were just thinking out loud,' Gilbert shrugged. 'Everyone wants Nigel dead, it seems, so that would solve the problem.'

'Not for Nigel, it wouldn't,' Cwen pointed out.

'Well, no.'

'You accept that William is up to something then?' Aveline asked.

'I suppose so,' Gilbert admitted. 'It does all seem a bit odd.'

'A bit odd? Yes, it's definitely a bit odd.' Cwen and Aveline shook heads in unison.

Hermitage felt the weight of events descend upon him once more. He had harboured the very slightest hope that Wat and Gilbert might have come up with a helpful suggestion, but no.

He could understand that Gilbert might seriously think that killing Nigel was a reasonable solution. After all, the man was a Norman, and another dead Saxon was probably neither here nor there. And it would make his problems go away; possibly. The king and the pope would see that the tax collector was dead and so carry on with whatever evil and deceitful scheme they had in mind.

Of course, he'd still get the blame for something or other, most likely. If he didn't kill Nigel he'd be blamed for keeping him alive, and if he did kill him, he'd be blamed for the death. This really was a dilemma with no obvious solution.

A thought then manifested itself in Hermitage's head. He considered the thought and wondered if it could be serious. He hadn't the first idea how to make it a reality, or even to speak it aloud without causing trouble. But if it could be done, it could work.

That was too many "coulds" for his liking, but he let the thought brew for a few moments while his eyes wandered the room, happy to let his mind get on with it.

'I don't like the way he's looking at me,' Nigel complained.

Hermitage hadn't realised he was looking at Nigel, but he did now.

'Hermitage?' Cwen asked carefully. 'What's going on?'

Hermitage didn't have any sensible answers at all; he only had a ridiculous suggestion. And he never liked a suggestion without an answer. Wat and Gilbert thinking aloud had not worked, but then they had been drunk.

He nodded at his own thought and decided to give it some air. 'We suspect that everyone wants Nigel dead, yes?'

'I think that's why we're here,' Aveline said sharply.

'But they only want him dead so that they can blame someone. William wants the tax collector dead so he can't collect the tax. The pope wants him dead so that he can blame William and take action against him. But then William will blame Gilbert for the whole situation.'

Nods all round.

'Or it's something even more deceitful and complicated that we can't even think of,' Hermitage added. 'The key feature is the death of Nigel. Or rather the death of the tax collector.'

Nigel moaned softly to himself.

'So, Wat and Lord Gilbert have come up with the answer.'

'Kill Nigel?' Cwen asked, sounding quite angry.

'Yes,' Hermitage said.

'What?' Everyone spoke at once, apart from Gilbert and Wat who had their eyes shut on their log-pile and were breathing very carefully through their mouths.

'Not really,' Hermitage urged. 'Of course, I don't mean really kill Nigel. I mean make everyone believe that Nigel has been killed.'

'How?' Cwen asked the awkward question.

'I don't know,' Hermitage admitted.

'Well, that's no good, is it?'

'I can't think of everything,' Hermitage protested. 'All I'm saying is that the only way out of this that we can think of is for Nigel to die. That way, Raegnald and the Normans will leave us alone, as will Father Baldice and the church.'

'Until they start allocating the blame,' Aveline pointed out.

'I don't want to die,' Nigel bleated.

'No one's going to make you die,' Cwen said firmly. She faced Hermitage. 'You mean we pretend he's dead?'

'That's it. Although there may have to be more to it than that. If we simply said, "it's all right, Nigel is dead now," we might not be believed.'

'You are the King's Investigator,' Cwen pointed out. 'If you said so, it might be fine.'

Hermitage shook his head slowly as the implications of this ridiculous idea sank in. 'We are talking about the king and the church, they'd probably want to see the body.'

'Eek,' Nigel said.

'Oh, do be quiet,' Cwen said with some irritation. 'If you

haven't got anything useful to contribute to your own murder, don't say anything.'

And that gave Hermitage another idea. 'Raegnald was right.'

'Right about what?'

'He said we'd dealt with so many murders, we must be able to do this one for him.'

'So?'

'We have dealt with many murders,' Hermitage said. 'So we should know how to arrange one, shouldn't we?'

Cwen thought about this for a moment. 'And get away with it?'

'Exactly. So many times we've worked out how people did their murder, we must know where they went wrong.'

'So we do it right?' Cwen checked.

'We make it look like it's been done right,' Hermitage corrected. 'And we make everyone else think that it's been done right.'

'Even if we don't have a body?'

'That could be a problem,' Hermitage admitted. 'But I haven't thought it through completely. Perhaps together, we could work out what needs to happen.'

'And when they come to blame my father for the murder?' Aveline asked.

'We have to make sure no one can. Gilbert cannot be responsible.'

Gilbert stirred at the sound of his name, but that was all he could manage.

There were a few moments of silence as everyone tried to take this in.

'It's asking a lot,' Cwen said. 'Persuade everyone that there's been a murder when there hasn't. Make sure the one man to blame doesn't get the blame and all walk out of it alive.'

'As I said, I haven't thought through the details, and we'll all need to work things through to make sure we haven't forgotten something.'

There was a grunt from Wat, who had obviously fallen asleep again, and he lifted his head to look at everyone with a wide yawn.' 'Have I missed anything?' he asked, scratching his head and looking puzzled at the horrible taste he had just found in his mouth.

'We're all going to murder Nigel,' Cwen said.

'Ah, right you are.' Wat took breath and licked his lips. 'I don't suppose anyone's got any wine, have they?'

Caput XIX: The Plan Is Planned

'Excuse me.' Nigel uttered these words in the tone that said he wasn't asking to be excused at all, rather he was asking other people to excuse themselves. 'Far be it from me to interfere in my own murder.'

'What is it?' Cwen asked brusquely. 'We're doing all this for your benefit, you know. Unless you'd rather be murdered in real life?'

'We're not murdering him in real life?' Wat sounded puzzled.

'Shut up,' Cwen advised.

'Of course, I don't want to be murdered,' Nigel confirmed. 'And I am grateful that you're even bothering to help. We're grateful.' He squeezed Alyssa's hand. 'After all, there's no reason any of you should be involved.'

'That's what I said,' Wat put in.

Cwen stood from her chair, walked over to the pile of logs Wat was sitting on and kicked them. They rolled and collapsed under him, and he finished in a heap on the floor.

'One more word and we'll put you on the fire with your friends,' Cwen indicated the logs. 'Because they're the only friends you've got at the moment.'

Wat extricated himself from the logs.

'And you can put them all back where they came from,' Aveline instructed.

'My murder?' Nigel reminded them of the real problem at hand. 'What happens to me?'

'You survive,' Hermitage said. 'If we can work out how to do any of this.'

'And do what? I can hardly go back to Lincoln, what with being dead and all.'

'You can make a new life.'

'I liked the one I had.'

'Father,' Alyssa instructed. 'You have taken on a role that requires your death. Either you have to give up everything and stay alive, or you have to give up everything including life.'

Nigel's shoulders sank. 'All those fine positions,' he mumbled. 'My house.'

'Alyssa can return,' Hermitage said. 'No one is suggesting killing her.'

Alyssa nodded that this was a bright spot.

'And where will I be?' Nigel moaned.

'Alive,' Hermitage said. 'Somewhere or other.' He could understand that Nigel was losing a lot by this plan, but it wasn't as much as he could lose. ''There are many Saxons who have already given their blood to the Normans, or had it taken.'

'I know,' Nigel admitted. 'But things were working so nicely. The Normans had settled in Lincoln and life was getting back to normal. Now this.'

'It's not as if you had any choice,' Hermitage assured him. 'If the king had your name, that was that. Believe me, I speak from personal experience.'

Nigel could only shake his head sadly.

Of course, Hermitage thought, could Nigel do what so many others in the country seemed to be doing? 'Do you have a brother?' he asked enthusiastically.

'A brother? What does that have to do with anything?'

'Do you?'

'Well, no. I have a sister, but she went north with her husband, into the wild lands, so we'll never see her again.'

'Wild lands?'

'Yorkshire.'

'You have no brother, then.'

'No.' Nigel could not see where this was leading.

'There you are.'

'There I am, what?'

Hermitage thought everyone would know this, but perhaps he had wider experience than most. 'Nigel is murdered, yes?'

'Yes,' Nigel accepted wearily.

'So you can appear as his long lost brother, erm, Norbert.'

'Norbert?'

'It's nicely foreign and would explain why you'd been away. You heard about your brother's death and so you came back to look after Alyssa.'

'It's ridiculous,' Nigel scoffed.

'You'd be surprised how many people are doing it,' Hermitage said. 'Go off and fight the Normans, lose and rather than re-appear and be harried by the victors, turn up as your own long-lost brother.'

Aveline gave a little growl of disapproval.

'If this plan doesn't work,' Cwen said quite harshly. 'Lord Gilbert might have to be coming back as his own brother as well; once William gets hold of him. And then he won't be lord of anywhere.'

Aveline said no more.

'We don't even have a plan,' Hermitage fretted. 'Not even the bones of one. All we know is that Nigel must appear to die, and Gilbert must not be held responsible.'

'Can I point out,' Wat said with some confidence, 'that this was my idea in the first place. Well, mine and Lord Gilbert's. And it's no good you two glaring at me like that.' He widened his eyes and glared in exaggerated fashion at Cwen and

Aveline. 'It doesn't sound to me as if any of you had a plan at all. Wasted your night sleeping, if you ask me. Now that we've given you our idea, you don't know how to put it into action.'

The way that Aveline and Cwen were shifting on their seats made Hermitage fear for Wat's safety.

Wat continued. 'Just ask yourself, who would you turn to if you wanted a clever and ingenious scheme to deceive some important people?'

Hermitage hoped that he couldn't come up with a single name for that question.

Cwen looked thoughtful. 'Aethelthryth,' she said enthusiastically.

'Aethelthryth?' Wat was disappointed. 'No, not Aethelthryth, me.'

'You?' Cwen's single word said that her reaction was mixed; surprised, amused and mocking, all at once.

'Yes, me.'

'Your days of cleverness and ingenuity are long behind you,' Cwen gave a snort of laughter. 'If we wanted an important person to drink a lot of ale and sit around all day doing nothing, we'd come to you.'

'I didn't get where I am today without extracting a lot of money from rich, important people. And you can't do that without being clever and ingenious.'

'That was years ago. And in case you hadn't noticed, the important people you dealt with are all dead. The Normans are here now. And we're talking about the king and the pope.'

'I sold a lot of tapestry to King Harold,' Wat boasted.

'What's your plan, then?' Aveline asked from behind a face as solid as a rock inside a block of ice.

'Ah, well, I haven't had a chance to think through the

details yet.'

'No plan. I see.'

'All right,' Wat said firmly. 'Let's begin.' He rubbed his hands. 'First things first, Nigel is dead.' He looked at Nigel as if measuring him up. He nodded to himself slowly. 'Does anyone actually know what he looks like? Would they recognise dead Nigel if they saw him?'

Hermitage didn't want Wat to start off on the wrong foot. In this case, the wrong foot seemed to be stepping in the direction of needing a body of some sort. 'Yes, of course they would.'

'Who?' Wat asked plainly.

'Us, for a start. We all know what he looks like.' Hermitage nodded towards Nigel to indicate the truth of this statement.

'Yes, but we're not the ones being deceived into thinking he's dead. I can't imagine the king or the pope know him.'

'I can't imagine the king or the pope are going to come looking themselves,' Hermitage said. 'The men in Lincoln know him, whoever they were.'

'Hm,' Wat wasn't happy about that.

'And Raegnald?' Hermitage suggested.

Wat shook his head. 'I don't think so. He came straight to us and didn't really care who Nigel even was.'

'There's the voice in the night,' Cwen reminded them. 'Someone in or around the castle knows who he is and what's supposed to happen to him.'

Nigel moaned quietly.

Hermitage's mind leapt ahead to the moment he was standing over a body and the king was asking him if this was Nigel. And he wouldn't know how to lie. 'I hope you're not suggesting that a dead body is involved in any of this,' he said to Wat.

'Don't know yet,' Wat said in an offhand manner.

'Wat, we can't.'

'We wouldn't kill anyone,' Wat assured him. 'We'd use someone who's already dead. They wouldn't mind.'

'It's out of the question.' Hermitage tried to sound as firm as he possibly could.

Wat obviously saw that Hermitage was going to be difficult over this. 'It'll be hard to persuade people that anyone is dead if we don't have someone dead to show them.'

'And people die all the time,' Aveline offered. 'Well, they seem to.'

'Probably something to do with the Normans,' Cwen retorted.

'How did he die, then?' Wat asked. 'Nigel is dead, but we don't actually have him to hand? What did he do, wander off?'

'It could be anything,' Hermitage insisted. 'He could have been washed away in a flood.'

'A flood? In Nottingham?'

'The river is broad and deep.'

'But it tends to wash the bodies up,' Aveline explained helpfully. 'On a bend to the east.' She glanced at her father. 'Or so I've heard. Chat amongst the soldiers, you know.'

'A fire?' Hermitage suggested.

'Bones,' Wat countered.

'We could use any bones,' Cwen put in. 'A cow?'

'A cow?' Wat was dismissive. 'You think people aren't going to notice the difference between dead Nigel and a cow?'

'They're not going to look that closely, are they?' Cwen was defiant. 'And we don't have to use the head.'

Wat snorted 'Either that or we have to explain that Nigel of Lincoln had horns.'

'This is all getting completely out of hand,' Hermitage complained. Talking about a deceit to save Nigel's life was one thing, going through the details was only increasing his worry.

'Why can't he be simply killed by robbers?' he asked. 'He was travelling home from Nottingham and was taken by men of the woods. After that, he was never seen again.'

'It does happen,' Gilbert admitted. 'There are unruly men on the loose.'

'It's a bit dull,' Wat complained.

'Dull is good,' Hermitage pressed. 'Dull doesn't interest people. Dull doesn't get the king's men searching and him sending people to question events.'

'You are the person the king sends to question events,' Cwen pointed out. 'And what would you do if William told you to investigate a man who disappeared into the woods?'

'Go and look in the woods, I suppose.'

'They are very big woods,' Alyssa said. 'I had to get through them, and they go on for miles.'

'Didn't come across any unruly men?' Was asked.

'No, but then I avoided any contact.'

'Then you'd do your three things,' Cwen ignored the diversion.

'My three things?' Hermitage asked. 'Oh, yes, method, motive and opportunity.'

'Who, what?' Gilbert asked.

'How was Nigel killed, who wanted to kill him and who had the opportunity?'

'Very clever,' Gilbert commented.

'Will we be talking about something else soon?' Nigel asked.

'This is the problem of the day,' Cwen reminded him. 'Go

on, Hermitage.'

Hermitage thought through the process and warmed to the idea of murder in the woods. 'How was he killed? We don't know, he just vanished in the woods. Who wanted to kill him? The robbers in the woods, obviously. Did they have the opportunity? Of course they did. He was in the woods and so were they.'

'But he was the holder of Peter's Purse,' Gilbert pointed out. 'Before he was murdered in the woods, he was a man of some importance.'

'I'm starting to feel sick,' Nigel complained.

'Important people don't get killed by passing robbers,' Gilbert pressed on.

'But he was Saxon,' Wat pointed out. 'So not that important. Would you have a sent a troop of guards to keep him safe?'

'Probably not,' Gilbert admitted.

'It is a bit of a coincidence though, isn't it,' Cwen said. 'The holder of Peter's Purse makes it all the way from Lincoln to Nottingham on his own, but then gets murdered on his way back.'

Hermitage nodded. 'It would raise the possibility that the motive was connected to the purse.' He rubbed his chin thoughtfully. The puzzle was usually who had done the murder after the event. Working out who could have done it beforehand was quite intriguing. Especially as no one was really dead, the death bit being the most disturbing aspect of any murder.

'It wouldn't be Gilbert,' he said. 'The appointment had only just been made and that was at the king's instruction. Why would Gilbert want Nigel dead? And if he did, why do it in the woods?

'We might then cast suspicion back in the direction of the king himself.'

'And he wouldn't like that,' Cwen said.

Hermitage agreed. 'He would certainly not want the business of the purse looked into if our speculations are correct.'

'There we are then,' Wat smiled. 'All agreed. Nigel goes home and gets killed on the way, Alyssa escapes and makes it back to Lincoln to report the event.'

'And what about us?' Cwen asked.

Wat did his best to sound mysterious and knowing. 'We were never here,' he intoned. 'We know nothing of Nigel or Lincoln or Peter or purses.'

'What if the king asks me to investigate?' Hermitage saw that his innate honesty could be a real problem.

'You confirm exactly what happened,' Cwen said. 'Lord Gilbert appointed Nigel who set off for Lincoln and vanished on the way. What more is there?'

Hermitage grimaced at all the other things there were.

'Unless you want to say that you made the whole thing up to deceive the king and the pope?'

Obviously, Hermitage didn't want to say that, but it was the truth, which he did always want to say.

'And with Nigel dead, the king and the pope can get on with business,' Cwen said. 'The purse-holder is just as dead as they wanted him in the first place. And it wasn't Gilbert's fault.'

Hermitage supposed that he should be grateful that they had concluded this awful situation so quickly. Now, he was struggling to remember quite how they'd got into this awful situation at all.

He couldn't help but think what would have happened if

he had never asked Gunnlaug to find out what was happening in Lincoln, They would all still be at home, none the wiser.

None the wiser sounded like the best sort of wise just at the moment.

'And what do I do?' Nigel asked plaintively.

Hermitage had almost forgotten about the victim.

'Easy,' Wat said brightly. 'Do exactly as expected. Head off back to Lincoln and vanish into the woods. Stay there for a while, I'd give it a couple of months, if I were you. Then you can reappear in Lincoln as Norbert, asking after your brother.'

'Stay in the woods,' Nigel seemed to have trouble understanding the most simple step of all.

'That's it.'

Nigel drew himself up and recovered some of his pride. 'I have never stayed in the woods in my life,' he protested with some disgust at the prospect.

'Well, you can't really go to Lincoln,' Cwen pointed out. 'Not with the men there wanting you dead.'

'And you can't stay here,' Gilbert said. 'There's obviously someone nearby who intends to do the deed.'

'I'd die if I stayed in the woods,' Nigel said.

'That would help,' Wat said. 'We wouldn't have to lie to anyone then.'

'Wat!' Hermitage cautioned.

'I am a man of the town,' Nigel said. 'A man of some modest significance. I don't know how to live in the woods like some ne'er-do-well.'

'You can start a fire, surely?' Wat asked.

Nigel admitted with a nod that he could start a fire.

'And catch rabbits,' Cwen suggested.

'My butcher provides the rabbit,' Nigel replied. 'And I don't have enough clothes for a week, let alone two months.'

Wat ran a hand over his face.

'You escaped the voice in the night and managed to get into a sack, father,' Alyssa said.

'Only because I gave that Ingolf fellow a coin to help.'

'Well,' Hermitage said. 'There's only one thing for it.'

'And that is?' Wat asked.

'Nigel will come back to Derby with us.'

'Over my dead body will he.' Wat folded his arms.

'There's nothing else to be done,' Hermitage said. 'He can't really go to Lincoln, someone will kill him. He can't stay here for the same reason, and he can't fend for himself.'

Wat seemed to sag under this assault of good reason.

'It'll only be for a while,' Hermitage assured him, although he had no confidence in this. 'Just long enough for him to come back as his own brother.'

Wat shook his head. 'Why do these things happen to me?' he asked no one in particular.

'You deserve them,' Cwen explained.

Wat wandered over to Lord Gilbert. 'I don't suppose there's any more wine anywhere?' he asked.

Gilbert looked rather suspicious but then whispered something in Wat's ear.

'We'll be leaving soon,' Cwen called. 'You've got to be able to walk.'

Wat waved her away and went with Lord Gilbert. As he did so he spoke quietly to the Norman. 'I wonder if you might do me a favour,' he said. 'There's someone I want you to send word to, but quietly.'

Gilbert cast a worried look over his shoulder.

'Don't tell Aveline. Especially not Aveline. Or Cwen.

Especially not Cwen as well.'

Lord Gilbert of Nottingham swallowed hard.

'Oh, and don't mention it to Hermitage, he can't keep a secret.'

Gilbert nodded.

'And for God's sake don't tell Nigel. In fact, best keep it to ourselves eh?'

Caput XX: A Little Annoyance

'I'm going to take him into the woods and kill him myself,' Wat said.

It was only a week later, but Nigel had proved to be a rather trying guest.

Even Hermitage had to call upon his depths of patience and charity to smile upon a difficult character.

'And no one will mind, because they think he's dead already,' Wat continued with passion. 'It won't be anything to do with any purses, it'll be because he's the most annoying man in Christendom.'

Hermitage nodded with some sympathy, naturally assuming that Wat was only jesting.

'Then you can investigate and tell the world that I did it,' Wat went on. 'I'll probably get a reward.'

'He does still seem to think of himself as a person of some importance.'

'Instead of thinking of himself as a corpse of no importance.'

The time for the noon meal was approaching and the anxiety in the workshop had increased daily until Hermitage could see that a breaking point was close at hand.

'Let me tell you, Hermitage,' Wat said seriously. 'If that man instructs that his meal be served him in his private chamber today, I shall personally see that he travels into town and eats with the pigs.'

Hermitage had nothing to say.

'No, better than that, I'll feed him to the pigs.'

There was a quick clatter on the stairs and Cwen appeared. She did not look happy.

'I assume you're planning to feed Nigel to the pigs,' she

said.

'It's a thought,' Wat agreed grimly.

Cwen shook her head. 'You can't be that cruel to a pig. The poor things would probably die in agony while he talked at them.'

'He has had a trying time,' Hermitage tried to be sympathetic to Nigel, who had lost everything, after all.

'Not for the last week, he hasn't,' Wat said. 'He's created a trying time for everyone else, that's what he's done.'

'He does seem to consider that he still holds positions of some importance,' Hermitage admitted.

'You've got to talk to him,' Cwen said.

'Me?' Hermitage asked with a quiver.

'It was your idea to bring him here, you can sort him out.'

'But..,'

'I've tried talking to him,' Cwen continued. 'I've tried explaining to him. I've tried telling him and I've tried giving him some very explicit instructions. And you know that there is no one in the workshop like me for issuing explicit instructions.'

The two men nodded their agreement to this.

'And it's like talking to a tree. He looks at you as if you're babbling Greek and then tells you that he will have some wine now. I really think that he can't actually hear the words of other people at all unless they're talking about him.'

'And he was such a shivering wreck in Nottingham,' Wat complained. 'Why can't he go back to hiding in a sack?'

'We're not good enough for him,' Cwen said. 'That's the truth of it. With anyone more important than him he becomes a fawning oaf. Mere tradespeople like us should be grateful for his presence. We don't even have any titles, for heaven's sake.'

'No wonder he jumped at the chance of being a purse holder to the Normans.'

'Is it too soon to send him back to Lincoln?' Hermitage asked.

'It's never too soon,' Wat replied. 'Of course, he'll doubtless be spotted, reported to the king or the pope and then killed, but would that be such a bad thing?'

'Wat! Of course, it would.'

Wat looked disappointed at this answer.

Hermitage knew that he would be no good dealing with Nigel, but he had to try. He would begin with the best intentions but would soon find himself striving to avoid any difficulty or awkwardness. As Nigel was the most difficult and awkward person for miles around, avoidance would triumph and nothing would be achieved.

'I'll have a word with him,' he said meekly.

'Make sure it's a proper one,' Cwen urged. 'Not your normal long and difficult words that mean whatever the person listening to them decides. Just tell him.'

'Just tell him,' Hermitage repeated the hopeless instruction. He tried to recall whether he'd ever just told anyone anything.

There was a clatter at the front door and Wat sprang to his feet. 'Ah, Ern with the meal.'

Hermitage and Cwen watched with some confusion as Wat jumped over to the stairs and headed down.

'I, er, just need to pay Ern.'

Hermitage and Cwen simply looked at one another.

'What's he up to?' Cwen asked.

Wat voluntarily paying anyone was unheard of. It was more usual for him to hide in the chimney when traders came knocking for their money. And as he had plenty of it,

Hermitage didn't understand the problem.

'He's cooking something up with Ern,' Cwen said with only moderate interest. 'We'll probably find out when it all goes wrong.'

At the bottom of the stairs, Wat found Ern and sidled up close, checking that there was no one about to hear. He even moved them away from the bottom of the stairs.

'Has my, erm, package arrived?'

'Yes,' Ern said, sounding grateful that he could now stop answering this daily question.

'Well?' Wat asked. 'Where is it?' He looked around.

'Let's see,' Ern was thoughtful. 'Where did I put your payment for the last month's meals?'

'Ern.' Wat sounded disappointed at the innkeeper. 'You know I'm good for it.'

'I do,' Ern agreed. 'I know you're good for it. I also know you don't pay it.'

Wat shook his head sadly. 'Are you saying that I have to pay before I can have delivery?'

'Well,' Ern said slightly reluctantly, 'when you put it like that...,'

'Yes?'

'It's a good summary. That's exactly what I'm saying.'

'Ern, Ern, Ern,' Wat intoned. Nonetheless, he turned his back, delved into the purse at his waist and found some coins for Ern, which he very reluctantly handed over. He even gave an involuntary shiver as they left his hand.

'Thank you,' Ern said brightly. 'You know, I've had a good idea for our arrangement going forward.'

'Oh yes, what's that?'

'I call it payment in advance.'

Wat went very pale.

'You give me next month's money now, and then I deliver the meals. Good, isn't it?'

'Good?' Wat croaked the word out.

'This way, I owe you instead of you owing me. And I'm much better at paying up than you.'

'It's..,'

'Agreed? Then I can get back and not have to worry about it. I can concentrate on other business, like making your delivery.'

'Ern, I am very disappointed in you.'

'I'm learning from the best,' Ern winked.

Wat paused for a very long time. 'One week,' he offered.

'Three.'

'Two.'

'Done.'

Wat sighed as he reached into his purse once more.

'Nice doing business with you,' Ern smiled as he left. 'For once.'

Wat reappeared upstairs with the basket of food in his hand.

'You look terrible,' Cwen said. 'You really did pay Ern, didn't you?'

Wat could only nod.

'I don't know what you're up to, but it's already going wrong.' Cwen took the basket and started to unwrap the contents.

Hermitage sighed that the moment for his word with Nigel had probably arrived.

This repast was for the senior figures of the workshop only; the three of them and Hartle, the old weaving master; and now Nigel. And they all knew they needed to take their meal away from the workshop, in case any of the apprentices got wind of it.

Their food would be supplied by Mrs Grod, Wat's cook. Cook; that was a proper word that left no room for ambiguity. Quite how it came to be applied to Mrs Grod was more of a mystery than even Hermitage could resolve.

Taking ingredients, preparing them in some way and then delivering them for consumption would appear to be a simple process of three stages. Mrs Grod obviously had no interest in any of them. Things went into the pot, came out and were eaten. Whatever happened to them while they were in there did not bear thinking about.

Hermitage supposed that this was still three stages, but in Mrs Grod's hands, any resemblance to food preparation was entirely coincidental; and her hands didn't bear thinking about either.

And, of course, there was a fourth stage to any meal served by Mrs Grod; the one that prompted many of the apprentices to take their food as close to the privy as possible.

As if by magic, Nigel appeared at the top of the stairs. 'Oh dear,' he said with a disappointed sigh. 'Bread, cheese and meat again.' The word, "again" would make any passer-by think that Nigel had eaten nothing else for the last ten years.

'No,' Cwen said blankly.

This did cause Nigel to raise an eyebrow and consider her in his usual haughty manner.

'This is ours,' Cwen said. 'We've decided not to feed you anymore.'

Nigel only gave a snort at this very poor jest.

Hermitage scowled at where Cwen might be going with this.

'It's what with you being dead, you see,' Cwen explained helpfully. 'You can't be dead and be eating things at the same time. Ern at the tavern will be getting suspicious. Word will spread that there's someone else living here. Next thing you know, the king's men will be coming round.'

'I hardly think that's likely.' Nigel clearly thought that no one associated with the king would come anywhere near a place like Wat's workshop. The unspoken implication was that they should be grateful that he had deigned to grace the place with his presence.

'Hermitage is the King's Investigator, they come round all the time. You're just lucky they haven't been recently. We're probably overdue for a visit.'

Nigel looked momentarily worried but quickly recovered his poise. 'Then you will have to hide me.'

Cwen shook her head. 'Even that would be suspicious. They'd only search the place, find you and drag you off.'

Nigel's eyes darted to the others, looking for some refuge from this unwarranted attack.

'I'm sure it will not come to that,' Hermitage offered some reassurance.

Cwen growled at him. 'It could,' she said very plainly.

Wat found the middle ground. 'Perhaps if you behaved a bit more like a member of the workshop, you'd go unnoticed.'

'A member of the workshop?' Nigel clearly thought this was akin to being asked to clean the privy.

'Fit in?' Wat suggested. 'You know, not take your meals on your own. Not ask people to bring you wine. Not criticise everything quite so much?'

Nigel simply looked very confused.

'Look,' Cwen got down to the facts. 'You are a deeply unpleasant, condescending, rude and offensive individual. You care for no one but yourself, have shown not an ounce of gratitude for what we've done for you and are on the verge of being murdered by one of us.'

'Cwen!' Hermitage spoke up.

'Well, he is, we all know it. He doesn't, of course. Rescuing you from the attentions of the king and the pope seemed like a good idea at the time. Now, it doesn't.

'As far as I can see, you've got three choices.'

'Really?' Nigel was dismissive once more.

'One; everyone thinks you're dead, so you can get on and be dead for real.'

'That's outrageous,' Nigel spluttered.

'Two; you can leave. Word is probably out now that you're dead, anyway. You left Nottingham days ago and haven't arrived in Lincoln. For all we know, they've already appointed a new keeper of the purse.'

'They might have killed him as well,' Wat said brightly.

'Because,' Cwen stepped closer to Nigel and stared very hard into his eyes. 'Number three is you stay here. But if you carry on behaving the way you have, you won't need to worry about falsifying your murder, because it'll actually happen.'

'Well, I never,' Nigel complained.

'I'm sure you haven't, but you will now. Which is it to be? One, two or three?'

'There's not much of a choice, is there?'

'No, there isn't.'

'I'm certainly not planning to die,' Nigel insisted.

'That's one out of the way then.'

'And if I venture out, I may be spotted and taken.'

'There goes two. I was confident that you couldn't find your own way to Lincoln anyway. Three it is. Behave yourself.'

It was clear from Nigel's expression that he didn't favour option three, but he didn't favour it slightly less than he didn't favour the other two.

'I suppose we could start to make plans for my return to Lincoln,' Nigel suggested.

'There you go again,' Cwen said. 'We make plans? What's we got to do with it? You're the one who has to get to Lincoln. You have to make the plans.'

'But we do want him to go,' Wat pointed out.

'Hm.' Cwen wasn't happy about that.

'And if he's not capable of doing it himself…,' Wat left the question open.

'He's not capable of doing anything himself,' Cwen agreed. 'He's the reason we're all in this mess to begin with. Peter's Purse!' She considered Nigel with her most withering glare, the one that could shrivel nettles.

Nigel seemed to accept this defeat in his inimitable manner; by pretending it hadn't happened at all, or if it had, had actually been a great victory.

'Bread, cheese and meat it is then,' Wat said, sounding as relieved as Hermitage that this awkward situation was over. 'Taken together,' he added, nodding that Nigel should sit.

Nigel couldn't hide his look of rather disgusted resignation but sat anyway.

'Peter's Purse,' Hermitage said as he took a chunk of bread. 'It is a bit odd, don't you think?'

'The whole thing is odd,' Cwen agreed as they settled to the meal. 'But put the church and the Normans together and you probably get three kinds of odd. No,' she added with another look at Nigel. 'There isn't any wine. Not at noon.'

'Oh.' The disappointed sigh came from Wat.

Hermitage tore off a smaller piece of his bread and nibbled it thoughtfully.

'Why would the whole question of Peter's Purse end up in

the hands of Nigel? It is a matter of great importance to the most important people in the world.'

Nigel seemed to think that this made him the ideal candidate.

'A rather lowly and minor official in a town of limited significance,' Hermitage summarised.

'Here,' Nigel complained.

'Oh, sorry.' Hermitage hadn't really been thinking about what he was saying; which was perfectly normal, his thoughts being quite capable of making themselves heard without his intervention. 'I mean, if the king really wanted someone to take charge of the purse, he would appoint one of his own nobles.'

'We've been over this,' Cwen sighed. 'William only wanted to appoint someone who could be killed. That way he avoids paying the tax and the blame for not paying it at the same time.'

'But why not a noble he doesn't like?' Hermitage asked. 'It would be a good way of getting rid of someone.'

No one had any objection to this disgraceful idea.

'And why Nigel, of all people? Nobody outside of Lincoln would have heard of him, let alone the king.'

Again, Nigel took silent offence at his belittlement.

Cwen was nodding to herself as she gnawed on a chicken leg. 'It's as if the king went to great lengths to choose the most hopeless and ineffective person there was.'

'Do you mind?' Nigel spoke up.

'Be quiet,' Cwen instructed. 'Not only is he of no note whatsoever, he couldn't even defend himself if he were attacked. Alyssa would put up more of a fight.'

'How did the king even know of him?' Wat asked through a mouthful of everything at once.

Hermitage suddenly had a horrible thought. 'If it was the king who sent the instruction,' he said, mainly to himself.

'Gilbert said it was,' Cwen pointed out.

'Yes, but how did he know? I imagine all he got was a parchment of some sort with the king's seal on it. Anyone could have sent that. Ranulph de Sauveloy, for example.'

'There is a man who could talk a snake out of its skin.'

'Does it matter?' Wat asked. 'An instruction came from someone to appoint Nigel. Gilbert believed it was the king.'

Hermitage saw that this was true and but didn't help much. 'But,' he said as he thought on, 'it puts the whole business at a much lower level than the king. Down amongst people who might know of Nigel.'

'Ranulph?' Cwen asked. 'He's still a pretty important Norman, and Nigel is a no one.'

'I am not no one,' Nigel protested.

'And Ranulph is an inquisitive devil,' Wat said. 'The king instructed him to make a record of everything in the kingdom, he was bound to come across Nigel sooner or later.'[9]

'Does it matter though?' Hermitage asked. 'We still have people who want Nigel dead. I'm not sure this is getting us anywhere.'

'You started it,' Cwen complained.

Hermitage could only shrug.

As they all returned to their food, gloomier than when they started, there was a clatter from below and the front door crashed open.

'Wat, Wat!' A voice called out urgently.

'Ern?' Wat asked, rising from his seat. 'What is it? Forgotten the sweetmeats?'

[9] The king did do this, it's in The King's Investigator, a Chronicle of Brother Hermitage, so it must be true.

Ern's head appeared at the top of the stairs and it was very flushed.

'Soldiers,' he panted out. 'In town. And they're asking for Hermitage.'

'Oh Lord,' Hermitage sighed. 'Not more investigation?'

Ern shook his head and gasped. 'They say they want to know about Nigel of Lincoln.'

Caput XXI: Hide The Hider

'Oh well, that's that, then.' Cwen might have just discovered that a thread in her tapestry had broken.

'What do you mean, that's that, then?' Nigel squeaked. 'There are soldiers looking for me.'

'Looking for Hermitage, he said.'

'Only because they think he's got me.'

'Which is why I say that's that, then.'

Wat was nodding his agreement. 'We might as well take you to them now. Perhaps they'll be lenient.'

'Lenient?' Nigel could not believe his ears. 'They'll want to kill me.'

'Could be.'

'Could be? What is the matter with you people?'

'There's nothing the matter with us,' Cwen said. 'It's the soldiers that there's something the matter with. And then you. There'll probably be something the matter with you in a little while.'

Nigel looked ready to climb into another sack. 'You must hide me.'

Wat shook his head as if he'd just been asked for a refund on a tapestry. 'We can't do that.'

'You've spent the last week hiding me.' Pleading had returned to Nigel's voice.

'Yes,' Cwen agreed. 'But no one had actually come here asking for you.'

'What difference does that make?'

'It's Hermitage, you see,' Wat explained.

Nigel's panicky eyes darted over to Hermitage, who was just as confused by all this as Nigel.

'Honesty.' Cwen shook her head in disappointment.

'Honesty?' Nigel asked. 'What's that got to do with anything?'

'Hermitage's honesty, to be precise.'

'We've told him about it on more than one occasion,' Wat continued. 'But he will persist. It's a very disappointing trait.'

Hermitage now saw what the problem was. If soldiers came here asking if they had Nigel, he would have to say yes. He had no strong moral objection to telling a falsehood to some Norman soldiers; particularly Norman soldiers who wanted to kill someone. It was just that he wasn't capable of doing it.

If they asked the question directly, he would hum and ah for a while, then he'd gabble something about not understanding the question. Soon after that he'd collapse and confess all.

'He can tell them I'm not here,' Nigel insisted.

'That would be dishonest.'

Nigel looked quickly from one to the other as if trying to spot the one who was about to break down and say this was all a jest. He even gave a questioning look to Ern, who only shrugged his agreement. 'It was the only way I had to get Wat to pay his bill,' the innkeeper explained. 'I asked Hermitage if he had any money.'

'Well, that explains a lot,' Wat complained.

'You can't be serious,' Nigel pressed.

No one revealed the jolly trick they must be playing on poor Nigel.

Hermitage could only look apologetic. 'I am a man of God,' he offered by way of explanation.

'That's no use to me.' Nigel was now hopping about as if looking for a hole to vanish into.

'Of course,' Hermitage said thoughtfully, 'if I could tell the truth, but it was a useful truth, that might help.'

'What's he gabbling about?'

'You can imagine that investigating murder requires dealing with the most disreputable types,' Hermitage explained.

'How awful for you.' Nigel was clearly more worried about the disreputable types with Norman helmets and swords who were on their way.

'And so a measure of deception is required.'

'Well, measure some out now.'

Hermitage appreciated that Nigel found himself in an awkward situation, but patience was always a virtue.

'In these situations, given that I cannot tell a bare lie, we make sure that I can tell the truth, but perhaps not quite all of it.'

'What a shocking sinner you are,' Nigel sneered sarcastically.

'I know,' Hermitage bowed his head.

'Perhaps getting to the point would be a good skill to develop?' Nigel prompted.

'Ah, yes. Now, when the soldiers get here and ask if we are hiding Nigel, I need to be able to say no.'

'But you are.' Nigel was getting positively desperate now.

'We are now, yes. But when the soldiers ask, we won't be.'

'Eh?'

'We simply stop hiding you.'

Nigel ran a hand over his face. 'Forgive me if I'm not following this, but the whole point of the last week has been to hide me from the Normans.'

'And the pope,' Cwen added.

'Yes, him too. Now, when the Normans actually turn up, you stop hiding me?'

'That's it,' Hermitage was pleased that he understood.

'You're all mad.'

'I don't mean that we give you up,' Hermitage continued. 'I just mean that we are not hiding you.'

'And how is that going to help?'

'We could do as Wat said. You blend into the workshop. Become an apprentice or something.'

'I'm not teaching him,' Cwen said.

Hermitage ignored her. 'When the soldiers ask if we're hiding you, I can say no. Because we aren't. You're in plain sight. You see?'

'And when they ask if I'm in the workshop at all?'

'Ah.' Hermitage had to give that one some more thought. 'Don't be.'

'What? Do I wait outside and introduce myself to them?'

'No, of course not. That would be silly.'

'That would be silly! Ha.' Nigel appeared to be on the verge of a fit.

'Go and tend to the vegetables or something.'

'Hide in the privy,' Cwen suggested. 'Preferably the bottom bit.'

'If you're not in the workshop, I can honestly say that you are not here.'

'And all this makes you feel better, does it?'

'It's not a case of feeling better,' Hermitage said. 'It's just that when I lie, everyone can see that I'm lying. I can't help it. This way, I don't have to.'

'It still sounds pretty dishonest for a man of God.'

'You're right,' Cwen agreed seriously. 'Perhaps it would be best if you went outside and met the soldiers. That way they won't damage the workshop with their swords.'

Nigel cast one more look around, clearly searching for

anyone who had a half-decent idea, instead of this nonsense.

'And they don't know what you look like,' Wat added. 'Just carry some bales of thread around. Take some finished work to the store, make yourself useful.'

Cwen snapped her fingers. 'Got it.'

They all looked at her with interest.

'He would still be in the workshop, but not part of it. Would that work?' she asked Hermitage.

'I'm not sure I understand, but I suppose I could define "workshop" as the collection of people who, through their combined efforts produce tapestry. Instead of the building itself, do you see?'

'Near enough,' Cwen said, blinking at this nonsense.

'And just how can he be in the workshop without being part of the workshop?' Wat asked rather sarcastically.

'He can work with the one person who doesn't make tapestry. He can help Mrs Grod.'

Wat, Ern and Hermitage all crossed themselves, while Nigel looked very worried.

Wat took a breath and spoke with sincerity to Nigel. 'I'd go with the Normans if I were you.'

. . .

The approach to Mrs Grod's realm would have to be a cautious one; it didn't do to catch her by surprise. At the bottom of the stairs, Ern had made straight for the door and wished them luck as they went. He would try to delay the soldiers but didn't hold out much hope.

'Ern,' Wat called after him. 'Send up my delivery as well.'

Ern shook his head that this was a distraction from more important matters.

'What delivery?' Cwen asked

Wat ignored her and led down the corridor to the cooking area, where the figure of Mrs Grod held sway. She also held several dangerous tools as well as the contents of her pot, which could do even more damage.

Throughout the workshop, Mrs Grod was a figure of awe - looking as if someone had dug her up. Her size meant that she was not a person to be crossed, but the way she looked at people gave the most concern. It was the same way she looked at everything else; chickens, pigs, vegetables, people; all were equal in Mrs Grod's eyes.

Speculation about Mr Grod was rife in the workshop, some suggesting that as she brought her concoctions together, she put a little of her husband into every creation; diners just had to find it and leave it on the side of the plate.

She had only come up in conversation with Wat once when he had explained that she had been with him for years. Hermitage strongly suspected that this was not at the choice of the weaver. How anyone would get rid of Mrs Grod once she'd decided to stay, God only knew.

If Mrs Grod had a soft spot, it was for Wat, and even then, she hid it well. Only he could talk to her without immediate danger, and only he conjured the monosyllabic replies that constituted her conversation.

She seemed to look upon Cwen as some sort of annoying ingredient that had escaped her attention and was now bothering her precious Wat. Cwen's own fierceness and the ability to stare down most people appeared to maintain a fragile peace between the two women.

Hermitage only puzzled the cook. Whenever they met, she simply showed complete confusion at what a monk was doing here. And every time she saw him, she seemed freshly surprised.

Hermitage, Cwen and Nigel stood back as Wat approached.

The noon meal was finished now, and the low groans of the apprentices provided the usual backdrop. Anyone would think that this would be the time for the cooking area to be cleaned and tidied, ready for the next day. If anyone wanted to think that, they were welcome to get on with it.

'Aha, Mrs Grod,' Wat said as if coming upon her by accident.

Mrs Grod turned her head, saw Wat and smiled.

The four of them took another step back.

The smile was not one of a woman who is taking pleasure from a meeting; this was the smile of a woman who's just thought of something she'd like to do, but probably isn't allowed.

She was dressed in her usual simple cloth dress that fell from her shoulders to the floor. It had spent as long in the kitchen as she had, but had fared less well. Some apprentices suggested that if she served up her dress instead of her cooking, they'd probably be better fed.

She was of indeterminate age, but must be at least forty to Hermitage's eye, and those forty years had been hard ones. She was naturally tall, being well over five-and-a-half feet but was broad as well. More questions were raised over this, as she clearly didn't eat her own cooking.

'We've brought Nigel,' Wat said.

Cwen and Hermitage hauled Nigel forward, despite his attempts to go in the other direction.

'Yes,' Wat continued in the face of Mrs Grod's appraisal of Nigel, which was not comfortable. 'He's, erm, free to, ah, help. If there's anything you need doing at all?'

Mrs Grod's look now combined confusion and offence; as if she needed any help in her own kitchen.

'He can clean the floor?' Wat suggested.

'He can what?' Nigel whispered in horror as he looked at the floor. Or rather, he looked at the layers under which there must be a floor somewhere.

Mrs Grod also considered her kitchen floor and clearly looked upon it with some pride.

'The truth is,' Wat chanced a step forward and lowered his voice. 'We need him out of the way for a while. Some Normans might be looking for him, and we can't have him in the workshop. You'd really be helping me out.' And then he smiled.

The effect on Mrs Grod was quite alarming, She blushed. She was red-faced most of the time, but now her neck joined in. She immediately hid this reaction by turning back to her pot and forcing something down into its depths, which probably wanted to get out.

'Excellent,' Wat said quickly. 'In you go, then.'

Hermitage felt quite ashamed as he and Cwen pushed the reluctant cook's assistant into the kitchen and then stepped smartly back, in case they were sucked in as well.

This got a grunt from Mrs Grod, so the mission could be considered a success.

'We'll come and get him when the Normans have gone,' Wat said.

'If he's still here,' Cwen muttered with a rueful glance at the pot on the fire.

Wat breathed huge, deep breaths as they retreated from the cook's domain. 'That went well,' he said, his voice breaking slightly. 'A troop of Norman soldiers will be a piece of pie after that.'

'And now you can say that we are not hiding Nigel and that he is not in the workshop,' Cwen said.

'I can,' Hermitage confirmed. Nigel was in plain sight in the kitchen.

'Honestly, the things we do for you.' She glanced back towards the cooking area as if half expecting to see Nigel's feet as the rest of him slipped into Mrs Grod's next meal.

As they retreated to the upstairs room to await the inevitable Norman conquest, Hermitage recovered from his close encounter with the cook.

'How do they know?' he asked. 'How do these Normans know to come here? And who are they?'

'At least Nigel's not hiding and he's not in the workshop, remember?' Cwen reminded him.

'Of course. But what do they want?'

'We don't know how many Normans are involved in this, or what they want,' Wat said. 'This could be an entirely new band who have come to offer Nigel a parade, for all we know. Hurrah for the holder of Peter's Purse.'

Hermitage scowled that this was not helping his growing sense of panic; apart from helping it grow. 'They know he left Nottingham with us. They know he came here. They already know. Saying he isn't here is not going to be any good at all.'

'Calm down, for goodness' sake,' Cwen urged. 'They know nothing of the sort. All they might know is that we were at Nottingham and so was Nigel. He probably went to Lincoln and we came here. In fact, we saw him on the Lincoln road, didn't we?'

'But we didn't,' Hermitage fretted.

'Hermitage,' Cwen looked him in the eye. 'When we stepped out of the keep door and walked down the hill, remember?'

'Erm, yes.'

'Did that track lead to Lincoln, or here?'

Hermitage thought about it for a moment. 'Well, both, I suppose. You'd have to get to the lower gate and then choose your direction.'

'There you are then. We left Gilbert on the Derby road and saw Nigel on the Lincoln road.'

'That's rather a fine differentiation,' Hermitage protested.

There was a loud and very military thump on the door.

'It's all right,' Cwen said. 'Norman soldiers don't do anything fine.'

'Oh my,' Hermitage said.

'Better answer the door.' Wat stood. 'Look what happened to the last man who tried to stop the Normans coming in.
'

Caput XXII: Interrogation

'All right, where is he?' A large and nasty looking Norman soldier asked after Wat opened the door.

'Here I am,' Wat said with a smile, holding his arms wide.

The soldier scowled at him. 'Brother Hermitage?' he asked carefully. He scowled, obviously thinking that monks weren't supposed to look like this.

'No, Wat the Weaver.' Wat sounded confused but gave a little bow.

'We don't want you.' The large, nasty soldier was now irritated as well. 'We want Brother Hermitage.'

Wat shrugged. 'What's he look like?'

'Don't get clever with me.'

'Wouldn't dream of it,' Wat said sincerely.

'You know very well what he looks like. You're his disgusting weaver.'

'I'm the disgusting weaver,' Wat corrected. 'He's my monk.'

The soldier grunted as he pushed Wat aside and strode into the workshop.

'Do come in,' Wat said.

The soldier was followed by three of his fellows, equally large and equally nasty, and who looked at Wat as if he should be punished for the impudence of being in his own workshop.

Hermitage and Cwen arrived at the bottom of the stairs and considered the Norman invasion.

Cwen appeared to reluctantly conclude that these Normans were probably too big for her to take on her own.

Hermitage was fighting the urge to confess and throw himself on their mercy, which he was pretty confident they wouldn't have.

'Is this the monk?' The lead soldier asked, pointing at Hermitage.

'That monk?' Wat asked.

'Yes, that monk,' the soldier growled out slowly.

'Is that monk the monk?' Wat frowned.

Then he gurgled as the soldier took him by the throat. 'They said you'd be trouble,' he explained.

'I am Brother Hermitage.' Hermitage stepped forward quickly and Wat was released. 'King William's Investigator.'

Cwen went over to Wat and took his arm, daring the soldier to try that again.

'Good.' The soldier looked Hermitage up and down. 'Who is it, then?'

'Erm, who is what?' Hermitage asked. He had worried about a direct question, but this one confused him completely. When the soldier asked if Nigel was in the kitchen, he didn't know what he'd say. Well, he did, it would be yes, but he knew that wouldn't help.

'Who killed Nigel of Lincoln?' the soldier said. 'I won't ask twice.'

As this was not at all what Hermitage had expected, he didn't have an idea what to say.

'Who killed Nigel of Lincoln?' Cwen repeated the question, seeing that Hermitage had come to a halt.

'Yes. Come on, out with it. Who did it?'

'Is he dead?' Cwen asked.

'He'd have to be if he'd been murdered,' Wat explained.

'Oh yes,' Cwen nodded as if grateful for the clarification.

'Who did it?' Hermitage longed to say that no one had done it and that Nigel was fine. Perhaps that would make all this confusion go away.

'You are the King's Investigator,' the soldier confirmed.

'You said so yourself.'

Hermitage nodded that this was correct.

'We were told that the King's Investigator says who's done a murder.'

'Erm, yes, I suppose so.'

The soldier sighed his impatience. 'So, who murdered Nigel of Lincoln?'

"No one", was jumping around on the end of Hermitage's tongue, just waiting to be released. 'Has he been murdered?' he managed to ask.

'Has he been murdered?' The soldier was clearly not happy with this question. 'What do you mean, has he been murdered?'

'Well,' Hermitage tried to look confused and nonplussed, which was quite easy in the circumstances. 'He may be dead, but do we know he's been murdered? You're the first one who's suggested that he has been.' He managed to forget Raegnald asking for Nigel to be murdered, which was a completely different tense, after all.

'Do you want Hermitage to investigate?' Cwen asked. 'Is that why you've come?'

'I have come,' the soldier said very slowly and very carefully, 'so that the King's Investigator can tell us who killed Nigel of Lincoln.'

Cwen nodded that she understood. 'You want him to investigate. That's fine, he can do that, can't you Hermitage?'

Hermitage gave a sort of nod.

'So?' the soldier asked.

'So what?' Hermitage replied.

'I am losing my patience,' the solider reported.

Hermitage thought that the man hadn't demonstrated that he had any to begin with.

'So, who did it? It's quite simple, for God's sake. I shouldn't have to tell you how to do your own job. You're the investigator, you know who did a murder, tell us who did this one.'

Hermitage saw a glimmer of the misunderstanding that was at the root of this very confusing conversation; yet another one.

'Do you think that investigation means simply knowing who committed a murder?'

'Of course. Can't think what other use it would be.'

'How would I know?' Hermitage pleaded.

'I don't know, do I?' the soldier complained. 'I'm not the investigator. If I was, I'd know who'd done it.'

'How?' Hermitage hoped the question might bring some insight to this man. 'How would you know who'd done it?'

The soldier shrugged his large and nasty shoulders. 'I assume all killers have to send you word that they've killed someone, then you keep the records.'

Hermitage could only sag as he was once more surprised by just how wrong people could be about almost anything. He really would have to write that dictionarium. Or perhaps he could just put the single definition on a sheet of parchment and pin it to the workshop wall. By this means, anyone with completely the wrong idea would go away without bothering him.

The new problem was how to tell a rough and violent-looking Norman soldier that he was wrong.

'Actually, it means that I work out who did it.'

'Work it out?' The soldier frowned at this expression as if it was one he'd never even heard of before.

'Yes, I take all the evidence and information and put it together to come to a conclusion.'

'About who did the murder?' The soldier was starting to sound a bit lost in all this detail.

'That's right.' Hermitage was pleased that the man had got it.

The soldier nodded to himself as he processed this new information. 'Who did it, then?'

'I don't know,' Hermitage said blankly. 'I haven't investigated, er, worked it out yet.'

The soldier folded his arms and stared at Hermitage for a moment or two. 'Have you worked it out now?' he asked.

'It doesn't happen immediately,' Cwen explained with dangerous condescension. 'It takes time.'

'We can wait,' the soldier said. 'But we haven't got all day.'

'It could take weeks,' Cwen said.

'Weeks?' The soldier did not believe what he was hearing.

Hermitage nodded. 'We have to find out how Nigel was killed and who could have done the deed. Then we see who wanted him dead. If there are lots of them, we have to consider who is most likely.' As he said this, he had to remind himself that the murder victim was in the kitchen, probably trying to scrub the floor.

The soldier was shaking his head at this unnecessary complication.

'You were with him in Nottingham,' the soldier said suspiciously, apparently just remembering what he'd been told.

'We were,' Hermitage agreed, wondering who'd told him. 'And he was to leave for Lincoln.'

'And we came here,' Cwen added.

'And you haven't seen him since?'

'Absolutely,' Cwen spoke. 'That's exactly what we're saying. We're saying that we haven't seen him.'

Hermitage's mind wormed around as it tried to accept that this was true; that was what they were saying.

'Why don't you Saxons talk properly?' the soldier complained. He breathed out heavily, clearly disappointed that this mission was not as straightforward as he had hoped.

Hermitage had some sympathy.

'Well,' Wat said brightly. 'Now that we know what we've got to do, we can get on with it. Nice of you to call though.'

'Stop talking,' the soldier instructed Wat, who nodded happy compliance. 'I think we'd better take a look around.'

'What for?' Cwen asked innocently. 'If Nigel's been murdered, he's hardly likely to be here, is he, Hermitage?'

'If he's been murdered.' Hermitage repeated carefully. 'He is certainly not here.' He was in danger of tying his mind in knots.

'The King's Investigator doesn't get sent the bodies, you know,' Cwen clarified.

The soldier looked around the space and spotted the stairs. 'What's up there?' he demanded.

'Erm, upstairs,' Cwen said.

The lead soldier nodded at one of his men. 'Take a look.'

The new man drew his sword with pleasure and slowly ascended the stairs, clearly expecting an ambush, or at the very least, strong resistance.

A few moments later he descended again looking disappointed. 'Nothing,' he reported.

'What do you have an upstairs for anyway?' the main man asked. 'You Saxons all live in huts.'

Cwen shrugged. 'Wat saw an upstairs in an old Roman house one day and decided to get one himself.'

Wat nodded.

The soldier appraised them. 'Idiots,' he concluded.

'Right, let's have a look at the rest of the place.' He strode off down the corridor.

Hermitage swallowed hard to contain the small squeak that wanted to get out as they approached Mrs Grod's territory.

The cook looked up from her pot and deposited her gaze on the new arrivals. Even four fully grown Norman soldiers halted in their tracks.

'Erm,' the soldier seemed caught between the questions, "who is this", and "what is this".

'Our cook,' Cwen said. 'Mrs Grod.'

'A cook?' The soldier sounded alarmed at Mrs Grod having anything to do with food; quite wisely.

'She's been with us for years.'

'Really?' The soldier clearly wouldn't let Mrs Grod anywhere near him for any length of time.

Mrs Grod curled her lips as she considered the soldiers. Whether this was a threat or the preliminary step to seeing what soldier tasted like, was hard to tell.

Either way, the Normans seemed quite happy to leave Mrs Grod to her horrible business.

'And who's that?' The soldier asked, pointing at Nigel.

Nigel was under the table. It wasn't immediately clear whether he had been put there by Mrs Grod or had discovered it was the safest place to be.

'That?' Cwen bent down to look at the shape.

Mrs Grod also turned and stooped to look at Nigel. She grunted as if only now recalling that that was where she had put him.

'Kitchen drudge,' Cwen dismissed the unimportant figure.

'What's he doing under the table?'

'Some drudgery, I imagine. Probably on the floor.'

'He's very well dressed for a kitchen drudge.'

Cwen peered a little harder. She stood up straight and put her hands on her hips. 'Have you been stealing clothes again?' she demanded of Nigel who was cowering so much that he couldn't cower any further. 'We've told him about this before,' Cwen informed the soldier.

She addressed Nigel. 'When these nice men have gone, it's back in your rags for you.'

Nigel said nothing.

'Well?' Cwen demanded.

Nigel tried nodding.

'Yes mistress,' Cwen prompted.

'Yes, mistress,' Nigel managed.

Cwen tutted at the soldier. 'You just can't get the quality of drudge these days,' she complained. 'I don't know what the world's coming to when people think drudgery is too good for them.'

'Let's see the rest of the place.' The soldier sounded quite keen to move on from the kitchen.

As they left, he cast a last look at Mrs Grod, probably to confirm that his senses had not deceived him. As he did so, the cook tipped her head slightly, gave a smile that revealed the remainders of her teeth and even fluttered her eyelids; much as a bat flutters its wings in the dark, right by your ear. He quickly retreated from the kitchen.

Hermitage hoped that his breath of relief wasn't audible as they left Nigel behind. He couldn't really believe that they had got away with this. Surely, the soldier knew perfectly well that the man under the table was Nigel, and they would go back in a moment to collect him.

His confidence grew as Wat and Cwen led the way out under the covered walkway that led to the workshop proper.

The clattering and noise of the place was a huge relief from the terror of the kitchen. Hermitage was always impressed by the vitality of the room and had even selected a word most appropriate to the activity. From the Latin, naturally, industria, meaning diligence. Not that every apprentice was equally diligent, of course. And he didn't think the Normans would be interested in his etymological musings; no one ever was.

One thing that every one of these young men could do though, even with their backs turned, was detect when Cwen walked in.

Idle chatter came to a halt and was instantly replaced by detailed questions about some specific aspect of weaving. Hermitage was sure that one discussion close by began as the tale of an encounter with a maid of the town, and ended with the apprentice complaining that his warp was showing.

Hartle, the old weaving master, looked up from the chair in which he was resting.

As heads turned and the presence of four large Normans was noted, conversation died completely.

'These men are having a look around,' Cwen announced.

Heads looked but said nothing.

Once more, Hermitage's fragile state took charge. He had personally heard several of the apprentices list the things they would do to Nigel if he didn't stop treating them as his personal servants. He only hoped the Normans didn't ask them anything.

'Apparently, someone called Nigel of Lincoln has been murdered,' Cwen said as if imparting exciting news.

Hermitage could swear he heard one of the apprentices mutter, "good".

'How do we know one of these didn't do it?' one of the

other soldiers asked.

'Murder Nigel?' Cwen asked in disbelief. 'No,' she answered her own question. 'Nigel of Lincoln would be in Lincoln. These boys are all in Derby.'

To Hermitage's ear, that argument had more holes than one of poor Egland's tapestries; Egland being the newest apprentice, who Cwen had already recommended be replaced by a sheep, who would do a better job of weaving its own wool into something recognisable.

The Normans seemed to accept this reasoning, though. They did consider each of the faces in the room as if looking for some twitch of confession but appeared satisfied.

'And there's no one else here?' the lead soldier asked.

'That's it,' Cwen confirmed. 'You've seen us all. And none of us killed him. We only found out he was dead when you told us.'

Hermitage twitched as the half-truths circled him like pecking magpies.

'Hm,' the soldier was still not happy. Eventually, he nodded himself and gave a silent instruction to his companions that they should leave.

Hermitage breathed a sigh of relief.

'Come on then,' the soldier said. 'We'll take ale in your upstairs, and you can explain just what you were doing in Nottingham in the first place.'

Hermitage's sigh stopped, as did the rest of his breath.

'Not a problem at all,' Wat said, indicating that he would lead the way.

. . .

Back in the upper chamber, the soldiers settled

comfortably with mugs of ale. The three assistants, as Hermitage had come to think of them, put their feet up on stools and looked ready for a little sleep.

'So,' the lead Norman asked, 'Nottingham. What were you doing there?'

'Just trade,' Wat said. 'My tapestries go all over the country.'

'Your tapestries!' Cwen muttered.

'We've only just sent one to Lincoln,' Wat ignored the comment.

'How nice,' the soldier said nastily. 'Nottingham not being Lincoln. And what were you doing with Lord Gilbert?'

'Oh,' Wat was happy to explain this. 'We know Lord Gilbert from way back, don't we, Hermitage?'

Hermitage was happy to nod his agreement to this truth, it being one of the very few that had come his way.

'And the lovely Lady Aveline,' Wat added.

Hermitage noticed the hardened Norman warrior's shoulders shiver at that name.

'Just so I understand,' the soldier said, his sarcasm at the ready. 'The three of you, including King William's Investigator, go to Nottingham to sell some tapestry, and you happen to visit Lord Gilbert at the time Nigel of Lincoln is there.'

'That's it,' Wat agreed.

'And then you left at the same time as Nigel, but he went to Lincoln and you came here.'

'There you are,' Wat was happy that they were all agreed.

'I don't believe a word of it,' the soldier concluded.

Hermitage didn't blame him.

'We had no idea Nigel was going to be there, did we Hermitage?' Cwen asked.

'Erm, no.' Hermitage could agree with that one as well.

'We certainly didn't know anyone wanted to kill him.' Cwen continued.

'Why do you want to know who did?' Wat asked casually.

'I told you, that's our concern.'

'Now,' the soldier got back to the question in hand. 'What were you doing in Nottingham? The King's Investigator does not sell tapestry.'

'No, he doesn't,' Wat agreed. 'But we do and Hermitage wanted to go as well.'

'Why?'

Why, indeed? Hermitage thought. These questions were becoming far too specific and unavoidable. He felt the moment he was going to tell all was fast approaching. There were only so many truths he could wriggle around before the real ones got out.

But he knew that once he began, he would have to finish. The truth of going to Nottingham was precisely because of Nigel's appointment. If that one got out, the whole world would collapse around him. Raegnald, Father Baldice, Gilbert and worst of all, Nigel in the kitchen. What possible explanation could he come up with for going to Nottingham that bore any resemblance to the truth?

'It's nice to get out occasionally,' Cwen said.

'It's nice to get out?' the soldier asked with frank disbelief.

Hermitage sagged. If that was the best they could come up with, he might as well pray to God for deliverance.

The soldier turned to face Hermitage directly, opened his mouth to issue the fatal query, and then shut it again as there was a call from downstairs.

'I say,' a cultured voice cried out. 'Is anyone here?'

Hermitage recognised the voice. 'Father Baldice?' he asked,

more in disbelieving relief than as a genuine question. He'd never thought he would be glad to meet the priest again.

'Baldice?' the soldier asked angrily. 'What's he doing here?'

'It's nice to get out?' Cwen suggested.

The soldier pointed a warning finger at Cwen before getting up and heading to the stairs with dread purpose.

His companions, stirred by the commotion, followed him.

Cwen blew a long breath. 'Do you think we're likely to find out what on earth is really going on now?'

Wat shook his head. 'Not a chance. But it'll be interesting to watch.'

Caput XXIII: Church and State

They all gathered at the bottom of the stairs, audience to the encounter between the hardened and well-armed soldiers and one well-dressed priest.

Hermitage wondered if this might be symbolic of the conflict between church and state and the struggle for supremacy as new forces emerged across Europe following the demise of Anglo-Saxon power. He shook his head to get such nonsense out of the way and wondered if the soldiers would actually hit the priest with something.

'Baldice,' the lead soldier said as if pointing out woodworm in Wat's door.

'Ah, Captain Leslandes, we meet again.' Baldice responded brightly.

Hermitage hadn't thought to ask the soldier's name, it didn't seem to matter, somehow.

'And just what are you doing here?' Leslandes demanded.

'I might ask the very same question of you.'

Leslandes sneered. 'I am on the king's service, speaking to the King's Investigator.'

Baldice smiled, his confidence simmering through his calm tones. 'And I am on church business, come to speak to a brother monk.' He held his arms wide. 'We are all doing our duty as is right and proper.'

'I'm afraid the King's Investigator is currently occupied upon the king's business.' Leslandes seemed to think that this was final.

'Ah,' Baldice's smile didn't waver one jot. 'But there is no higher duty than that to God.'

Hermitage didn't like being in the middle of any of this, whatever it was. It was all sounding a bit too symbolic for his taste. He was certainly not going to take part in any conflict or struggle.

'I think God's anointed king takes precedence over a lowly priest,' Leslandes hit back.

Baldice nodded his agreement. 'A lowly priest following the instructions of his superiors in the church. As you are following the instructions of, who? Some other soldier, I imagine.'

Wat leaned forward and whispered through his grin. 'This is getting nasty.'

'I take my orders from the court of the king,' Leslandes sounded worryingly confident as well now. 'Which is where I got my fellows here.'

Leslandes' fellows stepped forward with a swagger, obviously to show that there were more of them than there were priests.

'And estimable companions they seem to be. Is that Carnac I see there?' Baldice smiled an acknowledgement to one of the soldiers. 'And how fares your sister in the convent? Still well and unharmed, I trust.'

'Ohh,' Wat hissed. 'Vicious.'

The soldier called Carnac suddenly looked a bit less swaggerfull.

'What's your business, Baldice?' Leslandes asked the blunt question.

Baldice acknowledged with a modest bow of the head that the preliminary skirmishes were now over. 'I am sent on a matter of concern. Concern for a dear servant of the church.'

'As you can see, he's fine.' Leslandes nodded towards Hermitage.

'Not Brother Hermitage, I fear.' Baldice shook his head in sadness at his news. 'A poor servant only recently appointed and now lost, it seems.'

Leslandes shook his head as if this meant nothing to him. 'You should be more careful with your servants.'

'Oh, the church suffers in this. We believe some other force has taken the devoted one and it is only proper that we discover the truth of the matter.'

'Quite right too,' Leslandes agreed. 'Unfortunately, the King's Investigator is rather tied up at the moment. Perhaps the king would be gracious enough to release him to you in a few months. If you make a suitable request.'

Hermitage had a horrible revelation. These people didn't actually care about him or his investigation, or Nigel, even, they were playing their own game and if he got in the way, it might not go well.

He recalled a new pastime that had come over with the Danes and also seemed popular with some Normans. It was played on a board with a number of pieces, the front row being called paons by the invaders. The Saxons pronounced this as pawns. These pieces could be thrown into the game as sacrifices, being of little value. Hermitage felt quite a lot like a pawn. He was quite pleased with the neat comparison.

'No need,' Baldice said, sending a chill down Hermitage's back as he felt as if he had just been taken by the bishop. 'For the purpose of this enquiry, I have been asked to, what shall we call it?' He glanced at Hermitage. 'Investigate?'

'The king already has an investigator,' Leslandes pointed out with malice.

'He does,' Baldice did his little bow once more. 'And Brother Hermitage may well be able to shed some light on the matter in question.

'However, we would not want to burden the king's appointee with onerous duties concerning a matter within the church's remit. With this in mind, his Holiness has graciously consented to contribute to the resolution of the question.' Now Baldice looked Leslandes in the eye. 'I shall be the Pope's Investigator.'

'You've just been outranked, Hermitage,' Cwen said.

Hermitage didn't know whether this was a good thing or a bad one. He naturally assumed bad.

'As you wish,' Leslandes didn't seem concerned about this development. 'You will do what you must. I shall continue to look into the issue of the king's appointed servant,' he said these words very precisely. 'Nigel of Lincoln.'

'Ah, wonderful,' Baldice beamed. 'Then we can aid one another.'

Leslandes shook his head as if disappointed that Baldice was getting this all wrong. 'The church need not concern itself with the king's man. We can let you know when we reach a conclusion.'

'A king's man, doing the work of the church,' Baldice corrected.

'Good Lord,' Wat whispered. 'They're really talking about what they're talking about.'

Hermitage gave him a very puzzled glance.

'Nigel,' Wat explained. 'It's taken long enough. Up until now, they've been talking about anything but. I think this means things have got pretty serious.'

Hermitage longed to put his hand up and say that Nigel was under the kitchen table. Perhaps that would make everyone go away. He suspected the consequences would be a lot worse than that.

'A king's man who will be investigated by the king,' Leslandes insisted.

'Under the watchful eye of his Holiness,' Baldice

countered.

'Who has no jurisdiction in the matter,' Leslandes bit back.

'Who will give what guidance he may.'

'When no guidance is required.'

'Excuse me,' Wat spoke up.

Leslandes and Baldice seemed to have come to a position where they could go on throwing sentences at one another without either of them moving an inch.

'What is it?' Leslandes demanded, clearly irritated by the interruption.

'Nigel.'

'What about him?'

'I'm confused. We're confused, I expect.'

Baldice and Leslandes considered him as some child who's just asked where babies come from.

Wat took a breath. 'Captain Leslandes, you have come here asking for the murder of Nigel to be investigated.'

'Definitely murder, then?' Baldice asked with some pleasure.

'And Father Baldice, it was only a few days ago that you turned up in our bushes suggesting that we shouldn't investigate Nigel's death.'

'Did he now?' It was Leslandes' turn to gloat.

'What nonsense,' Baldice smiled. 'The weaver is a good fabricator of many things. Tales included, it seems.'

'But, you...,' Hermitage began. He didn't like to call a priest a liar.

'I made no mention of anyone called Nigel. It was you who brought the name up,' Baldice pointed out.

'You were still in the bushes,' Cwen said. 'Strange place for a priest.'

Wat continued. 'It seems that you are both very concerned

about Nigel.'

'Quite right,' Leslandes said with an accusatory stare at Baldice.

'Absolutely,' Baldice returned the compliment.

'We are concerned for his well-being,' Leslandes offered.

'As are we,' Baldice agreed. 'We fear some harm may come to him.' He looked specifically at the Norman as he said this.

Cwen sighed. 'If you lot find him, his well-being has had it.'

'So, let's go upstairs and lay a few truths out, shall we? Instead of all this dancing about,' Wat said.

'An excellent suggestion,' Baldice said, clearly thinking that Leslandes was going to come out worse.

'I welcome it,' Leslandes said with a gesture that Baldice could go first.

In the upper chamber, Leslandes and Baldice all took seats while the soldiers stood by, waiting for something horrible to happen. Or waiting to make something horrible happen.

Wat began. 'I always find that in any negotiation, the time comes to speak plainly. Otherwise, everyone gets confused.'

Hermitage thought that time had come several days ago.

'When we were in Nottingham, we met Nigel and found that he had been appointed holder of Peter's Purse.'

'A great honour,' Baldice confirmed.

'At the king's appointment,' Leslandes specified.

'Soon after that, people started threatening him.'

'Shocking,' Baldice said, mainly at Leslandes.

'Outrageous,' Leslandes fired back.

'Quite. We left Gilbert's keep headed for Derby while Nigel went for Lincoln. After which, he was not seen again.'

Hermitage had to look at the floor.

'We can only assume this,' Wat said, 'because Captain Leslandes here has come asking about his murder.'

'Perhaps because Captain Leslandes was there at the time?' Baldice suggested.

'More like that Captain Leslandes is pursuing a wrong-doer who might be close at hand,' Leslandes responded.

'Can I assume that neither of you has actually been to Lincoln to see if he's home?' Wat asked.

It was clear from their glances that neither of them had.

Wat nodded at this piece of information. 'So, you both think that Nigel has come to some harm. Presumably at the hands of the other.'

This got no words, just some hard looks.

'If the holder of Peter's Purse has been, as it turns out, murdered? That would be an awful thing.'

'Terrible,' Leslandes agreed.

'Egregious,' Baldice nodded.

'And if it was done by a king's man, the pope would have to take some action.'

'He certainly would,' Baldice said.

'Ridiculous suggestion,' Leslandes dismissed it.

'But if it was done by a man of the church who sought to blame the king…,' Wat suggested.

'The king would be mighty in his vengeance,' Leslandes said.

'Such a thing would never happen,' Baldice concluded.

'Either way, Nigel has gone and you want to find out what happened to him.'

Both men nodded.

'Perhaps he's not missing at all,' Cwen suggested. 'It could be he just got lost.'

'Got lost?' Baldice found this hard to believe.

'He wasn't the most capable of men when it came to the

practicalities of life. But then you wouldn't know that never having met him, I assume.'

Both faces said that actually meeting the man they were so concerned about was hardly relevant.

'He could still be wandering around in the woods.'

Leslandes shook his head. 'We are concerned that some harm has already befallen him.'

'As are we,' Baldice agreed. 'We are sure of it.'

'Oh,' Wat said. 'That's interesting. How can you be sure?'

'We keep our eyes and ears open.' Baldice's accusation to Leslandes was quite clear.

'As do we,' Leslandes' own apportionment of blame was equally explicit.

'Could it be that you both have men out seeking to make sure that some harm befalls Nigel?'

'What a ridiculous suggestion,' Leslandes almost laughed.

Baldice shook his head. 'The weaver really does have an imagination.'

Wat stood and wandered over to the small window that looked out over the front of the workshop. He appeared to be using the distraction to think how he was going to take this forward.

He noticed something on the road and turned back to the room with a confident smile.

Hermitage considered the smile with some confusion. Had Wat gone mad? There was absolutely nothing to smile about in this situation.

'How are we ever going to resolve the matter?' Wat asked quite lightly as if inquiring whether they wanted ale or wine.

'We find the guilty party.' Leslandes considered Baldice and clearly saw a party of one.

'And we deal with them.' Baldice's was all for dealing in

Leslandes' direction.

'Or, oh, I don't know,' Wat was nonchalant. 'Engage more senior figures to direct matters?'

'Pah,' Baldice dismissed the suggestion that there was anyone with more authority than him.

'We can sort this out here and now,' Leslandes said with a glance at his men. 'It'll be quite simple. And quick.'

'Ah,' Wat said suddenly. 'I've got the very thing. Wait here.' He skipped off down the stairs leaving a room full of very confused people. Hermitage being chief among them.

There was a murmur of conversation from below before footsteps creaked the stairs and Wat's face reappeared. It had a horribly triumphant smirk on it. 'Just in time,' he said. 'I was waiting for Ern to let me know of the arrival.'

Another figure came up behind Wat and only when the weaver stepped aside was the new arrival revealed.

The noise Hermitage made was more of a shout than the scream he had intended and so wasn't too embarrassing.

Leslandes jumped to his feet and Baldice suddenly looked very pale indeed.

'Have you met?' Wat asked politely. 'Father Baldice, Leslandes, this is Ranulph de Sauveloy. He's come all the way from London.'

'And he has had a terrible time of it and is not at all happy,' Ranulph said. His unnervingly calm voice made it clear that his unhappiness was someone else's fault, and they were probably sitting in the room right now. And they would soon be extremely sorry about it

Caput XXIV: Surprise, Surprise!

'My Lord,' Leslandes managed to get out as he gestured his soldiers to try and look a bit more soldierly. 'I, I, I didn't know you were here.'

'Of course you didn't.'

Leslandes looked very confused and even glanced at the stairs to see if they were lying to him. 'But, you only just sent..,'

'I what?' Ranulph asked sharply.

'Nothing, my lord.'

'That's right.'

Hermitage considered this exchange and concluded that there was something going on that he didn't know about. But as that was quite normal for a murder investigation, he just saved the puzzle for later. He knew there was no chance of getting any of the Normans to give him a straight answer to anything.

Baldice gave a bow of the head but didn't get up.

The only thing Hermitage could safely conclude was that Ranulph de Sauveloy was here. In the workshop. With them. Right now. And it sounded as if Wat had sent for him. Not only had Wat gone mad, but the rest of the world had gone with him.

He managed to turn his head in Cwen's direction and saw that she was no better off. Her look of shock soon turned to one of anger, which made straight for Wat.

De Sauveloy himself simply stood there and instilled fear in everyone. He was modestly dressed, although his clothes were of the very highest quality. He was of no great stature or physical presence and could perhaps go unnoticed in a crowd, which the crowd would probably come to regret.

Hermitage shivered. King William looked upon most people as if they were already dead and if they didn't stop fidgeting, he would draw his sword and make it a reality. De Sauveloy's look was the same, but in his case, you'd probably want to do it yourself, so as not to cause him any bother. Or, if you didn't possess a sword, you would borrow one for the purpose.

Hermitage was used to feeling inadequate and insignificant, but in Ranulph de Sauveloy's presence, these words were simply not up to the task. He could only hope that the man didn't speak too much. There was not a person or a topic in the world upon which Ranulph de Sauveloy did not have some weary comment concerning its inadequacy.

If he discussed the creation with God himself, de Sauveloy would probably sigh, "resting on the seventh day? Really? Nothing more useful to do?"

Fortunately, Wat broke Hermitage's reverie, which was considering asking everyone if they'd like to come and see who they had in the kitchen.

'I think this is all a bit beyond humble folk like us, isn't it?' Wat suggested. 'Far better that the great and the good of the land handle matters of such importance.'

Hermitage couldn't immediately think of anything great or good about Ranulph de Sauveloy. What on earth was Wat thinking, bringing this man here? And what was de Sauveloy thinking? Leaving London and the king for Wat's workshop? And why had soldiers only just turned up asking about a murder? Surely de Sauveloy knew they were here if he hadn't actually sent them himself.

Wat couldn't contain his smile. 'Father Baldice here tells us that he's been appointed the Pope's Investigator.'

Ranulph cast half a glance in the direction of the priest, a glance that he didn't have any better use for just at the moment. 'Yes,' he drawled. 'I imagine that's the sort of thing he would say.'

Baldice was trying to look calm and confident but it wasn't working very well. 'I suppose it is as well,' he said, with another impudent bow of the head for de Sauveloy. 'Great harm befalls the servant of the church and the king's servant is here to address the problem.'

This insult didn't bother de Sauveloy. 'There are so many problems,' he said, clearly talking to one of them. 'Let us hope that all can be resolved in one fell swoop, could we say?'

Hermitage thought that a rather neat phrase that he would try to remember. The imagery of falconry was obvious; and Baldice was the prey.

'Leslandes?' Ranulph asked.

'My lord.' Leslandes bowed his head again, only he did it properly. 'We came to discover who murdered Nigel of Lincoln, as you directed.' Even he sounded confused as to why de Sauveloy sent them off on this task when he was right behind them.

'And who was it?'

'Erm,' Leslandes stuttered. 'We don't know yet.'

'Well, that's not very good, is it?'

'It, erm, takes time, my lord. It all has to be worked out.'

Ranulph moved an eyebrow slightly as if this didn't warrant a full raise.

Leslandes seemed to realise that there was someone else in the room he could blame for this. 'That's what the monk says.'

De Sauveloy dropped his gaze on Hermitage, who struggled under the weight. 'The King's Investigator who happened to be with Gilbert in Nottingham.' Although this wasn't spoken as a question, it clearly was one.

'We know Gilbert from long back,' Wat said. 'Soon after the, erm, arrival of the Normans. We helped him find his daughter, didn't we, Hermitage.'

Hermitage nodded his agreement to this.

'Aveline,' Wat confirmed the name.

The information seemed to have absolutely no effect on de Sauveloy.

'And the three of you simply happened to be passing by, eh?'

'Trade needs travel, as they say,' Wat said.

'Do they?' Ranulph had no interest in either trade, what people said, or the people who said it.

Hermitage could tell that Ranulph was not satisfied with this explanation, quite wisely, as it happened. He knew that if the Norman pressed them further, he would have to shout out the truth. He would even take them downstairs to show them the kitchen table. Anything to make this awful fear inside him retreat.

'Having come this far, I suppose we had best see the matter out,' Ranulph said with terrible resignation.

Hermitage prepared for the worst.

'Nottingham is not far,' de Sauveloy noted.

Hermitage breathed again.

'Oh, no,' Wat said brightly. 'Just around the corner, really. That's why we go there so frequently. You'll often find us in Nottingham.' He was starting to gabble and so stopped talking. Which was also wise.

'Then we will go to Nottingham,' Ranulph said. 'Everyone can tell their piece and then we shall see who bears a great weight of responsibility.' Ranulph's eyes didn't even have to move to make it quite clear that Father Baldice was now the chief holder of responsibility. 'I want to inspect Gilbert's performance anyway.'

'The King's Investigator can explain everything when we are there,' Ranulph announced nonchalantly.

The King's Investigator nodded that he would be happy to do so. As long as it got him out of this room, right now. After all, anything could happen before they got to Nottingham and he was asked to explain the things about which he had not the first idea. Judgement Day, another war, simply dropping dead by the side of the road; he could only hope.

As they gathered their things ready to leave for Nottingham yet again, Hermitage did try to start thinking about what he was going to say.

Gathering everyone in the room and walking up and down in front of them usually brought something to mind and he would often surprise himself by saying, "aha" as everything became clear. After which, he would reveal the truth and they could all go home again.

Unfortunately, this time, he knew the truth before they even set off. He was confident that saying, "aha, Nigel is alive after all. Here he is", would not be well received. Especially when so many important people wanted him dead.

And if there were no murder at all, how could he solve it? He reminded himself that Nigel was supposed to be dead in the woods. All he had to do was work out who might have done it if it had been done, which it hadn't.

No, this was not going to go at all well.

...

They all gathered outside Wat's workshop for the journey to Nottingham, Ranulph de Sauveloy being the only one with a horse. He showed not the slightest concern at riding while everyone else walked. Having people physically beneath him, as well as in every other way, probably made him feel comfortable.

He also had soldiers of his own, who joined Leslandes' band. It should have been expected, but Hermitage had somehow imagined that Ranulph de Sauveloy could simply appear wherever he wanted; usually behind you.

'What are you bringing him for?' de Sauveloy asked Wat.

Hermitage's blood tried to hide somewhere deep inside as he saw Nigel appear just behind Wat.

Wat turned back as if only just noticing. 'The drudge?' Got to have a drudge.'

'Why?'

'I am Wat the Weaver,' Wat explained, doing his own poor impression of Ranulph's self-importance. 'I do have standards. I can't just go wandering off to Nottingham without a servant.'

'You didn't have him last time,' Ranulph said, knowing an awful lot more about their previous visit to Nottingham than Hermitage was comfortable with.

'We didn't know we were going to stay,' Wat said lightly. 'We could be there for days this time.'

'Oh, I don't think we'll need that long.' Ranulph slipped this comment between Baldice's ribs. He showed no further interest in Wat's servant and nudged his horse into a walk along the track, heedless of whether anyone else was coming with him or not.

'Wat,' Cwen hissed.' What are you doing? Now and generally. In fact, explain yourself.'

Wat was unable to answer as Baldice joined them at the back of what was now Ranulph's train. The priest looked at

Wat and sniffed before indicating that they could go ahead. 'Wouldn't want anyone disappearing before we get there,' he said unpleasantly.

'Quite agree.' Wat implied that the priest might be one of the disappearances. 'Come on, drudge,' he ordered Nigel. 'Carry my pack.' He held his pack out for Nigel who looked as if he'd never seen one before, let alone knew what you did with it.

'Yes, Master Wat,' Cwen prompted with a clip around Nigel's ear.

'Yes, Master Wat,' Nigel repeated with the clear intention of returning this treatment at the very first opportunity.

As they walked along in smothering silence, Hermitage thought that he had better make use of this time. He was going to be asked to speak in Nottingham, so perhaps he could organise some words in advance. If he organised enough of them, people might get bored and forget about the whole business.

He had to admit that was unlikely.

Where to begin though? He couldn't even discuss things with Wat and Cwen, which was usually essential. They always had such sensible suggestions. Things like, "he's probably lying, Hermitage". But this was such a difficult situation, unlike anything he'd had to deal with before. His own formulation: method, motive and opportunity didn't even work here. After all, no one was actually dead.

A "what if". That's what he needed, a few "what ifs," to get his mind working. What if Nigel really had been killed on the road to Lincoln. Who could have done it?

He thought about this for a moment and concluded that anyone could have done it, which was no help at all. Ranulph de Sauveloy seemed to know an awful lot more than he was letting on, so he could be behind it.

Or Father Baldice. Where had he been since they last met?

And then there was Raegnald. This whole sorry business was that wretched man's fault. Hermitage was tempted to blame him anyway, which was a terrible thought to have.

He came back to the fundamental problem that Nigel wasn't actually dead, which was proving to be very inconvenient.

Perhaps that was the answer. He would confront all these people who wished the man dead with the fact that he wasn't. They would have to withdraw all their terrible accusations against one another, and he would be left in peace. Well, that was unlikely, but at least it would bring a pause to the whole situation.

Most likely, it would also bring death to Nigel, just a bit later than planned.

This whole situation was impossible. Impossible and ridiculous. He longed for there not to be any murders and here he was, investigating no murder and it wasn't at all as easy as it should be.

Lying, he thought. That was the other common theme of the troubles he had to deal with. And sometimes it was the most disappointing aspect. Murder was the worst of the sins, there was no doubt about that, but lying about it made it even more shameful, somehow.

And frequently, it wasn't even the people who had done the murder who were doing the lying. People seemed to lie about all sorts of things, many of them completely unnecessary. It was most disheartening.

So, if there were no actual murder, making investigation of it tricky, to say the least, could he find the liars in all of this and accuse them of something or other? Lying, probably.

But who was lying? And how could he tell? This was where he really needed Wat and Cwen. They were much better at spotting this sort of thing than he was.

In a leap of sorts, which he was concerned might cause more confusion rather than less, he wondered what the situation would be if everyone was lying. What if he took everything everyone had said about anything and assumed it was a lie?

Of course, this would mean remembering what everyone had said, but only the most significant statements, surely? He didn't need to assume that Lord Gilbert was lying when he said there was wine in the cave. Or that Wat hadn't really got drunk at all.

So, where to start? Raegnald? What if Raegnald was lying? And if he were lying, what was he lying about?

He saw that they had already come a fair step from Derby and thought that he might not have enough time to go through every liar before the time came for his announcement. And would it help anyway? It had to be better than simply walking to his doom.

He soon realised that the task of working all this out was not straightforward. Recalling everything of significance was difficult, assuming it was a lie and then fitting that into every other lie was taxing his mind.

It was further distracted when Father Baldice appeared at his arm.

'So, King's Investigator,' the priest said, making the title sound quite unpleasant. 'Doubtless, when you speak in Nottingham you will conclude that the king's arm is behind poor Nigel's death.'

Hermitage couldn't stop his eye wandering to the figure of Nigel, who was shuffling along under Cwen's constant gaze.

Hermitage gave the sort of nod that was intended to show that he had heard the words, not that he agreed with them.

'After all, the poor fellow was in Gilbert's care just before he came to his end. What more is there to be said?'

Hermitage thought that nothing was probably best, so he said it.

'And of course,' Baldice added as if it were a matter of fact. 'The church, to whom you have devoted your life, will not look favourably on any other suggestion.'

'King's Investigator,' Ranulph's voice now called out.

Hermitage gave an apologetic bow to Baldice and scurried off to walk at the side of de Sauveloy's horse.

'I do hope that priest has not been giving you falsehoods,' Ranulph said without looking down. 'There will be no doubt in your mind that this is all the church's doing. Sending poor Nigel to his doom simply to implicate the king.'

Hermitage moved his head around in what he hoped was a non-committal manner.

The fact that poor Nigel was walking right behind them was an increasing problem. Hermitage now saw that every step away from Derby made announcing Nigel's survival even more difficult. He should have spoken up back at the workshop. Why was he waiting until Nottingham?

Ranulph had said it himself. They needed to let everyone tell their piece. He was only following instructions.

Somehow, he felt that the excuse of only following orders was not going to help in the slightest.

Caput XXV: Safely Gathered In

Arrival at Nottingham was a huge disappointment for Hermitage. These were trying times in the country, what with bands of robbers and displaced Saxons roaming the land without hindrance. You would think at least one of them would have spotted the travellers and caused some trouble. Not an actual death, perhaps, but enough to distract the attention of the Normans for a few weeks.

But no, a straightforward walk from Derby to Nottingham without a single diversion delivered all of Hermitage's dilemmas with alacrity.

Granted, it had taken all afternoon to get here, and night had taken charge of the town, so there was a good chance they would get rest before the real trial began. Not that Hermitage expected any rest. The hours of darkness would only make his worries shine brighter.

Lord Gilbert was at the door of the keep to greet them, almost as if they were expected. Aveline was there as well and both gave bows to de Sauveloy, who waved them away as a formality.

'We are all gathered?' de Sauveloy asked.

'Indeed,' Gilbert replied. 'As you instructed.'

De Sauveloy dismounted his horse and handed the reins to one of the soldiers. 'We are not to be disturbed,' he instructed, which Hermitage took as a very bad sign.

'And if anyone tries to leave,' Ranulph continued, 'you have my permission to kill them.'

The soldier nodded at his instruction while Hermitage swallowed hard.

Ranulph entered the hall and the others followed.

'Where's he think he's going?' Leslandes asked of Nigel.

'Oh, I take him everywhere,' Wat explained.

'Not here, you don't.' Leslandes looked quite disgusted at the prospect. He glared at Wat, 'We Normans don't approve of slaves.'

'He's not a slave,' Wat replied. 'He's a drudge.'

'Whatever he is, he can sleep with the animals. This gathering is to discuss the fate of Nigel of Lincoln; we're not having some dirty servant in the room.' Leslandes took Wat's pack from Nigel and threw it at Wat's feet. 'Bloody Saxons,' he muttered. 'You still haven't worked out that you are the drudges now.'

Hermitage could only think that having the real Nigel of Lincoln in the gathering could be a significant contribution to its success. It seemed too late to mention his presence now, and with each passing moment, it became later still. He could only hope that whatever it was Wat had done, he knew what he was doing when he did it. Or something like that.

'Come then,' de Sauveloy called back. 'Let's get to the root of this, hold Baldice to blame, and then back to work.'

Were they not even to get a night's rest, then? Hermitage's last hopes of this business simply going away were dashed.

As these hopes were already lying in crumbs beneath his feet, there was no further for them to go when he saw who was in the hall.

At least he managed to keep his mouth shut as he noted Alyssa and Raegnald standing on opposite sides of the fire. Alyssa looked at them with desperate eyes.

'As you can see, I've had all the interested parties brought together,' Ranulph announced. 'No one is sneaking away from this one.' These words were aimed straight at Baldice, who looked as if he had no idea what Ranulph was talking about.

Ranulph removed his fine riding gloves and addressed Gilbert. 'You may take me to my chamber,' he said. 'Is it up here?' He walked towards the stairs with a confused and disconcerted Gilbert on his heels.

Aveline folded her arms and gave Ranulph a stare as he went to take her sleeping chamber.

'Well, really,' she said when the man was obviously out of earshot. She then turned to the new arrivals. 'What are you doing here again?'

'Yes, Wat,' Cwen repeated in a low and hard voice. 'What are we doing here again?'

Wat smiled at them. He then nodded to Leslandes and Baldice. 'Better find somewhere to rest, I suppose. I imagine Ranulph will deal with us all in the morning.'

Gilbert now reappeared, looking no less confused. 'Lord Ranulph says that he will deal with us all in the morning.'

Baldice tutted at this poor behaviour and lack of respect for the church.

Leslandes simply looked around for the most comfortable spot to settle.

'Wise move,' Wat said quietly. 'Put the fear of God up everyone and let us stew overnight.'

'Talking of stewing,' Cwen said. 'I see the pot on the fire is bubbling nicely. Would you like to get in?'

Wat held his hands out low, indicating that they should not discuss anything while Baldice and Leslandes were within earshot.

Making great play of wandering around the keep looking for space that met his standards, Wat eventually decided that just to the left of the fire was best. This had the advantage that it was a relatively small space, and they could talk with quiet voices and not be overheard.

He gave a subtle nod that the others should follow.

The three of them, plus Aveline, Alyssa and Gilbert made quite a gathering; naturally Baldice, Leslandes and Raegnald watched what was going on with interest.

'Leslandes,' Gilbert ordered. 'Take a place by the door, in case anyone decides to take a walk in the night.'

Leslandes gave a sharp nod and headed for the door.

'You, priest,' Gilbert addressed Baldice, who raised his head with mild interest. 'Just clear off and stay away from me.' Gilbert rested his hand on the pommel of his sword to give his instruction added weight.

Baldice tried to look as if he wouldn't come near Gilbert if the man shone with the holy spirit.

'And whoever you are,' Gilbert spoked to Raegnald. 'Just go away.'

Raegnald gave an obsequious bow and did as he was told.

'Right,' Gilbert spoke softly when he was content Baldice and Raegnald were far enough away. 'I sent word to de Sauveloy as you asked and you bring him here?' His anger with Wat seemed even more effective when it was expressed with quiet malice.

'Look,' Wat began as he sat cross-legged on the floor and the others followed suit. 'In the whole of this situation, one thing is perfectly clear. We are all completely out of our depth, yes? Can we agree on that?'

Hermitage was very ready to agree.

'A conflict between the king and the pope?' Wat asked. 'What chance do we stand of coming out of it unscathed? Even Gilbert, a Norman noble, is at risk.'

Gilbert nodded sadly at this.

'But de Sauveloy?' Cwen said this as if Wat putting poison in their food might have been a kinder way of getting out of this.

'He must know what's going on if he isn't actually at the bottom of it all himself.'

'So why send for him?' Cwen demanded.

'And why did he come?' Hermitage asked.

'Good question,' Wat said. 'The second one, not the first,' he explained to Cwen who gave a little snarl in reply. 'What else could I do but send for him? If we're in this on our own, we'll get the blame.'

'For the death of Nigel?' Cwen asked.

Alyssa gave a little jump.

'It's all right,' Hermitage whispered. 'He's fine. He's outside sleeping with the animals.'

Alyssa nodded. 'He won't like that,' she observed.

'Of course for the death of Nigel,' Wat hissed. 'The king and the pope, remember? Do you think either of them is going to take any responsibility for any of this? If Nigel is dead, it must be our fault, we saw him last.'

'I thought the king was going to blame Gilbert,' Hermitage said, trying to keep up.

'Possibly, but now he's got us, hasn't he? The Saxon weavers and that monk, who conveniently walked into the middle of the whole thing.' This was clearly a criticism of Hermitage.

'We had to help Nigel,' he said.

'And now we have to help ourselves,' Wat insisted. 'And the only way of doing that is choosing a side. Church or king?'

Gilbert clearly thought the answer was obvious.

'If there is anyone more deceitful, conniving, slippery and downright deadly than the king, it's the pope,' Wat said.

Hermitage could only think that this was not an

appropriate way to consider the leaders of the modern world.

'And whose kingdom are we in?' Wat asked. 'Who is the one with all the soldiers and the swords?'

The answer to that one really was obvious.

'Sending word of all this to de Sauveloy gave him the upper hand over Baldice, which answers Hermitage's question of why he came.' Wat explained. 'Why on earth would the great Ranulph de Sauveloy answer the call of Wat the Weaver? Why not simply leave us to our fates?

'Because I told him that Father Baldice had been skulking around taking more than a passing interest in the fate of Nigel of Lincoln. Hence, Ranulph gets the chance to blame Baldice, with us as witnesses.'

'Oh dear,' Hermitage said for so many reasons.

'We are witnesses,' Wat assured him. 'You saw him in the bushes yourself.'

'Yes,' Hermitage agreed. 'But he was very circumspect about what he said. I'm sure he'll come up with a perfectly reasonable explanation.'

'Ha,' Wat coughed. 'If Ranulph de Sauveloy can't lay siege to a perfectly reasonable explanation and leave it begging for mercy, he's not the man I think he is.'

Deceitful, conniving and slippery occurred to Hermitage in another respect. 'And you even sending word to Ranulph put him in an awkward position.'

'Quite,' Wat agreed. 'Be difficult for him to blame us when we'd already told him everything.'

'The church is not going to be happy,' Cwen commented, reluctantly accepting that Wat's actions might have been for the best.

'The church is only Baldice, so far,' Wat said.

'We also know about Raegnald,' Hermitage reminded

them. 'He started all this off by saying that it was the Normans who wanted Nigel dead. What's Baldice going to say when he discovers that?'

'He's not going to discover it, is he?' Wat said quite firmly. 'We don't need to go telling everyone everything, do we?'

'You mean we lie,' Hermitage said, knowing that Wat was perfectly aware that this was out of the question.

'Not at all. We just don't mention him.'

'He's sitting over there,' Cwen pointed out. 'What's he doing here anyway? Why would Ranulph send for him?'

'He's probably been busy ingratiating himself while we were putting up with Nigel. He could be Ranulph's chief saddle polisher by now.'

'It's a bit of a coincidence, isn't it?' Hermitage asked. 'He did claim he overheard the Normans saying they wanted Nigel dead and now he's here at the end?'

Wat shrugged. 'Ranulph might need him here to deny that he ever heard anything about any Norman wishing Nigel anything but the best.'

'More lies,' Hermitage said sadly.

'By people who are used to lying,' Wat explained.

Hermitage glanced over at Raegnald and Baldice who seemed to exchange one quiet word and then studiously ignore one another; it was probably a rude word.

He despaired at the frailties of human nature and at the sheer venality on display. And all of this was from people who were supposed to be in charge. If everyone followed their example, what state would the world be in?

Then he despaired even further as he realised it wasn't even the leaders who were doing their own venality. They were using others. People they could blame if ever it became necessary.

Ranulph would surely sacrifice Raegnald if responsibility showed the slightest sign of getting anywhere near Ranulph himself.

And the leaders of the church would doubtless consign Baldice to some awful fate if the same happened to them.

Was this really the best the world could manage? Why were people of such sin, there was no better word for it, allowed to lead everyone else?

Of course, there was no question of anyone asking permission to be a leader, they simply took it upon themselves, and the strongest won. Perhaps there ought to be some method whereby the people who wanted to be in charge were given permission by everyone else?

He had heard that the Holy Roman Emperors were elected, but as they only ever elected the son of the previous emperor, it hardly seemed worth the effort.

The church had actually taken a great step forward with the election of Pope Alexander II. The first ever election of a pope by the cardinals had taken place only a few years previously.

But that hadn't seemed to work either. The pope was elected, yet here they were, dealing with this appalling situation. Perhaps the problem was that people only got elected who wanted to be leaders. The guile, deceit and downright force used in the past to get them in charge, was now used to get them elected.

Hermitage could see that electing someone who didn't want to be elected would have its own problems.

'Thinking of anything useful?' Cwen interrupted his reverie.

'Erm.' Hermitage considered the question. 'No, not really.'

'Thought so. Can I bring our attention back to this

predicament and what exactly we are planning to do in the morning?'

'We tell the truth,' Wat said. 'All the bits of it that anyone needs to know.'

Hermitage was confident that he would not be able to keep track of them.

'Ranulph is expecting me to explain everything,' he bleated.

'There you are then,' Wat said. 'You explain that Baldice appeared in the bushes and seemed very interested in the death of Nigel. That prompted us to come to Nottingham and find out what was going on. Then we met Nigel, went our separate ways and that's that.'

'That's that?' Hermitage could hardly believe the summary. 'What about Raegnald?'

'Ancient history,' Wat dismissed the problem. 'No need to bother everyone with the little details.'

'Little details!' Hermitage only just managed to keep his voice down. 'What if Baldice already knows? What if he's very aware that the Normans want Nigel dead and that Raegnald is their servant in that?'

Wat considered this for a moment. 'Look confused,' he said.

'Look what?'

'Confused.'

'You can manage that,' Cwen added.

'Just look at them like a poor, innocent monk who has no idea about the ways of the world. Say something like, "I have no recollection,".'

'No recollection?' Hermitage was shocked. 'Now that is a straightforward lie. Of course, I have a recollection. I was there.'

'Let Ranulph and Raegnald answer then.'

'The man wanted us to kill Nigel,' Hermitage explained slowly and carefully.

'Hermitage,' Wat cautioned. 'If you're going to be all difficult about this, you're best off not saying anything.'

'Difficult? What world do we live in where the truth has become "difficult"? And I'm the one who has to say everything,' Hermitage reminded him.

'Then you better start practising, make sure you get it right.'

'And no, "aha" this time,' Cwen added.

Hermitage must have looked very lost. He certainly felt it.

'The last thing we want is you working out what's really going on and then telling everyone about it.'

'Oh God, no,' Wat agreed.

The others all seemed to concur that this would be a very bad idea indeed.

Hermitage shook his head at all of this. 'And what about Nigel? The dead man who is actually outside.

'Best not mention him,' Aveline said.

'Not mention him?' Hermitage felt his despair could not get any more desperate.

'Everyone wants him dead anyway, it would only confuse things if he turns up.'

There were nods and murmurs of agreement to this; from everyone but Hermitage. Even Alyssa gave him a pleading look to keep her father out of this. Which seemed ridiculous, when he was the subject of the whole problem.

The gathering seemed to think there was no more to be said about this situation when Hermitage thought there was a whole book still to write. His arguments had failed even to be seen as arguments. He couldn't understand why people couldn't understand the problems.

There was no way he was going to be able to lie. If someone asked him a straight question he would have to answer. He knew this, and Wat and Cwen knew it as well. He just had to hope that they would step in before he did something particularly stupid.

As he watched the night darken through the windows, he felt his spirit go with it. He'd never thought that there could be anything worse than investigating a murder. Now he knew different.

Caput XXV: Time To Tell

The next morning was not really a next morning at all for Hermitage. Rather, it was a continuation of the night before with a bit less darkness.

He had only managed to sleep fitfully and that sleep had been full of strange dreams. He was naked in a castle, desperately trying to pull his habit over his head, only to find there was no hole for it to go through. Then he had to organise parchment in a library, which began very well until the parchment started catching fire as soon as he touched it.

Finally, he found himself standing before King William about to deliver a talk he had prepared on the Lexicography of the Post-Exodus prophets. When the king said he wanted a song about a talking deer instead, he woke up and concluded that sleep was not for him.

He didn't even feel that he could use the time to order his thoughts. From the discussion the night before, he concluded that most of his thoughts weren't wanted. And anything that bore even a passing resemblance to the truth should be avoided.

The explanation for all this was quite simple, but he wasn't allowed to say it. The very easiest path would be to open the discussion by saying that they had all come to discuss the death of Nigel of Lincoln but there was no need. Nigel wasn't dead at all.

Then he would go on to say that the Normans had wanted him dead, at least according to Raegnald, but that the church, in the shape of Baldice, wasn't concerned about him dying either.

He would roundly castigate both sides for their deplorable behaviour and send them home to think about what they'd done.

And why should he not do that? Why try and twist the twists until the only thing that remained standing was confusion?

They were the innocent parties in all of this, after all. Even Gilbert and Aveline had been put in a difficult position by the king.

And he had been sitting under a tree when Raegnald turned up with his outrageous request. Then Baldice had been hiding in the bushes. Why should he have to explain their misdeeds?

He should make his own decision in this matter and not be persuaded by Wat, who he sometimes thought would rather spin a deceit than a yarn of wool.

But if he did reveal Nigel, would that lead to that poor man's death?

Oh dear, he was just going round in the same circle once more. His preferred option would be to say nothing, keep out of the way and hope it all turned out all right in the end. But this time, he was the one who was expected to do the talking.

Perhaps, as in so many of his investigations, if he stood up and opened his mouth, something would occur to him.

But if it didn't, the worst that could happen would probably be quite horrible.

With the light of dawn, a clatter from above his head told him that Ranulph de Sauveloy was on the move and that the moment of revelation was close at hand. Maybe the ground would open up and the thrones of the twenty-four elders would appear; the apocalypse effectively distracting everyone from what Hermitage might have to say.

With much less ado than he would have appreciated, de Sauveloy came down the stairs and considered the room.

'Come on, then,' he said. 'We haven't got all day.'

Most of those in the room were still asleep and so took time to realise what was going on.

Cwen was instantly alert and looked ready to respond in kind to the one who had disturbed her.

The rest rose according to their habit, some looking confused and bleary, others quite ready for the day.

Only Alyssa had to be shaken awake by Aveline, and she did not look happy at this inconvenience.

Gilbert nodded at Aveline and indicated that she should see to the fire, which was now a smouldering glow after the passage of the night.

Looking very much as if this were an imposition too far, she nevertheless went over and poked it into life with an iron. She then added some fresh logs and made sure they were ready to take.

Ranulph de Sauveloy wandered over and took the seat closest to the fire as if this was simply his normal morning routine.

Lord Gilbert produced a mug of ale from somewhere and gave it to Ranulph.

Baldice and Raegnald wandered over and the rest of the room stood around waiting for whatever was about to come.

'So, Master Investigator,' de Sauveloy called to Hermitage. 'Let's have the truth of all this.'

The truth, Hermitage thought. No one in this room wanted the truth. If people weren't actually lying themselves, they wanted him to do it for them.

Nigel was alive and well but that must be hidden. The actions of Raegnald must be kept back. Baldice's motivations were completely unclear and the role of the Normans in all of this was probably despicable at best. And they wanted the truth?

He considered all the faces now looking to him and thought that not one of them would welcome the truth if it came through the door bearing gifts.

And how could he possibly keep track of which bit of what fact was supposed to go with who?

Perhaps it would be best, after all, to simply tell the whole truth to everyone. Well, the truth as far as he knew it, which probably wasn't the truth at all, given that everyone here wanted to lie about something or other.

There was one thing that had turned out to be correct; his assumption that everyone was lying. Even Wat and Cwen wanted to avoid the inconvenient bits of the truth.

His usual process in these situations was to walk about in front of all those gathered and lead them through his thinking until the guilty party was identified.

As he thought about this, he realised that it was quite a dangerous step to take. What if the guilty one didn't want to be mentioned and stopped Hermitage before he could speak?

At least this situation was different. Everyone in the room was guilty of something and their overriding desire was to make sure all that guilt fell on someone else.

Inconveniently, no one was guilty of Nigel's murder at all, as it hadn't even happened. This seemed to be the biggest lie of the lot.

As he considered this sad fact, a whole new level of dishonesty opened before him. His mouth dropped open as he hated to even consider the possibility that now occurred. He looked from one person in the room to the next with eyes at once confused and extremely disappointed.

'Hermitage?' Cwen asked slowly and cautiously. 'What are you up to?'

Usually, revelation was about what individual had done the single deed. This time, a whole panoply presented itself. Lies within lies within deceptions. Did he dare give any of it air?

He considered the chief protagonists and concluded that he had to. The web of deceit that he was supposed to be deceitful about was simply too much for him to manage. He'd get it wrong somewhere along the way and things would turn out for the worse.

And these people needed to be told. Not only did they need to be told, but others needed to see that they were told. The light of day should be shone upon them and he was the man to do it. He took a breath at this quite surprising and rather alarming conclusion. This wasn't like him at all.

'Hermitage,' Cwen sounded a warning.

He gestured that everything was under control. It wasn't, but he made the gesture anyway.

'Nigel of Lincoln,' he began.

Ranulph sighed his disappointment that Hermitage hadn't immediately accused Baldice.

'Poor Nigel,' Hermitage continued. 'Appointed by the king to be the holder of Peter's Purse. To gather the payments due to his holiness, Pope Alexander.'

Baldice nodded that this sounded quite right so far.

'An appointment made by Lord Gilbert, who sent word to Lincoln.'

Gilbert gave a curt nod that this was correct.

'Nigel responded to the call and was immediately threatened for it, both in Lincoln and Nottingham. He left to return to Lincoln, but never arrived.' True so far, Hermitage thought to himself.

'And what is at the root of all this?' Hermitage asked. 'Dishonesty,' he answered.

He could hear Wat and Cwen holding their breath.

'I'm not surprised,' Ranulph commented as he looked at Baldice.

'Very disappointing,' Baldice responded.

Hermitage closed his eyes so he wouldn't have to see the response to his next words. 'Dishonesty from everyone.'

He couldn't keep his eyes shut forever, so he glanced out to see that yes, Baldice and Ranulph were now looking at him.

'Let us go back to the beginning,' Hermitage said.

'Let's not,' he heard Wat whisper quite urgently.

'This all began with master Raegnald.' Hermitage nodded towards the man, who looked confused about why he was being mentioned.

'He came to me asking that I investigate the murder of Nigel.'

Raegnald shrugged.

'But he had completely the wrong idea of investigation, as everyone does, it seems. In fact, he wanted me to murder Nigel myself.'

Baldice shook his head sadly at this.

'He said that he had overheard some Normans saying that they wanted it done. Possibly Lords de Sauveloy and Le Pedvin.'

'Hermitage,' Cwen now hissed. 'Remember whose side we decided to be on.'

'I think the investigator has the truth of it,' Baldice said with smug satisfaction.

Hermitage didn't dare look at de Sauveloy. 'Except,' he went on quickly, 'when I consider all the information, I don't think that was true.'

'Naturally,' Ranulph said comfortably.

'There is so much dishonesty in this whole situation that

the only way to make any sense of it is to consider that everyone is lying. If not about everything, then certainly about something. The truth has been buried so deep, I don't think any of those involved can even see it anymore.

'I asked myself how Raegnald, a servant of the old Saxon king, got to hear sensitive information about William's plans at all? And how would he hear about the King's Investigator and my dealings with murder? Even I don't get told why I'm investigating something; and I am the King's Investigator. I am confident that I am not a common topic of conversation in the king's inner circle.

'Raegnald reported that he overheard a discussion between lords Le Pedvin and de Sauveloy, in which I was mentioned and the requirement for Nigel's death was specifically mentioned.

'Two of the most important men in the kingdom happen to be discussing the most important and sensitive matters within earshot of a Saxon?

'Not only are they discussing relations between the king and the pope, but they happen to mention the King's Investigator and all the murders I've done? Lord Ranulph is a careful man, particularly when it comes to matters of state.'

Ranulph bowed his head to acknowledge this compliment.

'That Raegnald should overhear is simply not credible,' Hermitage concluded.

'So, Raegnald didn't hear it at all?' Cwen asked, now taken up by the tale. 'He made it up?'

'I did not,' Raegnald protested.

'I think he did hear it,' Hermitage said. 'Otherwise, why would he come to me at all? Raegnald's report was completely true. That is exactly what he heard.'

'Thank you,' Raegnald said.

'There we have it, then,' Baldice concluded.

'But,' Hermitage went on, 'he was meant to hear it. I think I have shown that it is highly unlikely he really heard it by chance, so, that overhearing must have been deliberate. The words were planted in his ear, those in court knowing and wanting him to act upon them.'

'Why?' Wat asked.

'And why involve the King's Investigator?' Cwen asked. 'Commit a murder but let the investigator know you're doing it? Seems a bit odd.'

'Another conclusion from the wider dishonesty,' Hermitage said. 'If we accept that Raegnald was given the information on purpose, those at court would expect him to get the deed done and so they made it quite clear that I would be the one to help. After all, I had "done" so many murders in my time.'

'I say,' Hermitage had a fresh moment of revelation. 'This information fed to Raegnald was false. Would you think it unreasonable if we described it as dis-information? From the Latin, dis, opposite?'

He looked at the room and managed to discern quite quickly that no one was as excited about this possibility as he was. He got back to the question at hand.

'Sending him to me, with the dis-information that I murdered people, was bound to arouse my interest. When Nigel really was murdered, I would immediately know who did it.'

Cwen frowned. 'The Normans sent him to do the murder and get caught for it at the same time?'

'A pawn,' Hermitage said.

'Beg pardon?'

'It's from a new game that's very popular. The pawn is a

piece that gets sacrificed for the greater cause.'

'Charming.'

'I suspect that Lord de Sauveloy sent Leslandes out to get the result of my investigation before he even knew whether one was underway.'

'This is truly shocking,' Baldice said sombrely.

'What is just as shocking,' Hermitage said purposefully, 'is that Father Baldice knew all this.'

'Oh dear,' Baldice said calmly. 'The investigator is making up stories.'

Hermitage now took to pacing around the room, his confidence growing that his thoughts actually made some sense; which was a bit of a surprise.

'We know from Alyssa that no one called Father Baldice came to Lincoln. Have you ever seen him before, Alyssa?'

Alyssa looked very hard at Baldice and then shook her head. 'Never.'

'Why, then, would Baldice appear at our workshop asking about Nigel of Lincoln, in his very roundabout manner?'

The room looked to him for the answer, which he found quite satisfying. 'Because he was told by Raegnald. Why else would he appear so soon afterwards?

'And I saw them exchange a word last night and it did not look like the exchange of strangers.'

'But, but, but...,' Cwen said, sounding confused. 'He could have heard it from anyone. The appointment of Nigel was common knowledge.'

'The appointment was, yes, but not the false Norman plans on his life. I suspect that Lord de Sauveloy and Lord Le Pedvin made sure that the only ears that ever heard that particular conversation were Raegnald's. Lord Gilbert certainly didn't know, and he's a Norman lord.'

'Oh, yes,' Cwen nodded.

Gilbert proudly nodded that he was completely in the dark.

Ranulph gave a little smile, which was all the confirmation Hermitage needed.

'So, the only person Baldice could have heard this from was Raegnald.

'In addition, I asked myself how Raegnald, who was obviously close to the old Saxon court, had managed to survive all this time under Norman rule? It was clear from what he said that the Normans had yet to use him, so how was he getting by? After all, he is very well-dressed and presented. Someone else must be paying for his services.

'The Saxon nobles are all gone. The only organisation that has continued through this time is the Church. Could the truth be that he is a servant of the great and good, but that those great and good are in the Church?'

'I'm not with you,' Cwen said.

'I'm not sure anyone is,' Baldice gave a short laugh.

'I suspect that the Normans knew Raegnald was working for the Church and so made sure that he heard about the plans for Nigel, plans that were entirely false.'

'Oh, what?' Raegnald complained. 'I am not working for the Church,' he said.

Hermitage ignored him. 'Baldice and Raegnald genuinely thought that the king was planning to appoint Nigel and then kill him in a desperate attempt to avoid paying the pope.

'But Raegnald, not knowing that they knew..,'

'What?' Cwen scowled.

'Raegnald didn't know that the Normans knew he was working for the Church.'

Cwen's scowl didn't lift.

'I did say it was all very deceitful,' Hermitage said.

'I think you might have to explain this one all over again later,' Cwen just shook her head.

'So,' Hermitage continued. 'Pretending that he was acting for the king, Raegnald and Baldice would have Nigel killed and could then blame William.

'Raegnald was genuinely disappointed that I didn't actually do the murders. They must have had to change their plans after that, hence Baldice's visit to us to put me off any investigation.

'If all went well, Nigel would be murdered and the king blamed for issuing the order. The pope would step in, probably seeking to depose William and hand England over to who? The Holy Roman Emperor, perhaps?'

'I said we were out of our depth, didn't I?' Wat muttered.

'This is all terribly complicated, Hermitage,' Cwen said. 'How do we know any of it is true?'

Baldice's laugh was fulsome. 'King's Investigator?' he asked. 'King's Jester, more likely. What a tale of nonsense.'

'It all sounds very sensible to me,' Ranulph noted. 'Do go on, Brother.'

Even Hermitage felt that he needed to remind himself of his own thinking as he was in danger of losing track of which lie went with which person. 'The Normans deliberately let Raegnald think they wanted Nigel dead, and they sent him to me.

'He thought I would do the killing, Lord Ranulph knew that I would, of course, refuse and that I would be compelled to investigate. I would conclude that Raegnald arranged the deed, who turns out to be the church's man. Hence the pope is to blame.'

'Why do they bother?' Wat complained. 'Why not simply

send a message to the pope saying, "I'm not paying", you don't need to go to all this trouble to avoid your debts. Believe me, I should know.'

'For a humble weaver, that may be the case,' Hermitage said. 'Popes and kings are different animals.'

Wat nodded at the truth of this but then realised something. 'Who are you calling humble?' he asked.

Hermitage couldn't afford to be distracted; there was a good chance he would lose what little sense he was making of all this.

'Raegnald reports our encounter to Baldice, who tries to put me off. If they can kill Nigel by their own means, they think they can quickly blame the king.'

'All very fanciful,' Baldice commented. 'The Brother's ramblings are entertaining, but no mention of who killed Nigel, I note.'

'It certainly wasn't me,' Raegnald protested. 'I never even found the man.'

'Ah, yes,' Hermitage said. 'What about Nigel? And why poor Nigel in the first place? We all asked why Nigel of Lincoln at some stage or another. He was a most insignificant figure to be engaged on such an important matter. He wasn't even the most important person in Lincoln, let alone the kingdom.

'Why on earth would King William select someone such as him to deal with Peter's Purse? And Peter's Purse doesn't even need dealing with really. If the king agrees to pay the pope, he simply does so. He doesn't need someone like Nigel in the middle of it all.'

'None of them even know who Nigel is,' Cwen pointed out.

'They don't. Lord Gilbert was the first man to meet him.

And that didn't last long. Lord Ranulph probably came upon his name through the enquiries he is conducting into the kingdom and its wealth.'

'So, who were the men who went to his house?' Wat asked.

Hermitage didn't actually know that, which was very annoying. He was about to admit this problem when the answer came to him, which was very satisfying.

'Alyssa,' he asked, 'when we first met, you said you knew about the King's Investigator and Wat's workshop? Where did you hear that?'

Alyssa's brow furrowed as she thought about this. 'It was the men who were looking for father. They were talking amongst themselves outside the door, laughing about Wat's tapestries. They also complained that the King's Investigator only found out about murders, he didn't do them. That's what made me think I needed to find you.'

'There you have it,' Hermitage said with shameful triumph. 'The men were from Baldice and Raegnald. Alyssa reported that they were rough types and not soldiers and they knew about me. How did they know that, if not from Raegnald?

'After all, the only action the Normans took towards the murder was telling Raegnald. All they really wanted was for Raegnald to be responsible.'

'What a fanciful tale,' Raegnald spoke up and stepped forward. 'As if I'd have anything to do with the Church. I only seek to offer my humble skills to the king. And do his bidding.' He said these last words quite deliberately.

'By overhearing snippets of conversation and then getting completely the wrong idea about everything,' de Sauveloy said. 'Fortunately, the King's Investigator has seen through your idiocy.'

Ranulph shook his head slowly in sad disappointment.

'Always loitering about trying to ingratiate yourself into the king's service. And of course, we knew why. So you could report to your master, the pope.

'If you misheard Lord Le Pedvin and I discussing our concern that Nigel might be murdered and that we would have to send the investigator, that is hardly our concern.'

'Misheard?' Raegnald sounded mightily offended.

'And then reported a confidential manner to such as Baldice? Well, this really is disappointing.'

'And what of Nigel?' Hermitage couldn't help but ask. 'What of an innocent man in all of this? A name picked out because he happened to be available and eager for position? An innocent man earmarked for murder.'

Ranulph appeared to dismiss this. 'King William remains committed to reducing the number of innocent people killed to the bare minimum.'

'What does that mean?' Hermitage complained, his irritation getting the better of his judgement. 'Remains committed? He shouldn't have any innocent people killed at all.'

'It is a priority,' de Sauveloy confirmed.

'Not killing innocent people is a priority?'

'To which we continue to be committed,' Ranulph explained it fully.

'Which means you're not actually going to do anything about it at all,' Wat noted.

Ranulph didn't bother responding.

'Well, someone killed Nigel,' Raegnald complained. 'And I'm not taking the blame because I didn't do it.'

'And I certainly am not capable of such a deed,' Baldice agreed.

Ranulph was lugubrious. 'The very idea that we would

wish harm to a king's appointee is ridiculous.'

'Ha!' Raegnald gave a rather desperate laugh.

'That,' Hermitage said with some satisfaction, 'is the problem you are all left with. This has been a murder investigation with no dead body. Wat,' he said. 'Perhaps your drudge could return and fetch us all some wine?'

Wat smiled. 'Good idea,' he said as he got up and went to the door.

Caput XXVI: Introducing…

'I've got servants of my own,' Gilbert complained.

'This one is special,' Cwen said carefully. She winked at Gilbert and gave a knowing look to Aveline and Alyssa.

'What do you mean, problem?' Raegnald asked. 'Nigel's been murdered and the only people who wanted it done were the Normans. They said so, and I heard them.'

'But there is no body,' Hermitage pointed out. 'There is no dead Nigel to see. How do we even know that he is dead?'

'They killed him,' Raegnald protested.

'But you sent men to his home, searching for him.'

'I most certainly did not,' Raegnald said, but he said it in the manner of someone who most almost certainly did.

'It doesn't really matter as they didn't find him. He had already left for Nottingham.'

'And who was threatening him in Nottingham?' Cwen asked. 'He said he heard a voice.'

'I suspect that was Raegnald again. He could have heard that Nigel of Lincoln had arrived, after all, Aethelthryth knew. He simply stood outside the castle wall calling out threats. As he thought the Normans would approve, he wouldn't see any problems.'

'Quite right,' Raegnald agreed. 'The Normans did want him dead. And do.' He glared at Ranulph which had no effect whatsoever. 'I was only following orders,' he complained miserably.

'Why didn't Raegnald simply knock on the door and introduce himself to Gilbert?' Cwen asked. 'If he thought the Normans were behind it all?'

'Share the glory?' Hermitage asked, accurately summarising Raegnald's nature. 'He wanted to report back that the deed had been done. And he probably wanted to make sure he got the credit.'

'But he works for the Church,' Cwen said. 'I'm confused again.'

'Sadly,' Hermitage said. 'I think Raegnald is the sort of person who will work for whoever gives him the greatest reward. If he really could get in the good favour of the king, that would be better than Baldice. Or, he might carry on working for both of them.'

Before Raegnald could protest his innocence, which he didn't look ready to do anyway, the door opened and Wat returned.

'Here we are then,' he said brightly.

Hermitage gave a careful look and saw that Gilbert, Aveline and Alyssa were containing their recognition.

'Of course,' Hermitage now said. 'With no dead body to see, we don't know that anyone killed Nigel at all. Raegnald can't be held responsible for a death that might not have happened. Nor can Baldice, or Lord de Sauveloy. Even though none of them has actually had any interest in whether Nigel was alive or dead.'

He hoped this last criticism stung, but he suspected it didn't.

'There is no action either the Church or the king can take against the other,' he said. 'Because after all, we don't know that anyone has done anything wrong. Apart from lie shamelessly, of course.'

'Hm,' Ranulph mused. 'Not so sure about that. Lots of people get killed and then the body gets lost. Look at King Harold.'

'In which case,' Hermitage said, thinking that this was getting more like a mummer's performance than an investigation. 'I think Wat's drudge had better introduce himself.'

Ranulph, Raegnald and Baldice all looked rather disgusted at this prospect.

Hermitage nodded at Nigel and gave him a short bow. 'Would you tell everyone who you are?

Nigel looked very concerned about this.

'It's all right,' Hermitage assured. 'Everything has been addressed, so you can say now.'

Nigel looked about the room and remained hesitant.

'Go on,' Alyssa encouraged kindly. 'You can tell.'

With another nervous glance, Nigel muttered something at his feet.

'Speak up!' Raegnald urged.

Nigel raised his head and with a last glance at Hermitage, spoke. 'Norbert,' he said.

'Fascinating,' Ranulph commented. 'Norbert seems to have forgotten the wine.'

'No, no,' Hermitage nodded rather frantically. 'You can say, it's perfectly safe.'

Nigel took a bit more confidence and spoke again. 'Norbert,' he repeated. 'Norbert of erm, Lincoln.'

'That's a coincidence,' Baldice said with little interest. 'Is this why we're being introduced to the servants?'

'Nigel,' Hermitage prompted. 'Nigel of Lincoln.'

De Sauveloy did raise an eyebrow at this.

'Oh, Nigel?' Nigel said hesitantly. 'Yes. I'm his brother, Norbert.'

Ranulph now considered him more closely. 'What's the brother of Nigel of Lincoln doing as the weaver's drudge?'

'I fell on hard times,' Nigel reported.

'I'll say,' Ranulph agreed. 'Did your brother know who you

were working for?' He looked to Wat. 'It's a bit odd, isn't it? You having Nigel's brother as a servant?'

'Erm, yes, I suppose it is,' Wat had to agree.

'I didn't like to mention it,' Nigel explained. 'The shame, you know.'

'I do.' Ranulph cast his glance up and down Wat. 'Working for the weaver is enough shame for anyone. Also a shame you didn't bring any wine.' He turned back to Nigel. 'How long has the weaver known who you are? You know your brother has caused us all a lot of trouble, don't you?'

'Oh, erm, yes. Wat, that is, Master Wat said we were, erm, going to Nottingham to sort out some business about Nigel, so I thought I'd better let him know that I was, erm, Norbert.'

Ranulph looked disappointed but not surprised. 'Bloody Saxons,' he sighed. 'When did you last see your brother?'

'My brother?'

'Nigel?' Ranulph reminded him wearily.

'Oh, not for a long time.'

'You don't happen to know who killed him?'

'If he's even dead,' Hermitage said quite plainly. He longed to announce that the Norbert standing before them was, in fact, Nigel. But if Nigel himself didn't want to do it, he didn't feel he could interfere.

Ranulph shrugged as if that really didn't matter anymore.

Somehow, that was more annoying than the callous manipulation of the man's possible murder. All this trouble for everyone and now it didn't matter? Ranulph de Sauveloy should be made to face the consequences of his scheming.

'Norbert,' Hermitage said gravely. 'You can be Nigel now.'

Nigel looked positively alarmed.

'He can be Nigel?' Baldice asked.

Ranulph was scowling. 'He can be Nigel?' He thought about this for a moment and then seemed to see the point. 'Your brother was not a noble.'

'A noble?'

'Yes, a noble. He owned no land, had no tenants,' de Sauveloy stated the facts.

'Oh, erm, no, I don't think so.'

'I can tell you that he didn't.'

'How do you know that?' Wat asked carefully.

'Me?' Ranulph tried to sound innocent, which he really shouldn't attempt. 'I know everything.' He shrugged. 'Do what you please then. We can't have Saxons passing their land and possessions on to their relatives, everything belongs to us now. But as Nigel didn't have anything, Norbert can do what he likes. He can even call himself Nigel as far as I'm concerned.'

Hermitage was confused and quite annoyed now. Exposing all of the horrible deceptions meant that Nigel was free of threat, and here he was, insisting he was Norbert. Not only that, but the chief protagonists in all the trouble they had gone through, didn't care one way or the other.

'I imagine, now that Nigel is gone,' Cwen said, 'Norbert could rejoin the family and go back to Lincoln?'

Neither Ranulph nor Baldice showed any interest in this at all. 'And he'd be safe from any interference,' Cwen went on. 'Not being the holder of Peter's Purse.'

Ranulph was yawning and picking at his teeth, and Baldice was clearly considering whether he could simply get up and go now.

Only Raegnald was looking at Nigel with a puzzled expression.

Alyssa skipped over and took Nigel's arm. 'Come, Uncle

Norbert,' she said. 'Come back with me to Lincoln.'

Nigel looked as if he wasn't sure what he should do, but went off to join Gilbert and Aveline

'There goes a perfectly good drudge,' Wat complained.

'Perhaps you could take over Peter's Purse in compensation,' Ranulph suggested with some malice.

'Glad to be rid of him,' Wat retreated quickly.

Hermitage could do nothing but shake his head sadly at this entire situation and the behaviour it had exposed. Behaviour that none of the exposed seemed at all concerned about.

'Well,' Ranulph clapped his hands and stood. 'This has all gone very well. Good work, Investigator.'

'Good work?' Hermitage could only repeat the words blankly.

'Absolutely. Raegnald and Baldice undone as the pope's men, the realm can rest at ease.'

'Not if you're a Saxon, it can't,' Cwen muttered.

'I think a quick word with the Archbishop of Canterbury will find them some suitable employment.'

Raegnald and Baldice exchanged looks that were awfully pale, even from a distance.

'Scheming against the crown,' Ranulph tutted. 'Quite shocking.'

'Can I ask one thing?' Hermitage could only speak quietly, such was his profound disappointment with those in positions of power.

'Ask away.'

'Is the king going to pay Peter's Pence? After all this? The appointment of Nigel, just so he could be murdered. The deception of Raegnald, dragging us into the whole sorry business. What is actually going to happen with the tax?'

Ranulph shrugged. 'The king will probably pay.'[10]

Hermitage had no words left at all.

. . .

'How can no murder at all have been so full of sin?' Hermitage complained as they happily left the keep behind.

'It's the people,' Cwen observed

'It certainly is,' Hermitage agreed. 'I don't think we should have anything to do with any of them anymore.'

'I've got a new one to add to my list,' Wat said.

'A new one?'

'Why people commit murder? Anger, revenge, greed and now, what can we call it; when the people in charge want people dead so that they can be a bit more in charge?'

'Sounds like greed to me,' Cwen said.

'You're the one with the words, Hermitage,' Wat said. 'Which one would you choose for this?'

Hermitage already had one in mind. 'I was going to suggest politics,' he said.

'From the Latin?' Cwen huffed.

'No, the Greek.'

'Well, that makes a change.'

'But now that you've defined it,' Hermitage mused, 'I think greed is probably right.'

'Still,' Wat said. 'Some good did come of it all. In the end.'

'What?' Hermitage asked. 'Oh, Nigel never was murdered and has gone home to live without interference. Yes, we must count that as a blessing. After all, it could have been so much

10 "Arrears would be sent to Rome as soon as possible". Stenton, F, (1971) The Oxford History of England, Volume II, Anglo-Saxon England, Third Edition pp675

worse.'

'No, no, not that.'

'What then?' Hermitage couldn't think of any other good to have come out of this at all.

Wat smiled broadly at them both. 'Gilbert's going to buy a tapestry.'

Finis.

Made in the USA
Monee, IL
04 October 2021

79375926R00173